C A R M I L L A

~

T H E   E V I L   G U E S T

KING'S WAY PRESS
DEFINITIVE CLASSICS
SERIES

C A R M I L L A

~

THE EVIL GUEST

Joseph Sheridan Le Fanu

KING'S WAY PRESS

ATLANTA

2016

King's Way Press
3721 New Macland Rd Suite 200-141
Powder Springs, GA 30127

www.kwp-books.com

Limited Edition Printing

ISBN-10: 069270065X
ISBN-13: 978-0692700655

TABLE OF CONTENTS

FOREWORD
Paul Little
7

INTRODUCTION:
WHY SUCKING IS COOL
Scott Nicholson
13

CARMILLA
Joseph Sheridan Le Fanu
27

THE EVIL GUEST
Joseph Sheridan Le Fanu
155

ACCOUNT OF A "REAL LIFE" VAMPIRE:
ARNOLD PAUL OR ARNOD PAOLE
Johannes Fluckinger
327

FOREWORD

Paul Little

I am very pleased to present Full Moon Press's first title in our Definitive Classics Series, "Carmilla" by Joseph Sheridan Le Fanu. When I decided that FMP would publish some classic horror novels, Carmilla came to mind as my first choice.

I was recently asked in an interview with Cemetery Dance why I decided to publish Carmilla and how I chose Carmilla as the first book in our Definitive Classics Series. In that Interview I gave the "short" answer.

With this foreword, I hope to give the reader a full explanation of why I chose "Carmilla" to kick off the series. I also hope to encourage the reader to embrace and enjoy "Carmilla" as much as I have over the years.

I have been a vampire fan ever since I can remember. My family used to gather around the television and watch "The Friday Night Frights" on our local TBS station. The show came on every Friday and consisted of old horror movie reruns. I still remember the first time I saw the original "Dracula" movie featured on "The

Friday Night Frights" and I was hooked on "Dracula" and vampires ever since.

I read and reread "Dracula" by Bram Stoker many times over the years following. I would likewise read any vampire stories or novels I could get my hands on. I must have read dozens of vampire novels and short story collections before I came across "Carmilla".

I first read "Carmilla" in a big book that my mother purchased for me when I was about 14. The book was titled "The Big Book of Dracula" or something close to that. Unfortunately, I have since lost that book somewhere over the years. Maybe I will find it again or come across another copy.

"The Big Book of Dracula" was a huge anthology of vampire stories with "Dracula" as the featured story and other smaller vampire novels and novellas included. "Carmilla" was one of the stories towards the back of the book. Of all the stories in the massive book, "Carmilla" caught my attention and captured my heart.

Of course I had read "Dracula" and most of the other stories before, but this book was my first introduction to "Carmilla". I was struck by Le Fanu's female vampire villainess. While on one hand she was very much the brutal predator, on the other hand she also seemed to be a lost soul seeking love or at least acceptance. Also, I had never thought of a vampire as beautiful before "Carmilla".

Over the years I read and reread "Carmilla" and "Dracula". Eventually I lost track of the "Big Book of Dracula" and "Carmilla". Over the years, I remained a staunch fan of the vampire genre, although I could not bear to read some of the books that characterized vampires as mainly male, very effeminate, almost girly-man, romantic souls seeking only love and acceptance and the latest fashion tips.

Some of the vampires being written about in modern fiction had lost their roots. Gone were the predatory heartless killers and a new brand of donated blood drinking, romantic, fashion savvy, undead had arrived on the fiction scene. That's enough to make a true vampire fan want to barf, right? My vampire interest waned over the years as vampire novels became less and less like horror novels and more like Harlequin romance novels.

Thankfully I was saved from the romantic, effeminate, girly-man, fashion savvy, vampire genre by Brian Lumley. On a routine visit to the local bookstore I spied "The Necroscope" staring out at me from the horror section.

With Bob Eggleton's horrific vampire skull with forked tongue rendered so strikingly on the cover, it was a sure bet to capture my interest. With "The Necroscope", Brian Lumley had finally resurrected the heartless beast that used to be known as a vampire! Lumley's vampire villains are known best for their brutality and disregard for human life instead of their keen fashion sense. Thank you, Brian, for returning the vampire to all of us who are true fans of the brutal beasts. After reading 14 books in the "Necroscope" series and I am still hooked on Brian's books!

Now, back to "Carmilla". When I was researching publishing and all aspects of the small press industry, I came upon someone who had previously been involved in the business. This guy told me he had always dreamed of doing "Carmilla" in a special Limited Edition format. At the time I did not equate "Carmilla" with that story that had so long ago captured my interest, after all it had been nearly 16 years since I had last read "Carmilla".

I decided to look into book and see what made "Carmilla" so special to him. Much to my surprise my own memories of "Carmilla" came flooding back! I had often thought of the story, but had forgotten the name of that haunting vampire novel that captured my heart and imagination so many years before. I knew then that if I were to open a small press, I would have to publish "Carmilla".

One of the greatest literary tragedies in my mind is the fact that "Carmilla" has long remained in the shadow of "Dracula". Many who have read and loved "Dracula" don't even know that "Carmilla" is by and large known as the inspiration for Bram Stoker's better known and much loved vampire novel. I couldn't even find a copy of "Carmilla" in print at my local bookstore for reference. How could a story like "Carmilla" go virtually unnoticed for so long? How could it be that this story, the story that inspired a masterpiece called "Dracula" could not be readily found in a bookstore? To me it seems a tragedy of epic literary proportions.

With the Full Moon Press Definitive Classic Series version of "Carmilla" I hope to right this wrong. Ihope that the readers will find "Carmilla" to be as tragic and yet fulfilling as I did so many years ago.

With the extra artwork found in the volume you now hold, the addition of Le Fanu's "The Evil Guest", and the bonus historical story of Arnold Paul, I hope that you as the reader will agree that I have added some delightful bonuses, although I want the spotlight to remain on the story. This is Carmilla's time to shine!

Lock the doors and windows, turn the television off, turn the lights down low, sit back, and read "Carmilla". Enjoy the story as Stoker must have before penning "Dracula".

Now,...what was that?.... listen..................could that be the light step of Carmilla at your bedroom door?

Paul Little
April 22, 2008

INTRODUCTION
WHY SUCKING IS COOL

Scott Nicholson

V ampires, God love 'em all.

I've spent many idle moments wondering why they are so appealing, but it wasn't until I actually became one that I felt their true power.

No, I didn't fall victim to an undead descendant of Vlad Dracul, nor did my peculiar set of mental disorders meld into a belief that I actually needed to drink fresh blood in order to survive. Instead, I came about it in my fantasy life—that of the prolific, bestselling, award-winning horror author whose words give you whiter teeth, fresher breath, and helps prevent cancer.

Before I actually popped pointy fangs in my mouth, I'd had an unimpressed view of the most instantly recognizable and universal horror trope. My first exposure to the myth was through The Count on Sesame Street and his commercial counterpart, Count Chocula, who adorned the front of a sweetened cereal that I lusted after to no end, largely due to my childhood of poverty and my usual rations of bland corn flakes or oatmeal.

It wasn't Chocula and his swept-up hair, radical cape collar, or rabbit teeth that seduced me—I was just as hot for Cocoa Pebbles and coo-coo for Cocoa Puffs.

So my youthful brush with the big bad bloodsucker was hardly the kind to spark fear, and I never put my head under my pillow and trembled through the night in fear of a vampire's fingernails scratching against the window. I just didn't really think of them as scary, since even at an early age I was fairly rational and had plenty of real-life horrors to choose from. Though I was a fan of the spooky stuff, vampires seemed way too one-dimensional and their stories had only two predictable outcomes—either the lover seducing the main character who(surprise!) turned out to be a vampire, or the vampire got a stake in its heart.

All that changed in 1972, when "Kolchak: The Night Stalker" made its appearance on network television. What made the most impact on my reeling prepubescent mind was that the vampire wasn't flapping around the sky above a crumbling European castle or sleeping in a coffin somewhere across the ocean. Instead, it was right there, next door, down the street, in a world with cars, hospitals, traffic lights, newspaper reporters, and actual dead people.

I didn't go on an instant orgy of vampire fiction, movies, or subculture, but I began paying more attention to them—Morbius, the creepy clown in whiteface of Marvel Comics fame, and the old Boris Karloff depictions—especially when I began writing horror. My trope of choice was often the ghost, because I found I could make up my own rules for their motives and behavior and, being willfully ignorant, I assumed all vampires had to do to survive was avoid the sun, garlic butter on toast, and pissed-off noblemen in top hats.

By the time I had made the jump from rock-n-roll to a dedicated writing career, Anne Rice, Poppy Z. Brite, Laurell K. Hamilton and others had rewritten the rules for vampires, and the established monster of centuries took a postpunk strut on the catwalk. The creatures of legend had gone into the closet and come back out again, wearing kick-ass heels, sunglasses, and attitudes. Less-skilled writers jumped in and added their own bland interpretations, which were little more than formulaic romance novels that could have been created with a template, simply putting fangs on the dark, handsome, and slightly dangerous stranger and changing his name from "Bradley" or "Percival" to "Andreas" or "Gregor." The wheel turned and soon readers began clamoring for the vicarious experience of the vampire's viewpoint. The vampire had become the protagonist, not the adversary, and often the reader was expected to sympathize with its plight. I didn't really get it—great sex, never have to sleep, and look awesome in black. What's there to whine about?

Yet the books popped up like mushrooms and were gobbled down like potato chips, and I admit to a slight bit of envy. Why couldn't I write one of those? It looked so easy, maybe too easy, and with the creation of a marketing category called "paranormal romance," the publishing industry had found a way to publish vampire books that didn't have to be hidden in the dark corners where the other horror books were shelved. That is, until the horror sections disappeared altogether.

My first major writing success featured a vampire, though it was much more a fantasy story than a horror story. I woke up one morning with the phrase "vampire shortstop" in my head, no doubt a sleep-induced pun off the word "umpire." I rattled the story off in a couple of days, using the typical stereotypes, and the story went on to win the international Writers of the Future contest and get reprinted five times. It was so easy I should have cranked out a series of novels featuring the character (I'd have to find a way to bring him back from the dead, but that's never a problem in vampire properties that sell well enough to merit a sequel).

Instead, I stayed aloof from the subgenre until years later my book editor asked, "Have you ever thought of writing a vampire novel?" Since my contract was expiring, and I figured the editor would enthusiastically push the project within the publisher's sales staff and boost my numbers, putting me in a better position to get the next deal, I replied, "Yeah, thought about it."

And thus was born my novel *They Hunger*, pitched as "Deliverance with vampires," even though my vampires are technically a mix of gargoyle, chupacabra, and traditional bat-creature. Always one to tweak conventions to suit my own peculiar fancy, I originally wanted my blood-drinkers to have one huge fang in the middle of their uppers, so instead of nuzzling, coaxing, and sucking, they'd punch into the victim like a can opener penetrating a pint of V-8. The visuals alone would have nailed a movie sale, and my script adaptation is a little more gruesome than the book (the script, along with the graphic novel, are being marketed under my original title of "The Gorge," but at one time I'd used the working title of "Running Red." Yeah, vampire titles can get pretty cheesy if you're not careful.)

Before I was much into *They Hunger*, I figured I'd better get around to reading the seminal vampire novel— Bram Stoker's classic. Yes, I confess that I had neglected

Dracula, mostly because of my misunderstanding and mild resentment toward the popularity of vampire books. The novel was very much what I expected, rather languid in style but with some genuinely creepy moments, and going to the original source material for much of the modern rules of expected conduct gave me a new appreciation for the beloved nightfeeders.

My reading about *Dracula* and Bram Stoker led me to Joseph Sheridan Le Fanu's "Carmilla," which is not the first vampire tale but is generally considered an inspiration for Bram Stoker's work. "Carmilla" predates *Dracula* by 25 years and itself draws on the work of many, compiling in its conclusion the learned text of "serious scholars" of the 1700s who often had a religious motive in explaining vampires while never fully acknowledging that such creatures were real. Though clearly no one has ever provided solid evidence the creatures exist, past hysteria was real, innocent people died because of it, and plenty of corpses were staked or beheaded "just to make sure." Whether reports of people rising from the grave came from hallucinations, premature burial, or sheer superstition, it made perfect sense to add an extra, though oversize, nail to the coffin. I don't know about you, but I'd just as soon have a stake driven through my somnambulant, comatose heart than risk waking up in a pine box with six feet of packed clay over me. Of course, some pious authorities eventually called the practice of staking "barbaric" and decided it was better to preempt any opportunity for afterlife frolicking by draining the blood and filling the veins full of pickle juice.

European jurisprudence aside, one of my more appealing discoveries was the promise of sly lesbian overtones in "Carmilla." While homosexuality is as latent in all races and nationalities as is the bloodsucking myth, it was just as slow to come out into the sunshine, and now the sensationalism seems a little silly, and though I'm not a Victorian scholar, I would be surprised if the book caused much of a stir back in the 1870s. For one thing, not all that many people read back then, and it was still to some degree the leisurely pursuit of the privileged class. For another, the lesbianism is subtle enough that it can easily be construed as the genuine sisterly affection that many females seem to share.

But screw that. Let's jazz it up a little and assume Le Fanu is engaging in pure and gleeful voyeurism. I won't give away the story, since you now hold it in your hot little hands and can decide for yourself, but aside from the sensual nature of Carmilla's feeding, the protagonist used one word several times to describe what Carmilla was attempting to do: "own" her.

That possession is a core element of the vampire's enduring appeal. The vampire's power helps the victim surrender more easily, and that same power is evident in many human love affairs, often with consequences that are just as dire. We often feel we must "surrender" to love, that we are helpless, that we are "falling in," and perhaps that powerlessness gives us the permission to engage in reckless behavior, i.e. trust another creature with our heart and soul and happiness. If we are madly in love, we feel possessed, and when our lover (a.k.a. our vampire) comes at us, the seductive eyes lead us to bare our throats and yield to whatever desires are inflicted upon us.

Love is love, and I believe all humans are by nature bisexual—after that, it just becomes a question of degree and where one falls on the scale. Since I accept bisexuality and homosexuality as perfectly healthy and normal, then a "lesbian vampire" holds no taboo to me, which would probably limit my prurient interest in "Carmilla" if not for my unending fascination with psychology and what makes people tick.

Le Fanu wasn't content to dole out a typical monster tale, though he was quite a prolific ghost-story writer, as you'll see the second work in this edition, "The Evil Guest." Ron Breznay, who writes the Old Masters of Horror column for Hellnotes.com, said Le Fanu counted on tone and effect, rather than shock, to convey horror:

> In "Carmilla," the narrator initiates the tone of the story by describing the loneliness of the castle— the isolation and the few people who live there, with occasional visits from distant neighbors—as well as the disarming beauty of the isolated, bucolic surroundings. The story continues in such a leisurely fashion, making the horror, when it arrives, all the more terrible by contrast.
>
> Le Fanu often followed a mystery format, as in "The Evil Guest." A common theme of his was that of a villain returning to society in a new form, such as by possessing a human body or in the form of a living corpse or an animal. Spectral illusions and haunted suicides were recurring devices.

"Carmilla" and "The Evil Guest" are both a bit dated because of their language, only natural given the speedy evolution or devolution of language that has occurred with the ever-more-rapid changes in communication technology. A bigger hurdle for modern readers is the narrative framework, in which the author relates much of the story through secondhand sources, with key action taking place offstage and other important information coming from letters. The narrative also jumps around instead of keeping the straight beginning-to-end timeline familiar to most readers, and of course today's commercial fiction is largely targeted to a seventh-grade reading level. "The Evil Guest," in particular, follows a "look behind the curtain" form of omniscient storytelling, in which Le Fanu often pulls aside his reader into a conspiratorial and universal "we."

All that aside, "Carmilla" is surprisingly easy to read and grasp today, particularly the vivid scenes when Carmilla so lustily approaches her far-too-acquiescent prey. Let's face it, most of us dig sex, and when there are teeth and breasts and hard breathing and soft hair involved, our hearts are going to beat a little faster, especially when we're supposed to feel a little naughtier than normal, as with any practice that could be considered daring, immoral, or antisocial.

In my unscientific inquiries on the subject, I've found that girl-on-girl is somehow more acceptable (and even understandable and expected) than boy-and-boy, and many heterosexual males consider "watching two chicks going at it" one of their fondest fantasies. Not to delve into my own bedroom antics any more than necessary, but I've come to believe that particular male fantasy springs from a very immature, erroneous, and self-centered view of the situation: the male thinks if he shows up on the scene, the ladies will instantly part and make him the focal point of a scorching *menage a trois*, while in reality the ladies would likely view him as an underinflated fifth wheel.

But, hey, it sells, and it also adds a little more intellectual juice to the proceedings, as explained by Jason Colavito, author of *A Hideous Bit of Morbidity: An Anthology of Horror Criticism from the Enlightenment to World War I.*

Colavito says "Carmilla" is both a bridge between early and modern vampires and an outsider to tradition not only because of the lesbianism, but also because of the males who would love to watch if given a chance, but if left out of the playing, tend to get a little oppressive:

John Polidori's Gothic novella *The Vampyre* (1819) had set the template for the aristocratic bloodsucker—the feudal nobleman as literal parasite on society—who preys on beautiful maidens, while the popular serial novel *Varney the Vampire* (1845-1847) had provided the fangs and gore to compliment the creature's strange glamour. Bram Stoker would draw from these works, and especially from "Carmilla," in assembling *Dracula* (1897), which he first wanted set in the same Austrian province as Le Fanu's tale. Le Fanu, clearly working in this tradition, transformed and transcended it by making his vampire aristocrat a woman and having her prey on another of her sex. But Le Fanu did more than this, creating in "Carmilla" a parallel structure where innocent Laura's experience of vampirism and her experience of homosexuality progress on twin tracks until the male heroes of the story must step in to destroy her unhealthy knowledge of horrors that dare not speak their names.

As early as the eighteenth century the French began referring to homosexuality as "the German vice," so it is entirely appropriate that Le Fanu placed his pair of female lovers in Styria, a German-speaking region of the Austro-Hungarian Empire. In "Carmilla," Laura's susceptibility to both lesbianism and vampirism is prefigured in her childhood dream of being bitten by a beautiful girl. Her gradual indoctrination at the hands of the vampire Carmilla into what Victorian audiences viewed as unnatural acts leads to her gradual decline and forces the men in the story to assert their control over Laura's fate by destroying the source of the psychic and physical corruption that threatens to overwhelm her, the vampire. The story ends with Laura sharing scholarly research on the habits and powers of vampires, which Le Fanu likely derived from Dom Augustin Calmet's 1751 treatise on vampires. When Laura says "it is difficult to deny, or even to doubt the existence of such a phenomenon as the Vampire," she is speaking not just of the otherworldly creature but also of the homosexuality it symbolized and of which polite audiences and especially well-bred young women were supposed to be ignorant.

Modern readers are jaded, of course, and there's not much new under the sun. Lesbian vampires were outed by low-budget film directors to the point of saturation and tedium, so that even an affair like Susan Sarandon's and Catherine Deneuve's in 1983's "The Hunger," hot enough to keep David Bowie on the sidelines, now seems as old-fashioned as Grandma's Sears & Roebuck corset. Still, the subgenre remains strong, and lesbian vampires will always draw a second glance on the bookstore shelves and often bear some greasy fingerprints before the product is sold. It may be a little benevolent to credit Le Fanu with launching the industry, as some publishing executive was bound to think of it sooner or later, but let's give the devil his due.

"Carmilla" will retain a place in the timeline that leads directly to "Buffy the Vampire Slayer" and beyond, into what controversial religious scholar and author of "The Vampire Book" J. Gordon Melton calls the ongoing evolution of the vampire myth to fit current social whims. In an interview on the blog TheoFantastique, Melton said, "The vampires have always had a symbolic function in society. In Eastern Europe, it explained unusual death and served to facilitate what today we know as the grief process. Over the centuries it has periodically mutated to serve a new generation's needs. Today it has become a symbol of what the average person finds so elusive—fulfilling sexuality, social power, and any hope of personal immortality. That's a heady trio of carrots to dangle in front of us."

Katherine Ramsland, author of *The Science of Vampires* and many other books, downplays the lesbian angle in "Carmilla" but notes, "I think it made a contribution, certainly, to the psychopathic female vampire and to the notion that vampires seek to infiltrate families to draw away the prize."

Jeffrey Bowden believes people are in it for the suffering: "I think this has to do with an innate sense that people have to express their individuality through painful ritualism. These vampire folks, they certainly embody individualism in a most radical way. I would imagine that, if possible, there would be plenty of angst-ridden youths that would opt to become vampires in a heartbeat. Of course, they wouldn't want to just wake up one day and be a vampire, they would prefer to be bitten in the neck as part of the process. I think there is a strong strain of masochism that runs through our culture. Unfortunately, these angst-ridden youths are stuck with, over the years, long hair, ear piercings, tongue piercings, tattoos, etc."

Once again going to my armchair research, I will offer my own spin, summed up by what I learned when I grew pointy teeth and a sickly complexion and learned firsthand the undying allure of the vampire. I shoot new promotional photos for each of my books, tying them in with the subject matter, so naturally I decided to stage a vampire shot for *They Hunger*. A friend in the funeral industry let me use an antique casket and a room in the local parlor, and I was to be a cheesy Victorian vampire killer hovering over an innocent, startled young female vampire, with the tag "Buy my book or I'll kill this vampire." Goofing around, we did a few outtakes where I climbed into the casket and pretended to play dead. A friend tricked up the photo to give me fangs and applied makeup and black nail polish, though my eyes are open and I have a sly grin.

I posted the photo on Myspace and immediately got a lot of comments about how "hot" I was. Now, I know I'm an acquired taste and not the kind of guy they'd pick for the cover of G.Q., so I was startled and a little dismayed at the reaction, since I looked much the same as before, only deader. So I began asking people (and these weren't just females, by the way) why the photo was so appealing. And the answer was "Power."

We love the idea of immortality, even if we lose our taste for chocolate and German beer. And we love the idea of taking whatever we want and getting away with it, with absolutely no punishment as long as we avoid the tip of the pointy wooden stake. Basically, we love the vehemence of vampires, the compulsion to say "You're hot, come get me, I can't help myself." Yeah, you know how it goes—the resistance of "Please...don't...stop..." gives way to "Please don't stop!"

Once we're bitten, we in turn go on to assert our power over other soon-to-be-willing mortals, even those who might have spurned us back when we warm-blooded and had a nice tan. So the flesh is a little cold, and I'm sure their abilities to lubricate leave a lot to be desired, but, hey, all we really want is to be loved for who we are, right?

Even if it's just a walking bag of hot, succulent hemoglobin.

Vampires.

They suck.

Where's the downside?

Scott Nicholson
April, 2008

SCOTT NICHOLSON is the author of seven novels, including *The Skull Ring* from Full Moon Press. He's written over 60 stories, five screenplays, and numerous articles. His Web site is www.hauntedcomputer.com.

CARMILLA

PROLOGUE

Upon a paper attached to the Narrative which follows, Doctor Hesselius has written a rather elaborate note, which he accompanies with a reference to his Essay on the strange subject which the MS. illuminates.

This mysterious subject he treats, in that Essay, with his usual learning and acumen, and with remarkable directness and condensation. It will form but one volume of the series of that extraordinary man's collected papers.

As I publish the case, in this volume, simply to interest the "laity," I shall forestall the intelligent lady, who relates it, in nothing; and after due consideration, I have determined, therefore, to abstain from presenting any précis of the learned Doctor's reasoning, or extract from his statement on a subject which he describes as "involving, not improbably, some of the profoundest arcana of our dual existence, and its intermediates."

I was anxious on discovering this paper, to reopen the correspondence commenced by Doctor Hesselius, so many years before, with a person so clever and careful as his informant seems to have been. Much to my regret, however, I found that she had died in the interval. She, probably, could have added little to the Narrative which she communicates in the following pages, with, so far as I can pronounce, such conscientious particularity.

CHAPTER I

An Early Fright

In Styria, we, though by no means magnificent people, inhabit a castle, or schloss. A small income, in that part of the world, goes a great way. Eight or nine hundred a year does wonders. Scantily enough ours would have answered among wealthy people at home. My father is English, and I bear an English name, although I never saw England. But here, in this lonely and primitive place, where everything is so marvelously cheap, I really don't see how ever so much more money would at all materially add to our comforts, or even luxuries.

My father was in the Austrian service, and retired upon a pension and his patrimony, and purchased this feudal residence, and the small estate on which it stands, a bargain.

Nothing can be more picturesque or solitary. It stands on a slight eminence in a forest. The road, very old and narrow, passes in front of its drawbridge, never raised in my time, and its moat, stocked with perch, and sailed over by many swans, and floating on its surface white fleets of water lilies.

Over all this the schloss shows its many-windowed front; its towers, and its Gothic chapel.

The forest opens in an irregular and very picturesque glade before its gate, and at the right a steep Gothic bridge carries the road over a stream that winds in deep shadow through the wood. I have said that this is a very lonely place. Judge whether I say truth. Looking from the hall door towards the road, the forest in which our castle stands extends fifteen miles to the right, and twelve to the left. The nearest inhabited village is about seven of your English miles to the left. The nearest inhabited schloss of any historic associations, is that of old General Spielsdorf, nearly twenty miles away to the right.

I have said "the nearest *inhabited* village," because there is, only three miles westward, that is to say in the direction of General Spielsdorf's schloss, a ruined village, with its quaint little church, now roofless, in the aisle of which are the moldering tombs of the proud family of Karnstein, now extinct, who once owned the equally desolate chateau which, in the thick of the forest, overlooks the silent ruins of the town.

Respecting the cause of the desertion of this striking and melancholy spot, there is a legend which I shall relate to you another time.

I must tell you now, how very small is the party who constitute the inhabitants of our castle. I don't include servants, or those dependents who occupy rooms in the buildings attached to the schloss. Listen, and wonder! My father, who is the kindest man on earth, but growing old; and I, at the date of my story, only nineteen. Eight years have passed since then.

I and my father constituted the family at the schloss. My mother, a Styrian lady, died in my infancy, but I had a good-natured governess, who had been with me from, I might almost say, my infancy. I could not remember the time when her fat, benignant face was not a familiar picture in my memory.

This was Madame Perrodon, a native of Berne, whose care and good nature now in part supplied to me the loss of my mother, whom I do not even remember, so early I lost her. She made a third at our little dinner party. There was a fourth, Mademoiselle De Lafontaine, a lady such as you term, I believe, a "finishing governess." She spoke French and German, Madame Perrodon French and broken English, to which my father and I added English, which, partly to prevent its becoming a lost language among us, and partly from patriotic motives, we spoke every day. The consequence was a Babel, at which strangers used to laugh, and which I shall make no attempt to reproduce in this narrative. And there were two or three young lady friends besides, pretty nearly of my own age, who were occasional visitors, for longer or shorter terms; and these visits I sometimes returned.

These were our regular social resources; but of course there were chance visits from "neighbors" of only five or six leagues distance. My life was, notwithstanding, rather a solitary one, I can assure you.

My gouvernantes had just so much control over me as you might conjecture such sage persons would have in the case of a rather spoiled girl, whose only parent allowed her pretty nearly her own way in everything.

The first occurrence in my existence, which produced a terrible impression upon my mind, which, in fact, never has been effaced, was one of the very earliest incidents of my life which I can recollect. Some people will think it so trifling that it should not be recorded here. You will see, however, by-and-by, why I mention it. The nursery, as it was called, though I had it all to myself, was a large room in the upper story of the castle, with a steep oak roof. I can't have been more than six years old, when one night I awoke, and looking round the room from my bed, failed to see the nursery maid. Neither was my nurse there; and I thought myself alone. I was not frightened, for I was one of those happy children who are studiously kept in ignorance of ghost stories, of fairy tales, and of all such lore as makes us cover up our heads when the door cracks suddenly, or the flicker of an expiring candle makes the shadow of a bedpost dance upon the wall, nearer to our faces. I was vexed and insulted at finding myself, as I conceived, neglected, and I began to whimper, preparatory to a hearty bout of roaring; when to my surprise, I saw a solemn, but very pretty face looking at me from the side of the bed. It was that of a young lady who was kneeling, with her hands under the coverlet. I looked at her with a kind of pleased wonder, and ceased whimpering. She caressed me with her hands, and lay down beside me on the bed, and drew me towards her, smiling; I felt immediately delightfully soothed, and fell asleep again. I was wakened by a sensation as if two needles ran into my breast very deep at the same moment, and I cried loudly. The lady started back, with her eyes fixed on me, and then slipped down upon the floor, and, as I thought, hid herself under the bed.

I was now for the first time frightened, and I yelled with all my might and main. Nurse, nursery maid, housekeeper, all came running in, and hearing my story, they made light of it, soothing me all they could meanwhile. But, child as I was, I could perceive that their faces were pale with an unwonted look of anxiety, and I saw them look under the bed, and about the room, and peep under tables and pluck open cupboards; and the housekeeper whispered to the nurse: "Lay your hand along that hollow in the bed; someone *did* lie there, so sure as you did not; the place is still warm."

I remember the nursery maid petting me, and all three examining my chest, where I told them I felt the puncture, and pronouncing that there was no sign visible that any such thing had happened to me.

The housekeeper and the two other servants who were in charge of the nursery, remained sitting up all night; and from that time a servant always sat up in the nursery until I was about fourteen.

I was very nervous for a long time after this. A doctor was called in, he was pallid and elderly. How well I remember his long saturnine face, slightly pitted with smallpox, and his chestnut wig. For a good while, every second day, he came and gave me medicine, which of course I hated.

The morning after I saw this apparition I was in a state of terror, and could not bear to be left alone, daylight though it was, for a moment.

I remember my father coming up and standing at the bedside, and talking cheerfully, and asking the nurse a number of questions, and laughing very heartily at one of the answers; and patting me on the shoulder, and kissing me, and telling me not to be frightened, that it was nothing but a dream and could not hurt me.

But I was not comforted, for I knew the visit of the strange woman was *not* a dream; and I was *awfully* frightened.

I was a little consoled by the nursery maid's assuring me that it was she who had come and looked at me, and lain down beside me in the bed, and that I must have been half-dreaming not to have known her face. But this, though supported by the nurse, did not quite satisfy me.

I remembered, in the course of that day, a venerable old man, in a black cassock, coming into the room with the nurse and housekeeper, and talking a little to them, and very kindly to me; his face was very sweet and gentle, and he told me they were going to pray, and joined my hands together, and desired me to say, softly, while they were praying, "Lord hear all good prayers for us, for Jesus' sake." I think these were the very words, for I often repeated them to myself, and my nurse used for years to make me say them in my prayers.

I remembered so well the thoughtful sweet face of that white-haired old man, in his black cassock, as he stood in that rude, lofty, brown room, with the clumsy furniture of a fashion three hundred years old about him, and the scanty light entering its shadowy atmosphere through the small lattice. He kneeled, and the three women with him, and he prayed aloud with an earnest quavering voice for, what appeared to me, a long time. I forget all my life preceding that event, and for some time after it is all obscure also, but the scenes I have just described stand out vivid as the isolated pictures of the phantasmagoria surrounded by darkness.

CHAPTER II

A Guest

I am now going to tell you something so strange that it will require all your faith in my veracity to believe my story. It is not only true, nevertheless, but truth of which I have been an eyewitness.

It was a sweet summer evening, and my father asked me, as he sometimes did, to take a little ramble with him along that beautiful forest vista which I have mentioned as lying in front of the schloss.

"General Spielsdorf cannot come to us so soon as I had hoped," said my father, as we pursued our walk.

He was to have paid us a visit of some weeks, and we had expected his arrival next day. He was to have brought with him a young lady, his niece and ward, Mademoiselle Rheinfeldt, whom I had never seen, but whom I had heard described as a very charming girl, and in whose society I had promised myself many happy days. I was more disappointed than a young lady living in a town, or a bustling neighborhood can possibly imagine. This visit, and the new acquaintance it promised, had furnished my day dream for many weeks.

"And how soon does he come?" I asked.

"Not till autumn. Not for two months, I dare say," he answered. "And I am very glad now, dear, that you never knew Mademoiselle Rheinfeldt."

"And why?" I asked, both mortified and curious.

"Because the poor young lady is dead," he replied. "I quite forgot I had not told you, but you were not in the room when I received the General's letter this evening."

I was very much shocked. General Spielsdorf had mentioned in his first letter, six or seven weeks before, that she was not so well as he would wish her, but there was nothing to suggest the remotest suspicion of danger.

"Here is the General's letter," he said, handing it to me. "I am afraid he is in great affliction; the letter appears to me to have been written very nearly in distraction."

We sat down on a rude bench, under a group of magnificent lime trees. The sun was setting with all its melancholy splendor behind the sylvan horizon, and the stream that flows beside our home, and passes under the steep old bridge I have mentioned, wound through many a group of noble trees, almost at our feet, reflecting in its current the fading crimson of the sky. General Spielsdorf's letter was so extraordinary, so vehement, and in some places so self-contradictory, that I read it twice over—the second time aloud to my father—and was still unable to account for it, except by supposing that grief had unsettled his mind.

It said, "I have lost my darling daughter, for as such I loved her. During the last days of dear Bertha's illness I was not able to write to you.

"Before then I had no idea of her danger. I have lost her, and now learn *all*, too late. She died in the peace of innocence, and in the glorious hope of a blessed futurity. The fiend who betrayed our infatuated hospitality has done it all. I thought I was receiving into my house innocence, gaiety, a charming companion for my lost Bertha. Heavens! what a fool have I been!

"I thank God my child died without a suspicion of the cause of her sufferings. She is gone without so much as conjecturing the nature of her illness, and the accursed passion of the agent of all this misery. I devote my remaining days to tracking and extinguishing a monster. I am told I may hope to accomplish my righteous and merciful purpose. At present there is scarcely a gleam of light to guide me. I curse my conceited incredulity, my despicable affectation of superiority, my blindness, my obstinacy—all—too late. I cannot write or talk collectedly now. I am distracted. So soon as I shall have a little recovered, I mean to devote myself for a time to enquiry, which may possibly lead me as far as Vienna. Some time in the autumn, two months hence, or earlier if I live, I will see you—that is, if you permit me; I will then tell you all that I scarce dare put upon paper now. Farewell. Pray for me, dear friend."

In these terms ended this strange letter. Though I had never seen Bertha Rheinfeldt my eyes filled with tears at the sudden intelligence; I was startled, as well as profoundly disappointed.

The sun had now set, and it was twilight by the time I had returned the General's letter to my father.

It was a soft clear evening, and we loitered, speculating upon the possible meanings of the violent and incoherent sentences which I had just been reading.

We had nearly a mile to walk before reaching the road that passes the schloss in front, and by that time the moon was shining brilliantly. At the drawbridge we met Madame Perrodon and Mademoiselle De Lafontaine, who had come out, without their bonnets, to enjoy the exquisite moonlight.

We heard their voices gabbling in animated dialogue as we approached. We joined them at the drawbridge, and turned about to admire with them the beautiful scene.

The glade through which we had just walked lay before us. At our left the narrow road wound away under clumps of lordly trees, and was lost to sight amid the thickening forest. At the right the same road crosses the steep and picturesque bridge, near which stands a ruined tower which once guarded that pass; and beyond the bridge an abrupt eminence rises, covered with trees, and showing in the shadows some grey ivy-clustered rocks.

Over the sward and low grounds a thin film of mist was stealing like smoke, marking the distances with a transparent veil; and here and there we could see the river faintly flashing in the moonlight.

No softer, sweeter scene could be imagined. The news I had just heard made it melancholy; but nothing could disturb its character of profound serenity, and the enchanted glory and vagueness of the prospect.

My father, who enjoyed the picturesque, and I, stood looking in silence over the expanse beneath us. The two good governesses, standing a little way behind us, discoursed upon the scene, and were eloquent upon the moon.

Madame Perrodon was fat, middle-aged, and romantic, and talked and sighed poetically. Mademoiselle De Lafontaine—in right of her father who was a German,

assumed to be psychological, metaphysical, and something of a mystic—now declared that when the moon
shone with a light so intense it was well known that it
indicated a special spiritual activity. The effect of the full
moon in such a state of brilliancy was manifold. It acted
on dreams, it acted on lunacy, it acted on nervous people,
it had marvelous physical influences connected with life.
Mademoiselle related that her cousin, who was mate of
a merchant ship, having taken a nap on deck on such a
night, lying on his back, with his face full in the light on
the moon, had wakened, after a dream of an old woman
clawing him by the cheek, with his features horribly
drawn to one side; and his countenance had never quite
recovered its equilibrium.

"The moon, this night," she said, "is full of idyllic
and magnetic influence—and see, when you look behind
you at the front of the schloss how all its windows flash
and twinkle with that silvery splendor, as if unseen hands
had lighted up the rooms to receive fairy guests."

There are indolent styles of the spirits in which,
indisposed to talk ourselves, the talk of others is
pleasant to our listless ears; and I gazed on, pleased with
the tinkle of the ladies' conversation.

"I have got into one of my moping moods tonight,"
said my father, after a silence, and quoting Shakespeare,
whom, by way of keeping up our English, he used to
read aloud, he said:

"'In truth I know not why I am so sad. It wearies
me: you say it wearies you; But how I got it—came
by it.'

"I forget the rest. But I feel as if some great
misfortune were hanging over us. I suppose the poor

General's afflicted letter has had something to do with it."

At this moment the unwonted sound of carriage wheels and many hoofs upon the road, arrested our attention.

They seemed to be approaching from the high ground overlooking the bridge, and very soon the equipage emerged from that point. Two horsemen first crossed the bridge, then came a carriage drawn by four horses, and two men rode behind.

It seemed to be the traveling carriage of a person of rank; and we were all immediately absorbed in watching that very unusual spectacle. It became, in a few moments, greatly more interesting, for just as the carriage had passed the summit of the steep bridge, one of the leaders, taking fright, communicated his panic to the rest, and after a plunge or two, the whole team broke into a wild gallop together, and dashing between the horsemen who rode in front, came thundering along the road towards us with the speed of a hurricane.

The excitement of the scene was made more painful by the clear, long-drawn screams of a female voice from the carriage window.

We all advanced in curiosity and horror; me rather in silence, the rest with various ejaculations of terror.

Our suspense did not last long. Just before you reach the castle drawbridge, on the route they were coming, there stands by the roadside a magnificent lime tree, on the other stands an ancient stone cross, at sight of which the horses, now going at a pace that was perfectly frightful, swerved so as to bring the wheel over the projecting roots of the tree.

I knew what was coming. I covered my eyes, unable to see it out, and turned my head away; at the same moment I heard a cry from my lady friends, who had gone on a little.

Curiosity opened my eyes, and I saw a scene of utter confusion. Two of the horses were on the ground, the carriage lay upon its side with two wheels in the air; the men were busy removing the traces, and a lady with a commanding air and figure had got out, and stood with clasped hands, raising the handkerchief that was in them every now and then to her eyes.

Through the carriage door was now lifted a young lady, who appeared to be lifeless. My dear old father was already beside the elder lady, with his hat in his hand, evidently tendering his aid and the resources of his schloss. The lady did not appear to hear him, or to have eyes for anything but the slender girl who was being placed against the slope of the bank.

I approached; the young lady was apparently stunned, but she was certainly not dead. My father, who piqued himself on being something of a physician, had just had his fingers on her wrist and assured the lady, who declared herself her mother, that her pulse, though faint and irregular, was undoubtedly still distinguishable. The lady clasped her hands and looked upward, as if in a momentary transport of gratitude; but immediately she broke out again in that theatrical way which is, I believe, natural to some people.

She was what is called a fine looking woman for her time of life, and must have been handsome; she was tall, but not thin, and dressed in black velvet, and looked rather pale, but with a proud and commanding countenance, though now agitated strangely.

"Who was ever being so born to calamity?" I heard her say, with clasped hands, as I came up. "Here am I, on a journey of life and death, in prosecuting which to lose an hour is possibly to lose all. My child will not have recovered sufficiently to resume her route for who can say how long. I must leave her: I cannot, dare not, delay. How far on, sir, can you tell, is the nearest village? I must leave her there; and shall not see my darling, or even hear of her till my return, three months hence."

I plucked my father by the coat, and whispered earnestly in his ear: "Oh! papa, pray ask her to let her stay with us—it would be so delightful. Do, pray."

"If Madame will entrust her child to the care of my daughter, and of her good gouvernante, Madame Perrodon, and permit her to remain as our guest, under my charge, until her return, it will confer a distinction and an obligation upon us, and we shall treat her with all the care and devotion which so sacred a trust deserves."

"I cannot do that, sir, it would be to task your kindness and chivalry too cruelly," said the lady, distractedly.

"It would, on the contrary, be to confer on us a very great kindness at the moment when we most need it. My daughter has just been disappointed by a cruel misfortune, in a visit from which she had long anticipated a great deal of happiness. If you confide this young lady to our care it will be her best consolation. The nearest village on your route is distant, and affords no such inn as you could think of placing your daughter at; you cannot allow her to continue her journey for any considerable distance without danger. If, as you say, you cannot suspend your journey, you must part with her tonight, and nowhere could you do so with more honest assurances of care and tenderness than here."

There was something in this lady's air and appearance so distinguished and even imposing, and in her manner so engaging, as to impress one, quite apart from the dignity of her equipage, with a conviction that she was a person of consequence.

By this time the carriage was replaced in its upright position, and the horses, quite tractable, in the traces again.

The lady threw on her daughter a glance which I fancied was not quite so affectionate as one might have anticipated from the beginning of the scene; then she beckoned slightly to my father, and withdrew two or three steps with him out of hearing; and talked to him with a fixed and stern countenance, not at all like that with which she had hitherto spoken.

I was filled with wonder that my father did not seem to perceive the change, and also unspeakably curious to learn what it could be that she was speaking, almost in his ear, with so much earnestness and rapidity.

Two or three minutes at most I think she remained thus employed, then she turned, and a few steps brought her to where her daughter lay, supported by Madame Perrodon. She kneeled beside her for a moment and whispered, as Madame supposed, a little benediction in her ear; then hastily kissing her she stepped into her carriage, the door was closed, the footmen in stately liveries jumped up behind, the outriders spurred on, the postilions cracked their whips, the horses plunged and broke suddenly into a furious canter that threatened soon again to become a gallop, and the carriage whirled away, followed at the same rapid pace by the two horsemen in the rear.

CHAPTER III

We Compare Notes

We followed the *cortege* with our eyes until it was swiftly lost to sight in the misty wood; and the very sound of the hoofs and the wheels died away in the silent night air.

Nothing remained to assure us that the adventure had not been an illusion of a moment but the young lady, who just at that moment opened her eyes. I could not see, for her face was turned from me, but she raised her head, evidently looking about her, and I heard a very sweet voice ask complainingly, "Where is mamma?"

Our good Madame Perrodon answered tenderly, and added some comfortable assurances.

I then heard her ask:

"Where am I? What is this place?" and after that she said, "I don't see the carriage; and Matska, where is she?"

Madame answered all her questions in so far as she understood them; and gradually the young lady remembered how the misadventure came about, and was glad to hear that no one in, or in attendance on, the carriage was hurt; and on learning that her mamma had left her here, till her return in about three months, she wept.

I was going to add my consolations to those of Madame Perrodon when Mademoiselle De Lafontaine placed her hand upon my arm, saying:

"Don't approach, one at a time is as much as she can at present converse with; a very little excitement would possibly overpower her now."

As soon as she is comfortably in bed, I thought, I will run up to her room and see her.

My father in the meantime had sent a servant on horseback for the physician, who lived about two leagues away; and bedroom was being prepared for the young lady's reception.

The stranger now rose, and leaning on Madame's arm, walked slowly over the drawbridge and into the castle gate.

In the hall, servants waited to receive her, and she was conducted forthwith to her room. The room we usually sat in as our drawing room is long, having four windows, that looked over the moat and drawbridge, upon the forest scene I have just described.

It is furnished in old carved oak, with large carved cabinets, and the chairs are cushioned with crimson Utrecht velvet. The walls are covered with tapestry, and surrounded with great gold frames, the figures being as large as life, in ancient and very curious costume, and the subjects represented are hunting, hawking, and generally festive. It is not too stately to be extremely comfortable; and here we had our tea, for with his usual patriotic leanings he insisted that the national beverage should make its appearance regularly with our coffee and chocolate.

We sat here this night, and with candles lighted, were talking over the adventure of the evening.

Madame Perrodon and Mademoiselle De Lafontaine were both of our party. The young stranger had hardly lain down in her bed when she sank into a deep sleep; and those ladies had left her in the care of a servant.

"How do you like our guest?" I asked, as soon as Madame entered. "Tell me all about her?"

"I like her extremely," answered Madame, "she is, I almost think, the prettiest creature I ever saw; about your age, and so gentle and nice."

"She is absolutely beautiful," threw in Mademoiselle, who had peeped for a moment into the stranger's room.

"And such a sweet voice!" added Madame Perrodon.

"Did you remark a woman in the carriage, after it was set up again, who did not get out," inquired Mademoiselle, "but only looked from the window?"

"No, we had not seen her."

Then she described a hideous black woman, with a sort of colored turban on her head, and who was gazing all the time from the carriage window, nodding and grinning derisively towards the ladies, with gleaming eyes and large white eyeballs, and her teeth set as if in fury.

"Did you remark what an ill-looking pack of men the servants were?" asked Madame.

"Yes," said my father, who had just come in, "ugly, hang-dog looking fellows as ever I beheld in my life. I hope they mayn't rob the poor lady in the forest. They are clever rogues, however; they got everything to rights in a minute."

"I dare say they are worn out with too long traveling," said Madame.

"Besides looking wicked, their faces were so strangely lean, and dark, and sullen. I am very curious, I own; but I dare say the young lady will tell you all about it tomorrow, if she is sufficiently recovered."

"I don't think she will," said my father, with a mysterious smile, and a little nod of his head, as if he knew more about it than he cared to tell us.

This made us all the more inquisitive as to what had passed between him and the lady in the black velvet, in the brief but earnest interview that had immediately preceded her departure.

We were scarcely alone, when I entreated him to tell me. He did not need much pressing.

"There is no particular reason why I should not tell you. She expressed a reluctance to trouble us with the care of her daughter, saying she was in delicate health, and nervous, but not subject to any kind of seizure—she volunteered that—nor to any illusion; being, in fact, perfectly sane."

"How very odd to say all that!" I interpolated. "It was so unnecessary."

"At all events it *was* said," he laughed, "and as you wish to know all that passed, which was indeed very little, I tell you. She then said, 'I am making a long journey of *vital* importance—she emphasized the word—rapid and secret; I shall return for my child in three months; in the meantime, she will be silent as to who we are, whence we come, and whither we are traveling.' That is all she said. She spoke very pure French. When she said the word 'secret,' she paused for a few seconds, looking sternly, her eyes fixed on mine. I fancy she makes a great point of that. You saw how quickly she was gone. I hope I have not done a very foolish thing, in taking charge of the young lady."

For my part, I was delighted. I was longing to see and talk to her; and only waiting till the doctor should give me leave. You, who live in towns, can have no idea how great an event the introduction of a new friend is, in such a solitude as surrounded us.

The doctor did not arrive till nearly one o'clock; but I could no more have gone to my bed and slept, than I could have overtaken, on foot, the carriage in which the princess in black velvet had driven away.

When the physician came down to the drawing room, it was to report very favorably upon his patient. She was now sitting up, her pulse quite regular, apparently perfectly well. She had sustained no injury, and the little shock to her nerves had passed away quite harmlessly. There could be no harm certainly in my seeing her, if we both wished it; and, with this permission I sent, forthwith, to know whether she would allow me to visit her for a few minutes in her room.

The servant returned immediately to say that she desired nothing more.

You may be sure I was not long in availing myself of this permission.

Our visitor lay in one of the handsomest rooms in the schloss. It was, perhaps, a little stately. There was a somber piece of tapestry opposite the foot of the bed, representing Cleopatra with the asps to her bosom; and other solemn classic scenes were displayed, a little faded, upon the other walls. But there was gold carving, and rich and varied color enough in the other decorations of the room, to more than redeem the gloom of the old tapestry.

There were candles at the bedside. She was sitting up; her slender pretty figure enveloped in the soft silk dressing gown, embroidered with flowers, and lined with thick quilted silk, which her mother had thrown over her feet as she lay upon the ground.

What was it that, as I reached the bedside and had just begun my little greeting, struck me dumb in a moment, and made me recoil a step or two from before her? I will tell you.

I saw the very face which had visited me in my childhood at night, which remained so fixed in my memory, and on which I had for so many years so often ruminated with horror, when no one suspected of what I was thinking.

It was pretty, even beautiful; and when I first beheld it, wore the same melancholy expression.

But this almost instantly lighted into a strange fixed smile of recognition.

There was a silence of fully a minute, and then at length she spoke; I could not.

"How wonderful!" she exclaimed. "Twelve years ago, I saw your face in a dream, and it has haunted me ever since."

"Wonderful indeed!" I repeated, overcoming with an effort the horror that had for a time suspended my utterances. "Twelve years ago, in vision or reality, I certainly saw you. I could not forget your face. It has remained before my eyes ever since."

Her smile had softened. Whatever I had fancied strange in it, was gone, and it and her dimpling cheeks were now delightfully pretty and intelligent.

I felt reassured, and continued more in the vein which hospitality indicated, to bid her welcome, and to tell her how much pleasure her accidental arrival had given us all, and especially what a happiness it was to me.

I took her hand as I spoke. I was a little shy, as lonely people are, but the situation made me eloquent, and even bold. She pressed my hand, she laid hers upon it, and her eyes glowed, as, looking hastily into mine, she smiled again, and blushed.

She answered my welcome very prettily. I sat down beside her, still wondering; and she said:

"I must tell you my vision about you; it is so very strange that you and I should have had, each of the other so vivid a dream, that each should have seen, I you and you me, looking as we do now, when of course we both were mere children. I was a child, about six years old, and I awoke from a confused and troubled dream, and found myself in a room, unlike my nursery, wainscoted clumsily in some dark wood, and with cupboards and bedsteads, and chairs, and benches placed about it. The beds were, I thought, all empty, and the room itself without anyone but myself in it; and I, after looking about me for some time, and admiring especially an iron candlestick with two branches, which I should certainly know again, crept under one of the beds to reach the window; but as I got from under the bed, I heard someone crying; and looking up, while I was still upon my knees, I saw you—most assuredly you—as I see you now; a beautiful young lady, with golden hair and large blue eyes, and lips—your lips—you as you are here.

"Your looks won me; I climbed on the bed and put my arms about you, and I think we both fell asleep. I was aroused by a scream; you were sitting up screaming. I was frightened, and slipped down upon the ground, and, it seemed to me, lost consciousness for a moment;

and when I came to myself, I was again in my nursery at home. Your face I have never forgotten since. I could not be misled by mere resemblance. *You are* the lady whom I saw then."

It was now my turn to relate my corresponding vision, which I did, to the undisguised wonder of my new acquaintance.

"I don't know which should be most afraid of the other," she said, again smiling—"If you were less pretty I think I should be very much afraid of you, but being as you are, and you and I both so young, I feel only that I have made your acquaintance twelve years ago, and have already a right to your intimacy; at all events it does seem as if we were destined, from our earliest childhood, to be friends. I wonder whether you feel as strangely drawn towards me as I do to you; I have never had a friend—shall I find one now?" She sighed, and her fine dark eyes gazed passionately on me.

Now the truth is, I felt rather unaccountably towards the beautiful stranger. I did feel, as she said, "drawn towards her," but there was also something of repulsion. In this ambiguous feeling, however, the sense of attraction immensely prevailed. She interested and won me; she was so beautiful and so indescribably engaging.

I perceived now something of languor and exhaustion stealing over her, and hastened to bid her good night.

"The doctor thinks," I added, "that you ought to have a maid to sit up with you tonight; one of ours is waiting, and you will find her a very useful and quiet creature."

"How kind of you, but I could not sleep, I never could with an attendant in the room. I shan't require any assistance—and, shall I confess my weakness, I am haunted with a terror of robbers. Our house was robbed once, and two servants murdered, so I always lock my door. It has become a habit—and you look so kind I know you will forgive me. I see there is a key in the lock."

She held me close in her pretty arms for a moment and whispered in my ear, "Good night, darling, it is very hard to part with you, but good night; tomorrow, but not early, I shall see you again."

She sank back on the pillow with a sigh, and her fine eyes followed me with a fond and melancholy gaze, and she murmured again "Good night, dear friend."

Young people like, and even love, on impulse. I was flattered by the evident, though as yet undeserved, fondness she showed me. I liked the confidence with which she at once received me. She was determined that we should be very near friends.

Next day came and we met again. I was delighted with my companion; that is to say, in many respects.

Her looks lost nothing in daylight—she was certainly the most beautiful creature I had ever seen, and the unpleasant remembrance of the face presented in my early dream, had lost the effect of the first unexpected recognition.

She confessed that she had experienced a similar shock on seeing me, and precisely the same faint antipathy that had mingled with my admiration of her. We now laughed together over our momentary horrors.

CHAPTER IV

Her Habits — A Saunter

I told you that I was charmed with her in most particulars.

There were some that did not please me so well.

She was above the middle height of women. I shall begin by describing her.

She was slender, and wonderfully graceful. Except that her movements were languid—very languid—indeed, there was nothing in her appearance to indicate an invalid. Her complexion was rich and brilliant; her features were small and beautifully formed; her eyes large, dark, and lustrous; her hair was quite wonderful, I never saw hair so magnificently thick and long when it was down about her shoulders; I have often placed my hands under it, and laughed with wonder at its weight. It was exquisitely fine and soft, and in color a rich very dark brown, with something of gold. I loved to let it down, tumbling with its own weight, as, in her room, she lay back in her chair talking in her sweet low voice, I used to fold and braid it, and spread it out and play with it. Heavens! If I had but known all!

I said there were particulars which did not please me. I have told you that her confidence won me the first night I saw her; but I found that she exercised with respect to herself, her mother, her history, everything in fact connected with her life, plans, and people, an ever wakeful reserve. I dare say I was unreasonable, perhaps I was wrong; I dare say I ought to have respected the solemn injunction laid upon my father by the stately lady in black velvet. But curiosity is a restless and unscrupulous passion, and no one girl can endure, with patience, that hers should be baffled by another. What harm could it do anyone to tell me what I so ardently desired to know? Had she no trust in my good sense or honor? Why would she not believe me when I assured her, so solemnly, that I would not divulge one syllable of what she told me to any mortal breathing.

There was a coldness, it seemed to me, beyond her years, in her smiling melancholy persistent refusal to afford me the least ray of light.

I cannot say we quarreled upon this point, for she would not quarrel upon any. It was, of course, very unfair of me to press her, very ill-bred, but I really could not help it; and I might just as well have let it alone.

What she did tell me amounted, in my unconscionable estimation—to nothing.

It was all summed up in three very vague disclosures:

First—Her name was Carmilla.

Second—Her family was very ancient and noble.

Third—Her home lay in the direction of the west. She would not tell me the name of her family, nor their armorial bearings, nor the name of their estate, nor even that of the country they lived in.

You are not to suppose that I worried her incessantly on these subjects. I watched opportunity, and rather insinuated than urged my inquiries. Once or twice, indeed, I did attack her more directly. But no matter what my tactics, utter failure was invariably the result. Reproaches and caresses were all lost upon her. But I must add this, that her evasion was conducted with so pretty a melancholy and deprecation, with so many, and even passionate declarations of her liking for me, and trust in my honor, and with so many promises that I should at last know all, that I could not find it in my heart long to be offended with her.

She used to place her pretty arms about my neck, draw me to her, and laying her cheek to mine, murmur with her lips near my ear, "Dearest, your little heart is wounded; think me not cruel because I obey the irresistible law of my strength and weakness; if your dear heart is wounded, my wild heart bleeds with yours. In the rapture of my enormous humiliation I live in your warm life, and you shall die—die, sweetly die—into mine. I cannot help it; as I draw near to you, you, in your turn, will draw near to others, and learn the rapture of that cruelty, which yet is love; so, for a while, seek to know no more of me and mine, but trust me with all your loving spirit."

And when she had spoken such a rhapsody, she would press me more closely in her trembling embrace, and her lips in soft kisses gently glow upon my cheek.

Her agitations and her language were unintelligible to me.

From these foolish embraces, which were not of very frequent occurrence, I must allow, I used to wish to extricate myself; but my energies seemed to fail me. Her murmured words sounded like a lullaby in my ear, and soothed my resistance into a trance, from which I only seemed to recover myself when she withdrew her arms.

In these mysterious moods I did not like her. I experienced a strange tumultuous excitement that was pleasurable, ever and anon, mingled with a vague sense of fear and disgust. I had no distinct thoughts about her while such scenes lasted, but I was conscious of a love growing into adoration, and also of abhorrence. This I know is paradox, but I can make no other attempt to explain the feeling.

I now write, after an interval of more than ten years, with a trembling hand, with a confused and horrible recollection of certain occurrences and situations, in the ordeal through which I was unconsciously passing; though with a vivid and very sharp remembrance of the main current of my story.

But, I suspect, in all lives there are certain emotional scenes, those in which our passions have been most wildly and terribly roused, that are of all others the most vaguely and dimly remembered.

Sometimes after an hour of apathy, my strange and beautiful companion would take my hand and hold it with a fond pressure, renewed again and again; blushing softly, gazing in my face with languid and burning eyes, and breathing so fast that her dress rose and fell with the tumultuous respiration. It was like the ardor of a lover; it embarrassed me; it was hateful and yet over-powering; and with gloating eyes she drew me to her, and her hot lips traveled along my cheek in kisses; and she would whisper, almost in sobs, "You are mine, you *shall* be mine, you and I are one for ever." Then she had thrown herself back in her chair, with her small hands over her eyes, leaving me trembling.

"Are we related," I used to ask; "what can you mean by all this? I remind you perhaps of someone whom you love; but you must not, I hate it; I don't know you—I don't know myself when you look so and talk so."

She used to sigh at my vehemence, then turn away and drop my hand.

Respecting these very extraordinary manifestations I strove in vain to form any satisfactory theory—I could not refer them to affectation or trick. It was unmistakably the momentary breaking out of suppressed instinct and emotion. Was she, notwithstanding her mother's volunteered denial, subject to brief visitations of insanity; or was there here a disguise and a romance? I had read in old storybooks of such things. What if a boyish lover had found his way into the house, and sought to prosecute his suit in masquerade, with the assistance of a clever old adventuress. But there were many things against this hypothesis, highly interesting as it was to my vanity.

I could boast of no little attentions such as masculine gallantry delights to offer. Between these passionate moments there were long intervals of commonplace, of gaiety, of brooding melancholy, during which, except that I detected her eyes so full of melancholy fire, following me, at times I might have been as nothing to her. Except in these brief periods of mysterious excitement her ways were girlish; and there was always a languor about her, quite incompatible with a masculine system in a state of health.

In some respects her habits were odd. Perhaps not so singular in the opinion of a town lady like you, as they appeared to us rustic people. She used to come down very late, generally not till one o'clock, she would then take a cup of chocolate, but eat nothing; we then went out for a walk, which was a mere saunter, and she seemed, almost immediately, exhausted, and either returned to the schloss or sat on one of the benches that were placed, here and there, among the trees. This was a bodily languor in which her mind did not sympathize. She was always an animated talker, and very intelligent.

She sometimes alluded for a moment to her own home, or mentioned an adventure or situation, or an early recollection, which indicated a people of strange manners, and described customs of which we knew nothing. I gathered from these chance hints that her native country was much more remote than I had at first fancied.

As we sat thus one afternoon under the trees a funeral passed us by. It was that of a pretty young girl, whom I had often seen, the daughter of one of the rangers of the forest. The poor man was walking behind the coffin of his darling; she was his only child, and he looked quite heartbroken.

Peasants walking two-and-two came behind, they were singing a funeral hymn.

I rose to mark my respect as they passed, and joined in the hymn they were very sweetly singing.

My companion shook me a little roughly, and I turned surprised.

She said brusquely, "Don't you perceive how discordant that is?"

"I think it very sweet, on the contrary," I answered, vexed at the interruption, and very uncomfortable, lest the people who composed the little procession should observe and resent what was passing.

I resumed, therefore, instantly, and was again interrupted. "You pierce my ears," said Carmilla, almost angrily, and stopping her ears with her tiny fingers. "Besides, how can you tell that your religion and mine are the same; your forms wound me, and I hate funerals. What a fuss! Why you must die- *everyone* must die; and all are happier when they do. Come home."

"My father has gone on with the clergyman to the churchyard. I thought you knew she was to be buried today."

"*She*? I don't trouble my head about peasants. I don't know who she is," answered Carmilla, with a flash from her fine eyes.

"She is the poor girl who fancied she saw a ghost a fortnight ago, and has been dying ever since, till yesterday, when she expired."

"Tell me nothing about ghosts. I shan't sleep tonight if you do."

"I hope there is no plague or fever coming; all this looks very like it," I continued. "The swineherd's young wife died only a week ago, and she thought something seized her by the throat as she lay in her bed, and nearly strangled her. Papa says such horrible fancies do accompany some forms of fever. She was quite well the day before. She sank afterwards, and died before a week."

"Well, *her* funeral is over, I hope, and *her* hymn sung; and our ears shan't be tortured with that discord and jargon. It has made me nervous. Sit down here, beside me; sit close; hold my hand; press it hard-hard-harder."

We had moved a little back, and had come to another seat.

She sat down. Her face underwent a change that alarmed and even terrified me for a moment. It darkened, and became horribly livid; her teeth and hands were clenched, and she frowned and compressed her lips, while she stared down upon the ground at her feet, and trembled all over with a continued shudder as irrepressible as ague. All her energies seemed strained to suppress a fit, with which she was then breathlessly tugging; and at length a low convulsive cry of suffering broke from her, and gradually the hysteria subsided. "There! That comes of strangling people with hymns!" she said at last. "Hold me, hold me still. It is passing away."

And so gradually it did; and perhaps to dissipate the somber impression which the spectacle had left upon me, she became unusually animated and chatty; and so we got home.

This was the first time I had seen her exhibit any definable symptoms of that delicacy of health which her mother had spoken of. It was the first time, also, I had seen her exhibit anything like temper.

Both passed away like a summer cloud; and never but once afterwards did I witness on her part a momentary sign of anger. I will tell you how it happened.

She and I were looking out of one of the long drawing room windows, when there entered the courtyard, over the drawbridge, a figure of a wanderer whom I knew very well. He used to visit the schloss generally twice a year.

It was the figure of a hunchback, with the sharp lean features that generally accompany deformity. He wore a pointed black beard, and he was smiling from ear to ear, showing his white fangs. He was dressed in buff, black, and scarlet, and crossed with more straps and belts than I could count, from which hung all manner of things.

Behind, he carried a magic lantern, and two boxes, which I well knew, in one of which was a salamander, and in the other a mandrake. These monsters used to make my father laugh. They were compounded of parts of monkeys, parrots, squirrels, fish, and hedgehogs, dried and stitched together with great neatness and startling effect. He had a fiddle, a box of conjuring apparatus, a pair of foils and masks attached to his belt, several other mysterious cases dangling about him, and a black staff with copper ferrules in his hand. His companion was a rough spare dog, that followed at his heels, but stopped short, suspiciously at the drawbridge, and in a little while began to howl dismally.

In the meantime, the mountebank, standing in the midst of the courtyard, raised his grotesque hat, and made us a very ceremonious bow, paying his compliments very volubly in execrable French, and German not much better.

Then, disengaging his fiddle, he began to scrape a lively air to which he sang with a merry discord, dancing with ludicrous airs and activity, that made me laugh, in spite of the dog's howling.

Then he advanced to the window with many smiles and salutations, and his hat in his left hand, his fiddle under his arm, and with a fluency that never took breath, he gabbled a long advertisement of all his accomplishments, and the resources of the various arts which he placed at our service, and the curiosities and entertainments which it was in his power, at our bidding, to display.

"Will your ladyships be pleased to buy an amulet against the oupire, which is going like the wolf, I hear, through these woods," he said dropping his hat on the pavement. "They are dying of it right and left and here is a charm that never fails; only pinned to the pillow, and you may laugh in his face."

These charms consisted of oblong slips of vellum, with cabalistic ciphers and diagrams upon them.

Carmilla instantly purchased one, and so did I.

He was looking up, and we were smiling down upon him, amused; at least, I can answer for myself. His piercing black eye, as he looked up in our faces, seemed to detect something that fixed for a moment his curiosity.

In an instant he unrolled a leather case, full of all manner of odd little steel instruments.

"See here, my lady," he said, displaying it, and addressing me, "I profess, among other things less useful, the art of dentistry. Plague take the dog!" he interpolated. "Silence, beast! He howls so that your ladyships can scarcely hear a word. Your noble friend, the young lady at your right, has the sharpest tooth,— long, thin, pointed, like an awl, like a needle; ha, ha! With my sharp and long sight, as I look up, I have seen it distinctly; now if it happens to hurt the young lady, and I think it must, here am I, here are my file, my punch, my nippers; I will make it round and blunt, if her ladyship pleases; no longer the tooth of a fish, but of a beautiful young lady as she is. Hey? Is the young lady displeased? Have I been too bold? Have I offended her?"

The young lady, indeed, looked very angry as she drew back from the window.

"How dares that mountebank insult us so? Where is your father? I shall demand redress from him. My father would have had the wretch tied up to the pump, and flogged with a cart whip, and burnt to the bones with the cattle brand!"

She retired from the window a step or two, and sat down, and had hardly lost sight of the offender, when her wrath subsided as suddenly as it had risen, and she gradually recovered her usual tone, and seemed to forget the little hunchback and his follies.

My father was out of spirits that evening. On coming in he told us that there had been another case very similar to the two fatal ones which had lately occurred. The sister of a young peasant on his estate, only a mile away, was very ill, had been, as she described it, attacked very nearly in the same way, and was now slowly but steadily sinking.

"All this," said my father, "is strictly referable to natural causes. These poor people infect one another with their superstitions, and so repeat in imagination the images of terror that have infested their neighbors."

"But that very circumstance frightens one horribly," said Carmilla.

"How so?" inquired my father.

"I am so afraid of fancying I see such things; I think it would be as bad as reality."

"We are in God's hands: nothing can happen without his permission, and all will end well for those who love him. He is our faithful creator; He has made us all, and will take care of us."

"Creator! *Nature!*" said the young lady in answer to my gentle father. "And this disease that invades the country is natural. Nature. All things proceed from Nature—don't they? All things in the heaven, in the earth, and under the earth, act and live as Nature ordains? I think so."

"The doctor said he would come here today," said my father, after a silence. "I want to know what he thinks about it, and what he thinks we had better do."

"Doctors never did me any good," said Carmilla.

"Then you have been ill?" I asked.

"More ill than ever you were," she answered.

"Long ago?"

"Yes, a long time. I suffered from this very illness; but I forget all but my pain and weakness, and they were not so bad as are suffered in other diseases."

"You were very young then?"

"I dare say, let us talk no more of it. You would not wound a friend?"

She looked languidly in my eyes, and passed her arm round my waist lovingly, and led me out of the room. My father was busy over some papers near the window.

"Why does your papa like to frighten us?" said the pretty girl with a sigh and a little shudder.

"He doesn't, dear Carmilla, it is the very furthest thing from his mind."

"Are you afraid, dearest?"

"I should be very much if I fancied there was any real danger of my being attacked as those poor people were."

"You are afraid to die?"

"Yes, every one is."

"But to die as lovers may—to die together, so that they may live together.

"Girls are caterpillars while they live in the world, to be finally butterflies when the summer comes; but in the meantime there are grubs and larvae, don't you see—each with their peculiar propensities, necessities and structure. So says Monsieur Buffon, in his big book, in the next room."

Later in the day the doctor came, and was closeted with papa for some time.

He was a skillful man, of sixty and upwards, he wore powder, and shaved his pale face as smooth as a pumpkin. He and papa emerged from the room together, and I heard papa laugh, and say as they came out:

"Well, I do wonder at a wise man like you. What do you say to hippogriffs and dragons?"

The doctor was smiling, and made answer, shaking his head—

"Nevertheless life and death are mysterious states, and we know little of the resources of either."

And so they walked on, and I heard no more. I did not then know what the doctor had been broaching, but I think I guess it now.

CHAPTER V

A Wonderful Likeness

This evening there arrived from Gratz the grave, dark-faced son of the picture cleaner, with a horse and cart laden with two large packing cases, having many pictures in each. It was a journey of ten leagues, and whenever a messenger arrived at the schloss from our little capital of Gratz, we used to crowd about him in the hall, to hear the news.

This arrival created in our secluded quarters quite a sensation. The cases remained in the hall, and the messenger was taken charge of by the servants till he had eaten his supper. Then with assistants, and armed with hammer, ripping chisel, and turnscrew, he met us in the hall, where we had assembled to witness the unpacking of the cases.

Carmilla sat looking listlessly on, while one after the other the old pictures, nearly all portraits, which had undergone the process of renovation, were brought to light. My mother was of an old Hungarian family, and most of these pictures, which were about to be restored to their places, had come to us through her.

My father had a list in his hand, from which he read, as the artist rummaged out the corresponding numbers. I don't know that the pictures were very good, but they were, undoubtedly, very old, and some of them very curious also. They had, for the most part, the merit of being now seen by me, I may say, for the first time; for the smoke and dust of time had all but obliterated them.

"There is a picture that I have not seen yet," said my father. "In one corner, at the top of it, is the name, as well as I could read, 'Marcia Karnstein,' and the date '1698'; and I am curious to see how it has turned out."

I remembered it; it was a small picture, about a foot and a half high, and nearly square, without a frame; but it was so blackened by age that I could not make it out.

The artist now produced it, with evident pride. It was quite beautiful; it was startling; it seemed to live. It was the effigy of Carmilla!

"Carmilla, dear, here is an absolute miracle. Here you are, living, smiling, ready to speak, in this picture. Isn't it beautiful, Papa? And see, even the little mole on her throat."

My father laughed, and said "Certainly it is a wonderful likeness," but he looked away, and to my surprise seemed but little struck by it, and went on talking to the picture cleaner, who was also something of an artist, and discoursed with intelligence about the portraits or other works, which his art had just brought into light and color, while I was more and more lost in wonder the more I looked at the picture.

"Will you let me hang this picture in my room, papa?" I asked.

"Certainly, dear," said he, smiling, "I'm very glad you think it so like. It must be prettier even than I thought it, if it is."

The young lady did not acknowledge this pretty speech, did not seem to hear it. She was leaning back in her seat, her fine eyes under their long lashes gazing on me in contemplation, and she smiled in a kind of rapture.

"And now you can read quite plainly the name that is written in the corner.

It is not Marcia; it looks as if it was done in gold. The name is Mircalla, Countess Karnstein, and this is a little coronet over and underneath A.D. 1698. I am descended from the Karnsteins; that is, mamma was."

"Ah!" said the lady, languidly, "so am I, I think, a very long descent, very ancient. Are there any Karnsteins living now?"

"None who bear the name, I believe. The family were ruined, I believe, in some civil wars, long ago, but the ruins of the castle are only about three miles away."

"How interesting!" she said, languidly. "But see what beautiful moonlight!" She glanced through the hall door, which stood a little open. "Suppose you take a little ramble round the court, and look down at the road and river."

"It is so like the night you came to us," I said.

She sighed; smiling.

She rose, and each with her arm about the other's waist, we walked out upon the pavement.

In silence, slowly we walked down to the drawbridge, where the beautiful landscape opened before us.

"And so you were thinking of the night I came here?" she almost whispered.

"Are you glad I came?"

"Delighted, dear Carmilla," I answered.

"And you asked for the picture you think like me, to hang in your room," she murmured with a sigh, as she drew her arm closer about my waist, and let her pretty head sink upon my shoulder. "How romantic you are, Carmilla," I said. "Whenever you tell me your story, it will be made up chiefly of some one great romance."

She kissed me silently.

"I am sure, Carmilla, you have been in love; that there is, at this moment, an affair of the heart going on."

"I have been in love with no one, and never shall," she whispered, "unless it should be with you."

How beautiful she looked in the moonlight!

Shy and strange was the look with which she quickly hid her face in my neck and hair, with tumultuous sighs, that seemed almost to sob, and pressed in mine a hand that trembled.

Her soft cheek was glowing against mine. "Darling, darling," she murmured, "I live in you; and you would die for me, I love you so."

I started from her. She was gazing on me with eyes from which all fire, all meaning had flown, and a face colorless and apathetic.

"Is there a chill in the air, dear?" she said drowsily. "I almost shiver; have I been dreaming? Let us come in. Come; come; come in."

"You look ill, Carmilla; a little faint. You certainly must take some wine," I said.

"Yes. I will. I'm better now. I shall be quite well in a few minutes. Yes, do give me a little wine," answered Carmilla, as we approached the door.

"Let us look again for a moment; it is the last time, perhaps, I shall see the moonlight with you."

"How do you feel now, dear Carmilla? Are you really better?" I asked.

I was beginning to take alarm, lest she should have been stricken with the strange epidemic that they said had invaded the country about us.

"Papa would be grieved beyond measure," I added, "if he thought you were ever so little ill, without immediately letting us know. We have a very skillful doctor near us, the physician who was with papa today."

"I'm sure he is. I know how kind you all are; but, dear child, I am quite well again. There is nothing ever wrong with me, but a little weakness. "People say I am languid; I am incapable of exertion; I can scarcely walk as far as a child of three years old: and every now and then the little strength I have falters, and I become as you have just seen me. But after all I am very easily set up again; in a moment I am perfectly myself. See how I have recovered."

So, indeed, she had; and she and I talked a great deal, and very animated she was; and the remainder of that evening passed without any recurrence of what I called her infatuations. I mean her crazy talk and looks, which embarrassed, and even frightened me.

But there occurred that night an event which gave my thoughts quite a new turn, and seemed to startle even Carmilla's languid nature into momentary energy.

CHAPTER VI

A Very Strange Agony

When we got into the drawing room, and had sat down to our coffee and chocolate, although Carmilla did not take any, she seemed quite herself again, and Madame, and Mademoiselle De Lafontaine, joined us, and made a little card party, in the course of which papa came in for what he called his "dish of tea."

When the game was over he sat down beside Carmilla on the sofa, and asked her, a little anxiously, whether she had heard from her mother since her arrival.

She answered "No."

He then asked whether she knew where a letter would reach her at present.

"I cannot tell," she answered ambiguously, "but I have been thinking of leaving you; you have been already too hospitable and too kind to me. I have given you an infinity of trouble, and I should wish to take a carriage tomorrow, and post in pursuit of her; I know where I shall ultimately find her, although I dare not yet tell you."

"But you must not dream of any such thing," exclaimed my father, to my great relief. "We can't afford to lose you so, and I won't consent to your leaving us, except under the care of your mother, who was so good as to consent to your remaining with us till she should herself return. I should be quite happy if I knew that you heard from her: but this evening the accounts of the progress of the mysterious disease that has invaded our neighborhood, grow even more alarming; and my beautiful guest, I do feel the responsibility, unaided by advice from your mother, very much. But I shall do my best; and one thing is certain, that you must not think of leaving us without her distinct direction to that effect. We should suffer too much in parting from you to consent to it easily."

"Thank you, sir, a thousand times for your hospitality," she answered, smiling bashfully. "You have all been too kind to me; I have seldom been so happy in all my life before, as in your beautiful chateau, under your care, and in the society of your dear daughter."

So he gallantly, in his old-fashioned way, kissed her hand, smiling and pleased at her little speech.

I accompanied Carmilla as usual to her room, and sat and chatted with her while she was preparing for bed.

"Do you think," I said at length, "that you will ever confide fully in me?"

She turned round smiling, but made no answer, only continued to smile on me.

"You won't answer that?" I said. "You can't answer pleasantly; I ought not to have asked you."

"You were quite right to ask me that, or anything. You do not know how dear you are to me, or you could not think any confidence too great to look for. But I am under vows, no nun half so awfully, and I dare not tell my story yet, even to you. The time is very near when you shall know everything. You will think me cruel, very selfish, but love is always selfish; the more ardent the more selfish. How jealous I am you cannot know. You must come with me, loving me, to death; or else hate me and still come with me, and *hating* me through death and after. There is no such word as indifference in my apathetic nature."

"Now, Carmilla, you are going to talk your wild nonsense again," I said hastily.

"Not I, silly little fool as I am, and full of whims and fancies; for your sake I'll talk like a sage. Were you ever at a ball?"

"No; how you do run on. What is it like? How charming it must be."

"I almost forget, it is years ago."

I laughed.

"You are not so old. Your first ball can hardly be forgotten yet."

"I remember everything about it—with an effort. I see it all, as divers see what is going on above them, through a medium, dense, rippling, but transparent. There occurred that night what has confused the picture, and made its colours faint. I was all but assassinated in my bed, wounded here," she touched her breast, "and never was the same since."

"Were you near dying?"

"Yes, very—a cruel love—strange love, that would have taken my life. Love will have its sacrifices. No sacrifice without blood. Let us go to sleep now; I feel so lazy. How can I get up just now and lock my door?"

She was lying with her tiny hands buried in her rich wavy hair, under her cheek, her little head upon the pillow, and her glittering eyes followed me wherever I moved, with a kind of shy smile that I could not decipher.

I bid her good night, and crept from the room with an uncomfortable sensation.

I often wondered whether our pretty guest ever said her prayers. I certainly had never seen her upon her knees. In the morning she never came down until long after our family prayers were over, and at night she never left the drawing room to attend our brief evening prayers in the hall.

If it had not been that it had casually come out in one of our careless talks that she had been baptized, I should have doubted her being a Christian. Religion was a subject on which I had never heard her speak a word. If I had known the world better, this particular neglect or antipathy would not have so much surprised me.

The precautions of nervous people are infectious, and persons of a like temperament are pretty sure, after a time, to imitate them. I had adopted Carmilla's habit of locking her bedroom door, having taken into my head all her whimsical alarms about midnight invaders and prowling assassins. I had also adopted her precaution of making a brief search through her room, to satisfy herself that no lurking assassin or robber was "ensconced."

These wise measures taken, I got into my bed and fell asleep. A light was burning in my room. This was an old habit, of very early date, and which nothing could have tempted me to dispense with.

Thus fortified I might take my rest in peace. But dreams come through stone walls, light up dark rooms, or darken light ones, and their persons make their exits and their entrances as they please, and laugh at locksmiths.

I had a dream that night that was the beginning of a very strange agony.

I cannot call it a nightmare, for I was quite conscious of being asleep.

But I was equally conscious of being in my room, and lying in bed, precisely as I actually was. I saw, or fancied I saw, the room and its furniture just as I had seen it last, except that it was very dark, and I saw something moving round the foot of the bed, which at first I could not accurately distinguish. But I soon saw that it was a sooty-black animal that resembled a monstrous cat. It appeared to me about four or five feet long for it measured fully the length of the hearthrug as it passed over it; and it continued to-ing and fro-ing with the lithe, sinister restlessness of a beast in a cage. I could not cry out, although as you may suppose, I was terrified. Its pace was growing faster, and the room rapidly darker and darker, and at length so dark that I could no longer see anything of it but its eyes. I felt it spring lightly on the bed. The two broad eyes approached my face, and suddenly I felt a stinging pain as if two large needles darted, an inch or two apart, deep into my breast. I waked with a scream. The room was lighted by the candle that burnt there all through the night, and I saw a female figure standing at the foot of the bed, a little at the right side. It was in a dark loose dress, and its hair was down and covered its shoulders. A block of stone could not have been more still. There was not the slightest stir of respiration. As I stared at it, the figure appeared to have changed its place, and was now nearer the door; then, close to it, the door opened, and it passed out.

I was now relieved, and able to breathe and move. My first thought was that Carmilla had been playing me a trick, and that I had forgotten to secure my door. I hastened to it, and found it locked as usual on the inside. I was afraid to open it—I was horrified. I sprang into my bed and covered my head up in the bedclothes, and lay there more dead than alive till morning.

CHAPTER VII

Descending

It would be vain my attempting to tell you the horror with which, even now, I recall the occurrence of that night. It was no such transitory terror as a dream leaves behind it. It seemed to deepen by time, and communicated itself to the room and the very furniture that had encompassed the apparition.

I could not bear next day to be alone for a moment. I should have told papa, but for two opposite reasons. At one time I thought he would laugh at my story, and I could not bear its being treated as a jest; and at another I thought he might fancy that I had been attacked by the mysterious complaint which had invaded our neighborhood. I had myself no misgiving of the kind, and as he had been rather an invalid for some time, I was afraid of alarming him.

I was comfortable enough with my good-natured companions, Madame Perrodon, and the vivacious Mademoiselle Lafontaine. They both perceived that I was out of spirits and nervous, and at length I told them what lay so heavy at my heart.

Mademoiselle laughed, but I fancied that Madame Perrodon looked anxious.

"By-the-by," said Mademoiselle, laughing, "the long lime tree walk, behind Carmilla's bedroom window, is haunted!"

"Nonsense!" exclaimed Madame, who probably thought the theme rather inopportune, "and who tells that story, my dear?"

"Martin says that he came up twice, when the old yard gate was being repaired, before sunrise, and twice saw the same female figure walking down the lime tree avenue."

"So he well might, as long as there are cows to milk in the river fields," said Madame.

"I daresay; but Martin chooses to be frightened, and never did I see fool more frightened."

"You must not say a word about it to Carmilla, because she can see down that walk from her room window," I interposed, "and she is, if possible, a greater coward than I."

Carmilla came down rather later than usual that day.

"I was so frightened last night," she said, so soon as were together, "and I am sure I should have seen something dreadful if it had not been for that charm I bought from the poor little hunchback whom I called such hard names. I had a dream of something black coming round my bed, and I awoke in a perfect horror, and I really thought, for some seconds, I saw a dark figure near the chimney-piece, but I felt under my pillow for my charm, and the moment my fingers touched it, the figure disappeared, and I felt quite certain, only that

GLENN CHADBOURNE

I had it by me, that something frightful would have made its appearance, and, perhaps, throttled me, as it did those poor people we heard of.

"Well, listen to me," I began, and recounted my adventure, at the recital of which she appeared horrified.

"And had you the charm near you?" she asked, earnestly.

"No, I had dropped it into a china vase in the drawing room, but I shall certainly take it with me tonight, as you have so much faith in it."

At this distance of time I cannot tell you, or even understand, how I overcame my horror so effectually as to lie alone in my room that night. I remember distinctly that I pinned the charm to my pillow. I fell asleep almost immediately, and slept even more soundly than usual all night.

Next night I passed as well. My sleep was delightfully deep and dreamless.

But I wakened with a sense of lassitude and melancholy, which, however, did not exceed a degree that was almost luxurious.

"Well, I told you so," said Carmilla, when I described my quiet sleep, "I had such delightful sleep myself last night; I pinned the charm to the breast of my nightdress. It was too far away the night before. I am quite sure it was all fancy, except the dreams. I used to think that evil spirits made dreams, but our doctor told me it is no such thing. Only a fever passing by, or some other malady, as they often do, he said, knocks at the door, and not being able to get in, passes on, with that alarm."

"And what do you think the charm is?" said I.

"It has been fumigated or immersed in some drug, and is an antidote against the malaria," she answered.

"Then it acts only on the body?"

"Certainly; you don't suppose that evil spirits are frightened by bits of ribbon, or the perfumes of a druggist's shop? No, these complaints, wandering in the air, begin by trying the nerves, and so infect the brain, but before they can seize upon you, the antidote repels them. That I am sure is what the charm has done for us. It is nothing magical, it is simply natural."

I should have been happier if I could have quite agreed with Carmilla, but I did my best, and the impression was a little losing its force.

For some nights I slept profoundly; but still every morning I felt the same lassitude, and a languor weighed upon me all day. I felt myself a changed girl. A strange melancholy was stealing over me, a melancholy that I would not have interrupted. Dim thoughts of death began to open, and an idea that I was slowly sinking took gentle, and, somehow, not unwelcome, possession of me. If it was sad, the tone of mind which this induced was also sweet.

Whatever it might be, my soul acquiesced in it.

I would not admit that I was ill, I would not consent to tell my papa, or to have the doctor sent for.

Carmilla became more devoted to me than ever, and her strange paroxysms of languid adoration more frequent. She used to gloat on me with increasing ardor the more my strength and spirits waned. This always shocked me like a momentary glare of insanity.

Without knowing it, I was now in a pretty advanced stage of the strangest illness under which mortal ever suffered. There was an unaccountable fascination in its earlier symptoms that more than reconciled me to the incapacitating effect of that stage of the malady. This fascination increased for a time, until it reached a certain point, when gradually a sense of the horrible mingled itself with it, deepening, as you shall hear, until it discolored and perverted the whole state of my life.

The first change I experienced was rather agreeable. It was very near the turning point from which began the descent of Avernus.

Certain vague and strange sensations visited me in my sleep. The prevailing one was of that pleasant, peculiar cold thrill which we feel in bathing, when we move against the current of a river. This was soon accompanied by dreams that seemed interminable, and were so vague that I could never recollect their scenery and persons, or any one connected portion of their action. But they left an awful impression, and a sense of exhaustion, as if I had passed through a long period of great mental exertion and danger.

After all these dreams there remained on waking a remembrance of having been in a place very nearly dark, and of having spoken to people whom I could not see; and especially of one clear voice, of a female's, very deep, that spoke as if at a distance, slowly, and producing always the same sensation of indescribable solemnity and fear. Sometimes there came a sensation as if a hand was drawn softly along my cheek and neck. Sometimes it was as if warm lips kissed me, and longer and longer and more lovingly as they reached my throat, but there the caress fixed itself. My heart beat faster, my breathing rose and fell rapidly and full drawn; a sobbing, that rose into a sense of strangulation, supervened, and turned into a dreadful convulsion, in which my senses left me and I became unconscious.

It was now three weeks since the commencement of this unaccountable state.

My sufferings had, during the last week, told upon my appearance. I had grown pale, my eyes were dilated and darkened underneath, and the languor which I had long felt began to display itself in my countenance.

My father asked me often whether I was ill; but, with an obstinacy which now seems to me unaccountable, I persisted in assuring him that I was quite well.

In a sense this was true. I had no pain, I could complain of no bodily derangement. My complaint seemed to be one of the imagination, or the nerves, and, horrible as my sufferings were, I kept them, with a morbid reserve, very nearly to myself.

It could not be that terrible complaint which the peasants called the oupire, for I had now been suffering for three weeks, and they were seldom ill for much more than three days, when death put an end to their miseries.

Carmilla complained of dreams and feverish sensations, but by no means of so alarming a kind as mine. I say that mine were extremely alarming. Had I been capable of comprehending my condition, I would have invoked aid and advice on my knees. The narcotic of an unsuspected influence was acting upon me, and my perceptions were benumbed.

I am going to tell you now of a dream that led immediately to an odd discovery.

One night, instead of the voice I was accustomed to hear in the dark, I heard one, sweet and tender, and at the same time terrible, which said,

"Your mother warns you to beware of the assassin."
At the same time a light unexpectedly sprang up, and I saw Carmilla, standing, near the foot of my bed, in her

white nightdress, bathed, from her chin to her feet, in one great stain of blood.

I wakened with a shriek, possessed with the one idea that Carmilla was being murdered. I remember springing from my bed, and my next recollection is that of standing on the lobby, crying for help.

Madame and Mademoiselle came scurrying out of their rooms in alarm; a lamp burned always on the lobby, and seeing me, they soon learned the cause of my terror.

I insisted on our knocking at Carmilla's door. Our knocking was unanswered.

It soon became a pounding and an uproar. We shrieked her name, but all was vain.

We all grew frightened, for the door was locked. We hurried back, in panic, to my room. There we rang the bell long and furiously. If my father's room had been at that side of the house, we would have called him up at once to our aid. But, alas! he was quite out of hearing, and to reach him involved an excursion for which we none of us had courage.

Servants, however, soon came running up the stairs; I had got on my dressing gown and slippers meanwhile, and my companions were already similarly furnished. Recognizing the voices of the servants on the lobby, we sallied out together; and having renewed, as fruitlessly, our summons at Carmilla's door, I ordered the men to force the lock. They did so, and we stood, holding our lights aloft, in the doorway, and so stared into the room.

We called her by name; but there was still no reply. We looked round the room. Everything was undisturbed. It was exactly in the state in which I had left it on bidding her good night. But Carmilla was gone.

CHAPTER VIII

Search

At sight of the room, perfectly undisturbed except for our violent entrance, we began to cool a little, and soon recovered our senses sufficiently to dismiss the men. It had struck Mademoiselle that possibly Carmilla had been wakened by the uproar at her door, and in her first panic had jumped from her bed, and hid herself in a press, or behind a curtain, from which she could not, of course, emerge until the majordomo and his myrmidons had withdrawn. We now recommenced our search, and began to call her name again.

It was all to no purpose. Our perplexity and agitation increased. We examined the windows, but they were secured. I implored of Carmilla, if she had concealed herself, to play this cruel trick no longer—to come out and to end our anxieties. It was all useless. I was by this time convinced that she was not in the room, nor in the dressing room, the door of which was still locked on this side. She could not have passed it. I was utterly puzzled. Had Carmilla discovered one of those secret passages which the old housekeeper said were known to exist in the schloss, although the tradition of their exact situation had been lost? A little time would, no doubt, explain all—utterly perplexed as, for the present, we were.

It was past four o'clock, and I preferred passing the remaining hours of darkness in Madame's room. Daylight brought no solution of the difficulty. The whole household, with my father at its head, was in a state of agitation next morning. Every part of the chateau was searched. The grounds were explored. No trace of the missing lady could be discovered. The stream was about to be dragged; my father was in distraction; what a tale to have to tell the poor girl's mother on her return. I, too, was almost beside myself, though my grief was quite of a different kind.

The morning was passed in alarm and excitement. It was now one o'clock, and still no tidings. I ran up to Carmilla's room, and found her standing at her dressing table. I was astounded. I could not believe my eyes. She beckoned me to her with her pretty finger, in silence. Her face expressed extreme fear.

I ran to her in an ecstasy of joy; I kissed and embraced her again and again. I ran to the bell and rang it vehemently, to bring others to the spot who might at once relieve my father's anxiety.

"Dear Carmilla, what has become of you all this time? We have been in agonies of anxiety about you," I exclaimed. "Where have you been? How did you come back?"

"Last night has been a night of wonders," she said.

"For mercy's sake, explain all you can."

"It was past two last night," she said, "when I went to sleep as usual in my bed, with my doors locked, that of the dressing room, and that opening upon the gallery. My sleep was uninterrupted, and, so far as I know, dreamless; but I woke just now on the sofa in the dressing room there, and I found the door between the rooms open, and the other door forced. How could all this have happened without my being wakened? It must have been accompanied with a great deal of noise, and I am particularly easily wakened; and how could I have been carried out of my bed without my sleep having been interrupted, I whom the slightest stir startles?"

By this time, Madame, Mademoiselle, my father, and a number of the servants were in the room. Carmilla was, of course, overwhelmed with inquiries, congratulations, and welcomes. She had but one story to tell, and seemed the least able of all the party to suggest any way of accounting for what had happened.

My father took a turn up and down the room, thinking. I saw Carmilla's eye follow him for a moment with a sly, dark glance.

When my father had sent the servants away, Mademoiselle having gone in search of a little bottle of valerian and salvolatile, and there being no one now in the room with Carmilla, except my father, Madame, and myself, he came to her thoughtfully, took her hand very kindly, led her to the sofa, and sat down beside her.

"Will you forgive me, my dear, if I risk a conjecture, and ask a question?"

"Who can have a better right?" she said. "Ask what you please, and I will tell you everything. But my story is simply one of bewilderment and darkness. I know absolutely nothing. Put any question you please, but you know, of course, the limitations mamma has placed me under."

"Perfectly, my dear child. I need not approach the topics on which she desires our silence. Now, the marvel of last night consists in your having been removed from your bed and your room, without being wakened, and this removal having occurred apparently while the windows were still secured, and the two doors locked upon the inside. I will tell you my theory and ask you a question."

Carmilla was leaning on her hand dejectedly; Madame and I were listening breathlessly.

"Now, my question is this. Have you ever been suspected of walking in your sleep?"

"Never, since I was very young indeed."

"But you did walk in your sleep when you were young?"

"Yes; I know I did. I have been told so often by my old nurse."

My father smiled and nodded.

"Well, what has happened is this. You got up in your sleep, unlocked the door, not leaving the key, as usual, in the lock, but taking it out and locking it on the outside; you again took the key out, and carried it away with you to some one of the five-and-twenty rooms on this floor, or perhaps upstairs or downstairs. There are so many rooms and closets, so much heavy furniture, and such accumulations of lumber, that it would require a week to search this old house thoroughly. Do you see, now, what I mean?"

"I do, but not all," she answered.

"And how, papa, do you account for her finding herself on the sofa in the dressing room, which we had searched so carefully?"

"She came there after you had searched it, still in her sleep, and at last awoke spontaneously, and was as much surprised to find herself where she was as any one else. I wish all mysteries were as easily and innocently explained as yours, Carmilla," he said, laughing. "And so we may congratulate ourselves on the certainty that the most natural explanation of the occurrence is one that involves no drugging, no tampering with locks, no burglars, or poisoners, or witches—nothing that need alarm Carmilla, or anyone else, for our safety."

Carmilla was looking charmingly. Nothing could be more beautiful than her tints. Her beauty was, I think, enhanced by that graceful languor that was peculiar to her. I think my father was silently contrasting her looks with mine, for he said:

"I wish my poor Laura was looking more like herself"; and he sighed.

So our alarms were happily ended, and Carmilla restored to her friends.

CHAPTER IX

The Doctor

As Carmilla would not hear of an attendant sleeping in her room, my father arranged that a servant should sleep outside her door, so that she would not attempt to make another such excursion without being arrested at her own door.

That night passed quietly; and next morning early, the doctor, whom my father had sent for without telling me a word about it, arrived to see me.

Madame accompanied me to the library; and there the grave little doctor, with white hair and spectacles, whom I mentioned before, was waiting to receive me.

I told him my story, and as I proceeded he grew graver and graver.

We were standing, he and I, in the recess of one of the windows, facing one another. When my statement was over, he leaned with his shoulders against the wall, and with his eyes fixed on me earnestly, with an interest in which was a dash of horror.

After a minute's reflection, he asked Madame if he could see my father.

He was sent for accordingly, and as he entered, smiling, he said:

"I dare say, doctor, you are going to tell me that I am an old fool for having brought you here; I hope I am."

But his smile faded into shadow as the doctor, with a very grave face, beckoned him to him.

He and the doctor talked for some time in the same recess where I had just conferred with the physician. It seemed an earnest and argumentative conversation. The room is very large, and I and Madame stood together, burning with curiosity, at the farther end. Not a word could we hear, however, for they spoke in a very low tone, and the deep recess of the window quite concealed the doctor from view, and very nearly my father, whose foot, arm, and shoulder only could we see; and the voices were, I suppose, all the less audible for the sort of closet which the thick wall and window formed.

After a time my father's face looked into the room; it was pale, thoughtful, and, I fancied, agitated.

"Laura, dear, come here for a moment. Madame, we shan't trouble you, the doctor says, at present."

Accordingly I approached, for the first time a little alarmed; for, although I felt very weak, I did not feel ill; and strength, one always fancies, is a thing that may be picked up when we please.

My father held out his hand to me, as I drew near, but he was looking at the doctor, and he said:

"It certainly is very odd; I don't understand it quite. Laura, come here, dear; now attend to Doctor Spielsberg, and recollect yourself."

"You mentioned a sensation like that of two needles piercing the skin, somewhere about your neck, on the night when you experienced your first horrible dream. Is there still any soreness?"

"None at all," I answered.

"Can you indicate with your finger about the point at which you think this occurred?"

"Very little below my throat—here," I answered.

I wore a morning dress, which covered the place I pointed to.

"Now you can satisfy yourself," said the doctor. "You won't mind your papa's lowering your dress a very little. It is necessary, to detect a symptom of the complaint under which you have been suffering."

I acquiesced. It was only an inch or two below the edge of my collar.

"God bless me!—so it is," exclaimed my father, growing pale.

"You see it now with your own eyes," said the doctor, with a gloomy triumph.

"What is it?" I exclaimed, beginning to be frightened.

"Nothing, my dear young lady, but a small blue spot, about the size of the tip of your little finger; and now," he continued, turning to papa, "the question is what is best to be done?"

"Is there any danger?" I urged, in great trepidation.

"I trust not, my dear," answered the doctor. "I don't see why you should not recover. I don't see why you should not begin immediately to get better. That is the point at which the sense of strangulation begins?"

"Yes," I answered.

"And—recollect as well as you can—the same point was a kind of center of that thrill which you described just now, like the current of a cold stream running against you?"

"It may have been; I think it was."

"Ay, you see?" he added, turning to my father. "Shall I say a word to Madame?"

"Certainly," said my father.

He called Madame to him, and said:

"I find my young friend here far from well. It won't be of any great consequence, I hope; but it will be necessary that some steps be taken, which I will explain by-and-by; but in the meantime, Madame, you will be so good as not to let Miss Laura be alone for one moment. That is the only direction I need give for the present. It is indispensable."

"We may rely upon your kindness, Madame, I know," added my father.

Madame satisfied him eagerly.

"And you, dear Laura, I know you will observe the doctor's direction."

"I shall have to ask your opinion upon another patient, whose symptoms slightly resemble those of my daughter, that have just been detailed to you—very much milder in degree, but I believe quite of the same sort. She is a young lady—our guest; but as you say you will be passing this way again this evening, you can't do better than take your supper here, and you can then see her. She does not come down till the afternoon."

"I thank you," said the doctor. "I shall be with you, then, at about seven this evening."

And then they repeated their directions to me and to Madame, and with this parting charge my father left us, and walked out with the doctor; and I saw them pacing together up and down between the road and the moat, on the grassy platform in front of the castle, evidently absorbed in earnest conversation.

The doctor did not return. I saw him mount his horse there, take his leave, and ride away eastward through the forest.

Nearly at the same time I saw the man arrive from Dranfield with the letters, and dismount and hand the bag to my father.

In the meantime, Madame and I were both busy, lost in conjecture as to the reasons of the singular and earnest direction which the doctor and my father had concurred in imposing. Madame, as she afterwards told me, was afraid the doctor apprehended a sudden seizure, and that, without prompt assistance, I might either lose my life in a fit, or at least be seriously hurt.

The interpretation did not strike me; and I fancied, perhaps luckily for my nerves, that the arrangement was prescribed simply to secure a companion, who would prevent my taking too much exercise, or eating unripe fruit, or doing any of the fifty foolish things to which young people are supposed to be prone.

About half an hour after my father came in—he had a letter in his hand—and said:

"This letter had been delayed; it is from General Spielsdorf. He might have been here yesterday, he may not come till tomorrow or he may be here today."

He put the open letter into my hand; but he did not look pleased, as he used when a guest, especially one so much loved as the General, was coming.

On the contrary, he looked as if he wished him at the bottom of the Red Sea. There was plainly something on his mind which he did not choose to divulge.

"Papa, darling, will you tell me this?" said I, suddenly laying my hand on his arm, and looking, I am sure, imploringly in his face.

"Perhaps," he answered, smoothing my hair caressingly over my eyes.

"Does the doctor think me very ill?"

"No, dear; he thinks, if right steps are taken, you will be quite well again, at least, on the high road to a complete recovery, in a day or two," he answered, a little dryly. "I wish our good friend, the General, had chosen any other time; that is, I wish you had been perfectly well to receive him."

"But do tell me, papa," I insisted, "what does he think is the matter with me?"

"Nothing; you must not plague me with questions," he answered, with more irritation than I ever remember him to have displayed before; and seeing that I looked wounded, I suppose, he kissed me, and added, "You shall know all about it in a day or two; that is, all that I know. In the meantime you are not to trouble your head about it."

He turned and left the room, but came back before I had done wondering and puzzling over the oddity of all this; it was merely to say that he was going to Karnstein, and had ordered the carriage to be ready at twelve, and that I and Madame should accompany him; he was going to see the priest who lived near those picturesque grounds, upon business, and as Carmilla had never seen them, she could follow, when she came down, with Mademoiselle, who would bring materials for what you call a picnic, which might be laid for us in the ruined castle.

At twelve o'clock, accordingly, I was ready, and not long after, my father, Madame and I set out upon our projected drive.

Passing the drawbridge we turn to the right, and follow the road over the steep Gothic bridge, westward, to reach the deserted village and ruined castle of Karnstein.

No sylvan drive can be fancied prettier. The ground breaks into gentle hills and hollows, all clothed with beautiful wood, totally destitute of the comparative formality which artificial planting and early culture and pruning impart.

The irregularities of the ground often lead the road out of its course, and cause it to wind beautifully round the sides of broken hollows and the steeper sides of the hills, among varieties of ground almost inexhaustible.

Turning one of these points, we suddenly encountered our old friend, the General, riding towards us, attended by a mounted servant. His portmanteaus were following in a hired wagon, such as we term a cart.

The General dismounted as we pulled up, and, after the usual greetings, was easily persuaded to accept the vacant seat in the carriage and send his horse on with his servant to the schloss.

CHAPTER X

Bereaved

It was about ten months since we had last seen him: but that time had sufficed to make an alteration of years in his appearance. He had grown thinner; something of gloom and anxiety had taken the place of that cordial serenity which used to characterize his features. His dark blue eyes, always penetrating, now gleamed with a sterner light from under his shaggy grey eyebrows. It was not such a change as grief alone usually induces, and angrier passions seemed to have had their share in bringing it about.

We had not long resumed our drive, when the General began to talk, with his usual soldierly directness, of the bereavement, as he termed it, which he had sustained in the death of his beloved niece and ward; and he then broke out in a tone of intense bitterness and fury, inveighing against the "hellish arts" to which she had fallen a victim, and expressing, with more exasperation than piety, his wonder that Heaven should tolerate so monstrous an indulgence of the lusts and malignity of hell.

My father, who saw at once that something very extraordinary had befallen, asked him, if not too painful to him, to detail the circumstances which he thought justified the strong terms in which he expressed himself.

"I should tell you all with pleasure," said the General, "but you would not believe me."

"Why should I not?" he asked.

"Because," he answered testily, "you believe in nothing but what consists with your own prejudices and illusions. I remember when I was like you, but I have learned better."

"Try me," said my father; "I am not such a dogmatist as you suppose. Besides which, I very well know that you generally require proof for what you believe, and am, therefore, very strongly predisposed to respect your conclusions."

"You are right in supposing that I have not been led lightly into a belief in the marvelous—for what I have experienced is marvelous—and I have been forced by extraordinary evidence to credit that which ran counter, diametrically, to all my theories. I have been made the dupe of a preternatural conspiracy."

Notwithstanding his professions of confidence in the General's penetration, I saw my father, at this point, glance at the General, with, as I thought, a marked suspicion of his sanity.

The General did not see it, luckily. He was looking gloomily and curiously into the glades and vistas of the woods that were opening before us.

"You are going to the Ruins of Karnstein?" he said.

"Yes, it is a lucky coincidence; do you know I was going to ask you to bring me there to inspect them. I have a special object in exploring. There is a ruined chapel, ain't there, with a great many tombs of that extinct family?"

"So there are—highly interesting," said my father. "I hope you are thinking of claiming the title and estates?"

My father said this gaily, but the General did not recollect the laugh, or even the smile, which courtesy exacts for a friend's joke; on the contrary, he looked grave and even fierce, ruminating on a matter that stirred his anger and horror.

"Something very different," he said, gruffly. "I mean to unearth some of those fine people. I hope, by God's blessing, to accomplish a pious sacrilege here, which will relieve our earth of certain monsters, and enable honest people to sleep in their beds without being assailed by murderers. I have strange things to tell you, my dear friend, such as I myself would have scouted as incredible a few months since."

My father looked at him again, but this time not with a glance of suspicion—with an eye, rather, of keen intelligence and alarm.

"The house of Karnstein," he said, "has been long extinct: a hundred years at least. My dear wife was maternally descended from the Karnsteins. But the name and title have long ceased to exist. The castle is a ruin; the very village is deserted; it is fifty years since the smoke of a chimney was seen there; not a roof left."

"Quite true. I have heard a great deal about that since I last saw you; a great deal that will astonish you. But I had better relate everything in the order in which it occurred," said the General. "You saw my dear ward—my child, I may call her. No creature could have been more beautiful, and only three months ago none more blooming."

"Yes, poor thing! when I saw her last she certainly was quite lovely," said my father. "I was grieved and shocked more than I can tell you, my dear friend; I knew what a blow it was to you."

He took the General's hand, and they exchanged a kind pressure. Tears gathered in the old soldier's eyes. He did not seek to conceal them. He said:

"We have been very old friends; I knew you would feel for me, childless as I am. She had become an object of very near interest to me, and repaid my care by an affection that cheered my home and made my life happy. That is all gone. The years that remain to me on earth may not be very long; but by God's mercy I hope to accomplish a service to mankind before I die, and to subserve the vengeance of Heaven upon the fiends who have murdered my poor child in the spring of her hopes and beauty!"

"You said, just now, that you intended relating everything as it occurred," said my father. "Pray do; I assure you that it is not mere curiosity that prompts me."

By this time we had reached the point at which the Drunstall road, by which the General had come, diverges from the road which we were traveling to Karnstein.

"How far is it to the ruins?" inquired the General, looking anxiously forward.

"About half a league," answered my father. "Pray let us hear the story you were so good as to promise."

CHAPTER XI

The Story

W ith all my heart," said the General, with an effort; and after a short pause in which to arrange his subject, he commenced one of the strangest narratives I ever heard.

"My dear child was looking forward with great pleasure to the visit you had been so good as to arrange for her to your charming daughter." Here he made me a gallant but melancholy bow. "In the meantime we had an invitation to my old friend the Count Carlsfeld, whose schloss is about six leagues to the other side of Karnstein. It was to attend the series of fetes which, you remember, were given by him in honor of his illustrious visitor, the Grand Duke Charles."

"Yes; and very splendid, I believe, they were," said my father.

"Princely! But then his hospitalities are quite regal. He has Aladdin's lamp. The night from which my sorrow dates was devoted to a magnificent masquerade. The grounds were thrown open, the trees hung with colored lamps. There was such a display of fireworks as Paris itself had never witnessed. And such music—music, you know, is my weakness—such ravishing music! The finest instrumental band, perhaps, in the world, and the finest singers who could be collected from all the great operas in Europe. As you wandered through these fantastically illuminated grounds, the moon-lighted chateau throwing a rosy light from its long rows of windows, you would suddenly hear these ravishing voices stealing from the silence of some grove, or rising from boats upon the lake. I felt myself, as I looked and listened, carried back into the romance and poetry of my early youth.

"When the fireworks were ended, and the ball beginning, we returned to the noble suite of rooms that were thrown open to the dancers. A masked ball, you know, is a beautiful sight; but so brilliant a spectacle of the kind I never saw before.

"It was a very aristocratic assembly. I was myself almost the only 'nobody' present.

"My dear child was looking quite beautiful. She wore no mask. Her excitement and delight added an unspeakable charm to her features, always lovely. I remarked a young lady, dressed magnificently, but wearing a mask, who appeared to me to be observing my ward with extraordinary interest. I had seen her, earlier in the evening, in the great hall, and again, for a few minutes, walking near us, on the terrace under the castle windows, similarly employed. A lady, also masked, richly and gravely dressed, and with a stately air, like a person of rank, accompanied her as a chaperon.

"Had the young lady not worn a mask, I could, of course, have been much more certain upon the question whether she was really watching my poor darling.

"I am now well assured that she was.

"We were now in one of the salons. My poor dear child had been dancing, and was resting a little in one of the chairs near the door; I was standing near. The two ladies I have mentioned had approached and the younger took the chair next my ward; while her companion stood beside me, and for a little time addressed herself, in a low tone, to her charge.

"Availing herself of the privilege of her mask, she turned to me, and in the tone of an old friend, and calling me by my name, opened a conversation with me, which piqued my curiosity a good deal. She referred to many scenes where she had met me—at Court, and at distinguished houses. She alluded to little incidents which I had long ceased to think of, but which, I found, had only lain in abeyance in my memory, for they instantly started into life at her touch.

"I became more and more curious to ascertain who she was, every moment. She parried my attempts to discover very adroitly and pleasantly. The knowledge she showed of many passages in my life seemed to me all but unaccountable; and she appeared to take a not unnatural pleasure in foiling my curiosity, and in seeing me flounder in my eager perplexity, from one conjecture to another.

"In the meantime the young lady, whom her mother called by the odd name of Millarca, when she once or twice addressed her, had, with the same ease and grace, got into conversation with my ward.

"She introduced herself by saying that her mother was a very old acquaintance of mine. She spoke of the agreeable audacity which a mask rendered practicable; she talked like a friend; she admired her dress, and insinuated very prettily her admiration of her beauty.

She amused her with laughing criticisms upon the people who crowded the ballroom, and laughed at my poor child's fun. She was very witty and lively when she pleased, and after a time they had grown very good friends, and the young stranger lowered her mask, displaying a remarkably beautiful face. I had never seen it before, neither had my dear child. But though it was new to us, the features were so engaging, as well as lovely, that it was impossible not to feel the attraction powerfully. My poor girl did so. I never saw anyone more taken with another at first sight, unless, indeed, it was the stranger herself, who seemed quite to have lost her heart to her.

"In the meantime, availing myself of the license of a masquerade, I put not a few questions to the elder lady.

"'You have puzzled me utterly,' I said, laughing. 'Is that not enough?

Won't you, now, consent to stand on equal terms, and do me the kindness to remove your mask?'

"'Can any request be more unreasonable?' she replied. 'Ask a lady to yield an advantage! Beside, how do you know you should recognize me? Years make changes.'

"'As you see,' I said, with a bow, and, I suppose, a rather melancholy little laugh.

"'As philosophers tell us,' she said; 'and how do you know that a sight of my face would help you?'

"'I should take chance for that,' I answered. 'It is vain trying to make yourself out an old woman; your figure betrays you.'

"'Years, nevertheless, have passed since I saw you, rather since you saw me, for that is what I am considering. Millarca, there, is my daughter; I cannot then be young, even in the opinion of people whom time has taught to be indulgent, and I may not like to be compared with what you remember me.

You have no mask to remove. You can offer me nothing in exchange.'

"'My petition is to your pity, to remove it.'

"'And mine to yours, to let it stay where it is,' she replied.

"'Well, then, at least you will tell me whether you are French or German; you speak both languages so perfectly.'

"'I don't think I shall tell you that, General; you intend a surprise, and are meditating the particular point of attack.'

"'At all events, you won't deny this,' I said, 'that being honored by your permission to converse, I ought to know how to address you. Shall I say Madame la Comtesse?'

"She laughed, and she would, no doubt, have met me with another evasion—if, indeed, I can treat any occurrence in an interview every circumstance of which was prearranged, as I now believe, with the profoundest cunning, as liable to be modified by accident.

"'As to that,' she began; but she was interrupted, almost as she opened her lips, by a gentleman, dressed in black, who looked particularly elegant and distinguished, with this drawback, that his face was the most deadly pale I ever saw, except in death. He was in no masquerade—in the plain evening dress of a gentleman; and he said, without a smile, but with a courtly and unusually low bow:—

"'Will Madame la Comtesse permit me to say a very few words which may interest her?'

"The lady turned quickly to him, and touched her lip in token of silence; she then said to me, 'Keep my place for me, General; I shall return when I have said a few words.'

"And with this injunction, playfully given, she walked a little aside with the gentleman in black, and talked for some minutes, apparently very earnestly. They then walked away slowly together in the crowd, and I lost them for some minutes.

"I spent the interval in cudgeling my brains for a conjecture as to the identity of the lady who seemed to remember me so kindly, and I was thinking of turning about and joining in the conversation between my pretty ward and the Countess's daughter, and trying whether, by the time she returned, I might not have a surprise in store for her, by having her name, title, chateau, and estates at my fingers' ends. But at this moment she returned, accompanied by the pale man in black, who said:

"'I shall return and inform Madame la Comtesse when her carriage is at the door.'

"He withdrew with a bow."

CHAPTER XII

A Petition

T hen we are to lose Madame la Comtesse, but I hope
only for a few hours,' I said, with a low bow.

"'It may be that only, or it may be a few weeks. It
was very unlucky his speaking to me just now as he did.
Do you now know me?'

"I assured her I did not.

"'You shall know me,' she said, 'but not at present.
We are older and better friends than, perhaps, you
suspect. I cannot yet declare myself. I shall in three
weeks pass your beautiful schloss, about which I have
been making enquiries. I shall then look in upon you for
an hour or two, and renew a friendship which I never
think of without a thousand pleasant recollections.
This moment a piece of news has reached me like a
thunderbolt. I must set out now, and travel by a devious
route, nearly a hundred miles, with all the dispatch I
can possibly make. My perplexities multiply. I am only
deterred by the compulsory reserve I practice as to my
name from making a very singular request of you. My

poor child has not quite recovered her strength. Her horse fell with her, at a hunt which she had ridden out to witness, her nerves have not yet recovered the shock, and our physician says that she must on no account exert herself for some time to come. We came here, in consequence, by very easy stages—hardly six leagues a day. I must now travel day and night, on a mission of life and death—a mission the critical and momentous nature of which I shall be able to explain to you when we meet, as I hope we shall, in a few weeks, without the necessity of any concealment.'

"She went on to make her petition, and it was in the tone of a person from whom such a request amounted to conferring, rather than seeking a favor.

"This was only in manner, and, as it seemed, quite unconsciously. Than the terms in which it was expressed, nothing could be more deprecatory. It was simply that I would consent to take charge of her daughter during her absence.

"This was, all things considered, a strange, not to say, an audacious request. She in some sort disarmed me, by stating and admitting everything that could be urged against it, and throwing herself entirely upon my chivalry. At the same moment, by a fatality that seems to have predetermined all that happened, my poor child came to my side, and, in an undertone, besought me to invite her new friend, Millarca, to pay us a visit. She had just been sounding her, and thought, if her mamma would allow her, she would like it extremely.

"At another time I should have told her to wait a little, until, at least, we knew who they were. But I had not a moment to think in. The two ladies assailed me together, and I must confess the refined and beautiful face of the young lady, about which there was something extremely engaging, as well as the elegance and fire of high birth, determined me; and, quite overpowered, I submitted, and undertook, too easily, the care of the young lady, whom her mother called Millarca.

"The Countess beckoned to her daughter, who listened with grave attention while she told her, in general terms, how suddenly and peremptorily she had been summoned, and also of the arrangement she had made for her under my care, adding that I was one of her earliest and most valued friends.

"I made, of course, such speeches as the case seemed to call for, and found myself, on reflection, in a position which I did not half like.

"The gentleman in black returned, and very ceremoniously conducted the lady from the room.

"'The demeanor of this gentleman was such as to impress me with the conviction that the Countess was a lady of very much more importance than her modest title alone might have led me to assume.

"Her last charge to me was that no attempt was to be made to learn more about her than I might have already guessed, until her return. Our distinguished host, whose guest she was, knew her reasons.

"'But here,' she said, 'neither I nor my daughter could safely remain for more than a day. I removed my mask imprudently for a moment, about an hour ago, and, too late, I fancied you saw me. So I resolved to seek an opportunity of talking a little to you. Had I found that you had seen me, I would have thrown myself on your high sense of honor to keep my secret some weeks. As it is, I am satisfied that you did not see me; but if you now suspect, or, on reflection, should suspect, who I am,

I commit myself, in like manner, entirely to your honor. My daughter will observe the same secrecy, and I well know that you will, from time to time, remind her, lest she should thoughtlessly disclose it.'

"She whispered a few words to her daughter, kissed her hurriedly twice, and went away, accompanied by the pale gentleman in black, and disappeared in the crowd.

"'In the next room,' said Millarca, 'there is a window that looks upon the hall door. I should like to see the last of mamma, and to kiss my hand to her.'

"We assented, of course, and accompanied her to the window. We looked out, and saw a handsome old-fashioned carriage, with a troop of couriers and footmen. We saw the slim figure of the pale gentleman in black, as he held a thick velvet cloak, and placed it about her shoulders and threw the hood over her head. She nodded to him, and just touched his hand with hers. He bowed low repeatedly as the door closed, and the carriage began to move.

"'She is gone,' said Millarca, with a sigh.

"'She is gone,' I repeated to myself, for the first time—in the hurried moments that had elapsed since my consent—reflecting upon the folly of my act.

"'She did not look up,' said the young lady, plaintively.

"'The Countess had taken off her mask, perhaps, and did not care to show her face,' I said; 'and she could not know that you were in the window.'

"She sighed, and looked in my face. She was so beautiful that I relented. I was sorry I had for a moment repented of my hospitality, and I determined to make her amends for the unavowed churlishness of my reception.

"The young lady, replacing her mask, joined my ward in persuading me to return to the grounds, where the concert was soon to be renewed. We did so, and walked up and down the terrace that lies under the castle windows.

"Millarca became very intimate with us, and amused us with lively descriptions and stories of most of the great people whom we saw upon the terrace. I liked her more and more every minute. Her gossip without being ill-natured, was extremely diverting to me, who had been so long out of the great world. I thought what life she would give to our sometimes lonely evenings at home.

"This ball was not over until the morning sun had almost reached the horizon. It pleased the Grand Duke to dance till then, so loyal people could not go away, or think of bed.

"We had just got through a crowded saloon, when my ward asked me what had become of Millarca. I thought she had been by her side, and she fancied she was by mine. The fact was, we had lost her.

"All my efforts to find her were vain. I feared that she had mistaken, in the confusion of a momentary separation from us, other people for her new friends, and had, possibly, pursued and lost them in the extensive grounds which were thrown open to us.

"Now, in its full force, I recognized a new folly in my having undertaken the charge of a young lady without so much as knowing her name; and fettered as I was by promises, of the reasons for imposing which I knew nothing, I could not even point my inquiries by saying that the missing young lady was the daughter of the Countess who had taken her departure a few hours before.

"Morning broke. It was clear daylight before I gave up my search. It was not till near two o'clock next day that we heard anything of my missing charge.

"At about that time a servant knocked at my niece's door, to say that he had been earnestly requested by a young lady, who appeared to be in great distress, to make out where she could find the General Baron Spielsdorf and the young lady his daughter, in whose charge she had been left by her mother.

"There could be no doubt, notwithstanding the slight inaccuracy, that our young friend had turned up; and so she had. Would to heaven we had lost her!

"She told my poor child a story to account for her having failed to recover us for so long. Very late, she said, she had got to the housekeeper's bedroom in despair of finding us, and had then fallen into a deep sleep which, long as it was, had hardly sufficed to recruit her strength after the fatigues of the ball.

"That day Millarca came home with us. I was only too happy, after all, to have secured so charming a companion for my dear girl."

CHAPTER XIII

The Woodman

There soon, however, appeared some drawbacks. In the first place, Millarca complained of extreme languor—the weakness that remained after her late illness—and she never emerged from her room till the afternoon was pretty far advanced. In the next place, it was accidentally discovered, although she always locked her door on the inside, and never disturbed the key from its place till she admitted the maid to assist at her toilet, that she was undoubtedly sometimes absent from her room in the very early morning, and at various times later in the day, before she wished it to be understood that she was stirring. She was repeatedly seen from the windows of the schloss, in the first faint grey of the morning, walking through the trees, in an easterly direction, and looking like a person in a trance. This convinced me that she walked in her sleep. But this hypothesis did not solve the puzzle. How did she pass out from her room, leaving the door locked on the inside? How did she escape from the house without unbarring door or window?

"In the midst of my perplexities, an anxiety of a far more urgent kind presented itself.

"My dear child began to lose her looks and health, and that in a manner so mysterious, and even horrible, that I became thoroughly frightened.

"She was at first visited by appalling dreams; then, as she fancied, by a specter, sometimes resembling Millarca, sometimes in the shape of a beast, indistinctly seen, walking round the foot of her bed, from side to side. "Lastly came sensations. One, not unpleasant, but very peculiar, she said, resembled the flow of an icy stream against her breast. At a later time, she felt something like a pair of large needles pierce her, a little below the throat, with a very sharp pain. A few nights after, followed a gradual and convulsive sense of strangulation; then came unconsciousness."

I could hear distinctly every word the kind old General was saying, because by this time we were driving upon the short grass that spreads on either side of the road as you approach the roofless village which had not shown the smoke of a chimney for more than half a century.

You may guess how strangely I felt as I heard my own symptoms so exactly described in those which had been experienced by the poor girl who, but for the catastrophe which followed, would have been at that moment a visitor at my father's chateau. You may suppose, also, how I felt as I heard him detail habits and mysterious peculiarities which were, in fact, those of our beautiful guest, Carmilla!

A vista opened in the forest; we were on a sudden under the chimneys and gables of the ruined village, and the towers and battlements of the dismantled castle, round which gigantic trees are grouped, overhung us from a slight eminence.

In a frightened dream I got down from the carriage, and in silence, for we had each abundant matter for thinking; we soon mounted the ascent, and were among the spacious chambers, winding stairs, and dark corridors of the castle.

"And this was once the palatial residence of the Karnsteins!" said the old General at length, as from a great window he looked out across the village, and saw the wide, undulating expanse of forest. "It was a bad family, and here its bloodstained annals were written," he continued. "It is hard that they should, after death, continue to plague the human race with their atrocious lusts. That is the chapel of the Karnsteins, down there."

He pointed down to the grey walls of the Gothic building partly visible through the foliage, a little way down the steep. "And I hear the axe of a woodman," he added, "busy among the trees that surround it; he possibly may give us the information of which I am in search, and point out the grave of Mircalla, Countess of Karnstein. These rustics preserve the local traditions of great families, whose stories die out among the rich and titled so soon as the families themselves become extinct."

"We have a portrait, at home, of Mircalla, the Countess Karnstein; should you like to see it?" asked my father.

"Time enough, dear friend," replied the General. "I believe that I have seen the original; and one motive which has led me to you earlier than I at first intended, was to explore the chapel which we are now approaching."

"What! see the Countess Mircalla," exclaimed my father; "why, she has been dead more than a century!"

"Not so dead as you fancy, I am told," answered the General.

"I confess, General, you puzzle me utterly," replied my father, looking at him, I fancied, for a moment with a return of the suspicion I detected before. But although there was anger and detestation, at times, in the old General's manner, there was nothing flighty.

"There remains to me," he said, as we passed under the heavy arch of the Gothic church—for its dimensions would have justified its being so styled—"but one object which can interest me during the few years that remain to me on earth, and that is to wreak on her the vengeance which, I thank God, may still be accomplished by a mortal arm."

"What vengeance can you mean?" asked my father, in increasing amazement.

"I mean, to decapitate the monster," he answered, with a fierce flush, and a stamp that echoed mournfully through the hollow ruin, and his clenched hand was at the same moment raised, as if it grasped the handle of an axe, while he shook it ferociously in the air.

"What?" exclaimed my father, more than ever bewildered.

"To strike her head off."

"Cut her head off!"

"Aye, with a hatchet, with a spade, or with anything that can cleave through her murderous throat. You shall hear," he answered, trembling with rage. And hurrying forward he said:

"That beam will answer for a seat; your dear child is fatigued; let her be seated, and I will, in a few sentences, close my dreadful story."

The squared block of wood, which lay on the grass-grown pavement of the chapel, formed a bench on which I was very glad to seat myself, and in the meantime the General called to the woodman, who had been removing some boughs which leaned upon the old walls; and, axe in hand, the hardy old fellow stood before us.

He could not tell us anything of these monuments; but there was an old man, he said, a ranger of this forest, at present sojourning in the house of the priest, about two miles away, who could point out every monument of the old Karnstein family; and, for a trifle, he undertook to bring him back with him, if we would lend him one of our horses, in little more than half an hour.

"Have you been long employed about this forest?" asked my father of the old man.

"I have been a woodman here," he answered in his patois, "under the forester, all my days; so has my father before me, and so on, as many generations as I can count up. I could show you the very house in the village here, in which my ancestors lived."

"How came the village to be deserted?" asked the General.

"It was troubled by revenants, sir; several were tracked to their graves, there detected by the usual tests, and extinguished in the usual way, by decapitation, by the stake, and by burning; but not until many of the villagers were killed.

"But after all these proceedings according to law," he continued—"so many graves opened, and so many vampires deprived of their horrible animation—the village was not relieved. But a Moravian nobleman, who happened to be traveling this way, heard how matters were, and being skilled—as many people are in his country—in such affairs, he offered to deliver the village from its tormentor. He did so thus: There being a bright moon that night, he ascended, shortly after sunset, the towers of the chapel here, from whence he could distinctly see the churchyard beneath him; you can see it from that window. From this point he watched until he saw the vampire come out of his grave, and place near it the linen clothes in which he had been folded, and then glide away towards the village to plague its inhabitants.

"The stranger, having seen all this, came down from the steeple, took the linen wrappings of the vampire, and carried them up to the top of the tower, which he again mounted. When the vampire returned from his prowlings and missed his clothes, he cried furiously to the Moravian, whom he saw at the summit of the tower, and who, in reply, beckoned him to ascend and take them. Whereupon the vampire, accepting his invitation, began to climb the steeple, and so soon as he had reached the battlements, the Moravian, with a stroke of his sword, clove his skull in twain, hurling him down to the churchyard, whither, descending by the winding stairs, the stranger followed and cut his head off, and next day delivered it and the body to the villagers, who duly impaled and burnt them.

"This Moravian nobleman had authority from the then head of the family to remove the tomb of Mircalla, Countess Karnstein, which he did effectually, so that in a little while its site was quite forgotten."

"Can you point out where it stood?" asked the General, eagerly.

The forester shook his head, and smiled.

"Not a soul living could tell you that now," he said; "besides, they say her body was removed; but no one is sure of that either."

Having thus spoken, as time pressed, he dropped his axe and departed, leaving us to hear the remainder of the General's strange story.

CHAPTER XIV

The Meeting

My beloved child," he resumed, "was now growing rapidly worse. The physician who attended her had failed to produce the slightest impression on her disease, for such I then supposed it to be. He saw my alarm, and suggested a consultation. I called in an abler physician, from Gratz.

"Several days elapsed before he arrived. He was a good and pious, as well as a learned man. Having seen my poor ward together, they withdrew to my library to confer and discuss. I, from the adjoining room, where I awaited their summons, heard these two gentlemen's voices raised in something sharper than a strictly philosophical discussion. I knocked at the door and entered. I found the old physician from Gratz maintaining his theory. His rival was combating it with undisguised ridicule, accompanied with bursts of laughter. This unseemly manifestation subsided and the altercation ended on my entrance.

"'Sir,' said my first physician, 'my learned brother seems to think that you want a conjuror, and not a doctor.'

"'Pardon me,' said the old physician from Gratz, looking displeased, 'I shall state my own view of the case in my own way another time. I grieve, Monsieur le General, that by my skill and science I can be of no use.

Before I go I shall do myself the honor to suggest something to you.'

"He seemed thoughtful, and sat down at a table and began to write.

"Profoundly disappointed, I made my bow, and as I turned to go, the other doctor pointed over his shoulder to his companion who was writing, and then, with a shrug, significantly touched his forehead.

"This consultation, then, left me precisely where I was. I walked out into the grounds, all but distracted. The doctor from Gratz, in ten or fifteen minutes, overtook me. He apologized for having followed me, but said that he could not conscientiously take his leave without a few words more. He told me that he could not be mistaken; no natural disease exhibited the same symptoms; and that death was already very near. There remained, however, a day, or possibly two, of life. If the fatal seizure were at once arrested, with great care and skill her strength might possibly return. But all hung now upon the confines of the irrevocable. One more assault might extinguish the last spark of vitality which is, every moment, ready to die.

"'And what is the nature of the seizure you speak of?' I entreated.

"'I have stated all fully in this note, which I place in your hands upon the distinct condition that you send for the nearest clergyman, and open my letter in his presence, and on no account read it till he is with you; you would despise it else, and it is a matter of life and death. Should the priest fail you, then, indeed, you may read it.'

"He asked me, before taking his leave finally, whether I would wish to see a man curiously learned upon the very subject, which, after I had read his letter, would probably interest me above all others, and he urged me earnestly to invite him to visit him there; and so took his leave.

"The ecclesiastic was absent, and I read the letter by myself. At another time, or in another case, it might have excited my ridicule. But into what quackeries will not people rush for a last chance, where all accustomed means have failed, and the life of a beloved object is at stake?

"Nothing, you will say, could be more absurd than the learned man's letter.

"It was monstrous enough to have consigned him to a madhouse. He said that the patient was suffering from the visits of a vampire! The punctures which she described as having occurred near the throat, were, he insisted, the insertion of those two long, thin, and sharp teeth which, it is well known, are peculiar to vampires; and there could be no doubt, he added, as to the well-defined presence of the small livid mark which all concurred in describing as that induced by the demon's lips, and every symptom described by the sufferer was in exact conformity with those recorded in every case of a similar visitation.

"Being myself wholly skeptical as to the existence of any such portent as the vampire, the supernatural theory of the good doctor furnished, in my opinion, but another instance of learning and intelligence oddly associated with some one hallucination. I was so miserable, however, that, rather than try nothing, I acted upon the instructions of the letter.

"I concealed myself in the dark dressing room, that opened upon the poor patient's room, in which a candle was burning, and watched there till she was fast asleep. I stood at the door, peeping through the small crevice, my sword laid on the table beside me, as my directions prescribed, until, a little after one, I saw a large black object, very ill-defined, crawl, as it seemed to me, over the foot of the bed, and swiftly spread itself up to the poor girl's throat, where it swelled, in a moment, into a great, palpitating mass.

"For a few moments I had stood petrified. I now sprang forward, with my sword in my hand. The black creature suddenly contracted towards the foot of the bed, glided over it, and, standing on the floor about a yard below the foot of the bed, with a glare of skulking ferocity and horror fixed on me, I saw Millarca. Speculating I know not what, I struck at her instantly with my sword; but I saw her standing near the door, unscathed. Horrified, I pursued, and struck again. She was gone; and my sword flew to shivers against the door.

"I can't describe to you all that passed on that horrible night. The whole house was up and stirring. The specter Millarca was gone. But her victim was sinking fast, and before the morning dawned, she died."

The old General was agitated. We did not speak to him. My father walked to some little distance, and began reading the inscriptions on the tombstones; and thus occupied, he strolled into the door of a side chapel to prosecute his researches. The General leaned against the wall, dried his eyes, and sighed heavily. I was relieved on hearing the voices of Carmilla and Madame, who were at that moment approaching. The voices died away.

In this solitude, having just listened to so strange a story, connected, as it was, with the great and titled dead, whose monuments were moldering among the dust and ivy round us, and every incident of which bore so awfully upon my own mysterious case—in this haunted spot, darkened by the towering foliage that rose on every side, dense and high above its noiseless walls— a horror began to steal over me, and my heart sank as I thought that my friends were, after all, not about to enter and disturb this triste and ominous scene.

The old General's eyes were fixed on the ground, as he leaned with his hand upon the basement of a shattered monument.

Under a narrow, arched doorway, surmounted by one of those demoniacal grotesques in which the cynical and ghastly fancy of old Gothic carving delights, I saw very gladly the beautiful face and figure of Carmilla enter the shadowy chapel.

I was just about to rise and speak, and nodded smiling, in answer to her peculiarly engaging smile; when with a cry, the old man by my side caught up the woodman's hatchet, and started forward. On seeing him a brutalized change came over her features. It was an instantaneous and horrible transformation, as she made a crouching step backwards. Before I could utter a scream, he struck at her with all his force, but she dived under his blow, and unscathed, caught him in her tiny grasp by the wrist. He struggled for a moment to release his arm, but his hand opened, the axe fell to the ground, and the girl was gone.

He staggered against the wall. His grey hair stood upon his head, and a moisture shone over his face, as if he were at the point of death.

The frightful scene had passed in a moment. The first thing I recollect after, is Madame standing before me, and impatiently repeating again and again, the question, "Where is Mademoiselle Carmilla?"

I answered at length, "I don't know—I can't tell—she went there," and I pointed to the door through which Madame had just entered; "only a minute or two since."

"But I have been standing there, in the passage, ever since Mademoiselle Carmilla entered; and she did not return."

She then began to call "Carmilla," through every door and passage and from the windows, but no answer came.

"She called herself Carmilla?" asked the General, still agitated.

"Carmilla, yes," I answered.

"Aye," he said; "that is Millarca. That is the same person who long ago was called Mircalla, Countess Karnstein. Depart from this accursed ground, my poor child, as quickly as you can. Drive to the clergyman's house, and stay there till we come. Begone! May you never behold Carmilla more; you will not find her here."

CHAPTER XV

Ordeal and Execution

As he spoke one of the strangest looking men I ever beheld entered the chapel at the door through which Carmilla had made her entrance and her exit. He was tall, narrow-chested, stooping, with high shoulders, and dressed in black. His face was brown and dried in with deep furrows; he wore an oddly-shaped hat with a broad leaf. His hair, long and grizzled, hung on his shoulders. He wore a pair of gold spectacles, and walked slowly, with an odd shambling gait, with his face sometimes turned up to the sky, and sometimes bowed down towards the ground, seemed to wear a perpetual smile; his long thin arms were swinging, and his lank hands, in old black gloves ever so much too wide for them, waving and gesticulating in utter abstraction.

"The very man!" exclaimed the General, advancing with manifest delight. "My dear Baron, how happy I am to see you, I had no hope of meeting you so soon." He signed to my father, who had by this time returned, and leading the fantastic old gentleman, whom he called the Baron to meet him. He introduced him formally, and they at once entered into earnest conversation. The stranger took a roll of paper from his pocket, and spread it on the worn surface of a tomb that stood by. He had a pencil case in his fingers, with which he traced imaginary lines from point to point on the paper, which from their often glancing from it, together, at certain points of the building, I concluded to be a plan of the chapel. He accompanied, what I may term, his lecture, with occasional readings from a dirty little book, whose yellow leaves were closely written over.

They sauntered together down the side aisle, opposite to the spot where I was standing, conversing as they went; then they began measuring distances by paces, and finally they all stood together, facing a piece of the sidewall, which they began to examine with great minuteness; pulling off the ivy that clung over it, and rapping the plaster with the ends of their sticks, scraping here, and knocking there. At length they ascertained the existence of a broad marble tablet, with letters carved in relief upon it.

With the assistance of the woodman, who soon returned, a monumental inscription, and carved escutcheon, were disclosed. They proved to be those of the long lost monument of Mircalla, Countess Karnstein.

The old General, though not I fear given to the praying mood, raised his hands and eyes to heaven, in mute thanksgiving for some moments.

"Tomorrow," I heard him say; "the commissioner will be here, and the Inquisition will be held according to law."

Then turning to the old man with the gold spectacles, whom I have described, he shook him warmly by both hands and said:

"Baron, how can I thank you? How can we all thank you? You will have delivered this region from a plague that has scourged its inhabitants for more than a century. The horrible enemy, thank God, is at last tracked."

My father led the stranger aside, and the General followed. I know that he had led them out of hearing, that he might relate my case, and I saw them glance often quickly at me, as the discussion proceeded.

My father came to me, kissed me again and again, and leading me from the chapel, said:

"It is time to return, but before we go home, we must add to our party the good priest, who lives but a little way from this; and persuade him to accompany us to the schloss."

In this quest we were successful: and I was glad, being unspeakably fatigued when we reached home. But my satisfaction was changed to dismay, on discovering that there were no tidings of Carmilla. Of the scene that had occurred in the ruined chapel, no explanation was offered to me, and it was clear that it was a secret which my father for the present determined to keep from me.

The sinister absence of Carmilla made the remembrance of the scene more horrible to me. The arrangements for the night were singular. Two servants, and Madame were to sit up in my room that night; and the ecclesiastic with my father kept watch in the adjoining dressing room.

The priest had performed certain solemn rites that night, the purport of which I did not understand any more than I comprehended the reason of this extraordinary precaution taken for my safety during sleep.

I saw all clearly a few days later.

The disappearance of Carmilla was followed by the discontinuance of my nightly sufferings.

You have heard, no doubt, of the appalling superstition that prevails in Upper and Lower Styria, in Moravia, Silesia, in Turkish Serbia, in Poland, even in Russia; the superstition, so we must call it, of the Vampire.

If human testimony, taken with every care and solemnity, judicially, before commissions innumerable, each consisting of many members, all chosen for integrity and intelligence, and constituting reports more voluminous perhaps than exist upon any one other class of cases, is worth anything, it is difficult to deny, or even to doubt the existence of such a phenomenon as the Vampire.

For my part I have heard no theory by which to explain what I myself have witnessed and experienced, other than that supplied by the ancient and well-attested belief of the country.

The next day the formal proceedings took place in the Chapel of Karnstein.

The grave of the Countess Mircalla was opened; and the General and my father recognized each his perfidious and beautiful guest, in the face now disclosed to view. The features, though a hundred and fifty years had passed since her funeral, were tinted with the warmth of life. Her eyes were open; no cadaverous smell exhaled from the coffin. The two medical men, one officially present, the other on the part of the promoter of the inquiry, attested the marvelous fact that there was a faint but appreciable respiration, and a corresponding action of the heart. The limbs were perfectly flexible, the flesh elastic; and the leaden coffin floated with blood, in which to a depth of seven inches, the body lay immersed.

Here then, were all the admitted signs and proofs of vampirism. The body, therefore, in accordance with the ancient practice, was raised, and a sharp stake driven through the heart of the vampire, who uttered a piercing shriek at the moment, in all respects such as might escape from a living person in the last agony. Then the head was struck off, and a torrent of blood flowed from the severed neck. The body and head was next placed on a pile of wood, and reduced to ashes, which were thrown upon the river and borne away, and that territory has never since been plagued by the visits of a vampire.

My father has a copy of the report of the Imperial Commission, with the signatures of all who were present at these proceedings, attached in verification of the statement. It is from this official paper that I have summarized my account of this last shocking scene.

CHAPTER XVI

Conclusion

I write all this you suppose with composure. But far from it; I cannot think of it without agitation. Nothing but your earnest desire so repeatedly expressed, could have induced me to sit down to a task that has unstrung my nerves for months to come, and reinduced a shadow of the unspeakable horror which years after my deliverance continued to make my days and nights dreadful, and solitude insupportably terrific.

Let me add a word or two about that quaint Baron Vordenburg, to whose curious lore we were indebted for the discovery of the Countess Mircalla's grave.

He had taken up his abode in Gratz, where, living upon a mere pittance, which was all that remained to him of the once princely estates of his family, in Upper Styria, he devoted himself to the minute and laborious investigation of the marvelously authenticated tradition of Vampirism. He had at his fingers' ends all the great and little works upon the subject.

"Magia Posthuma," "Phlegon de Mirabilibus," "Augustinus de cura pro Mortuis," "Philosophicae et Christianae Cogitationes de Vampiris," by John Christofer Herenberg; and a thousand others, among which I remember only a few of those which he lent to my father. He had a voluminous digest of all the judicial cases, from which he had extracted a system of principles that appear to govern—some always, and others occasionally only—the condition of the vampire. I may mention, in passing, that the deadly pallor attributed to that sort of revenants, is a mere melodramatic fiction. They present, in the grave, and when they show themselves in human society, the appearance of healthy life. When disclosed to light in their coffins, they exhibit all the symptoms that are enumerated as those which proved the vampire-life of the long-dead Countess Karnstein.

How they escape from their graves and return to them for certain hours every day, without displacing the clay or leaving any trace of disturbance in the state of the coffin or the cerements, has always been admitted to be utterly inexplicable. The amphibious existence of the vampire is sustained by daily renewed slumber in the grave. Its horrible lust for living blood supplies the vigor of its waking existence. The vampire is prone to be fascinated with an engrossing vehemence, resembling the passion of love, by particular persons. In pursuit of these it will exercise inexhaustible patience and stratagem, for access to a particular object may be obstructed in a hundred ways. It will never desist until it has satiated its passion, and drained the very life of its coveted victim. But it will, in these cases, husband and protract its murderous enjoyment with the refinement of an epicure, and heighten it by the gradual approaches of an artful courtship. In these cases it seems to yearn for something like sympathy and consent. In ordinary ones it goes direct to its object, overpowers with violence, and strangles and exhausts often at a single feast.

The vampire is, apparently, subject, in certain situations, to special conditions. In the particular instance of which I have given you a relation, Mircalla seemed to be limited to a name which, if not her real one, should at least reproduce, without the omission or addition of a single letter, those, as we say, anagrammatically, which compose it.

Carmilla did this; so did Millarca.

My father related to the Baron Vordenburg, who remained with us for two or three weeks after the expulsion of Carmilla, the story about the Moravian nobleman and the vampire at Karnstein churchyard, and then he asked the Baron how he had discovered the exact position of the long-concealed tomb of the Countess Mircalla? The Baron's grotesque features puckered up into a mysterious smile; he looked down, still smiling on his worn spectacle case and fumbled with it. Then looking up, he said:

"I have many journals, and other papers, written by that remarkable man; the most curious among them is one treating of the visit of which you speak, to Karnstein. The tradition, of course, discolors and distorts a little. He might have been termed a Moravian nobleman, for he had changed his abode to that territory, and was, beside, a noble. But he was, in truth, a native of Upper Styria. It is enough to say that in very early youth he had been a passionate and favored lover of the beautiful Mircalla, Countess Karnstein. Her early death plunged him into inconsolable grief. It is the nature of vampires to increase and multiply, but according to an ascertained and ghostly law.

"Assume, at starting, a territory perfectly free from that pest. How does it begin, and how does it multiply itself? I will tell you. A person, more or less wicked, puts an end to himself. A suicide, under certain circumstances, becomes a vampire. That specter visits living people in their slumbers; they die, and almost invariably, in the grave, develop into vampires. This happened in the case of the beautiful Mircalla, who was haunted by one of those demons. My ancestor, Vordenburg, whose title I still bear, soon discovered this, and in the course of the studies to which he devoted himself, learned a great deal more.

"Among other things, he concluded that suspicion of vampirism would probably fall, sooner or later, upon the dead Countess, who in life had been his idol. He conceived a horror, be she what she might, of her remains being profaned by the outrage of a posthumous execution. He has left a curious paper to prove that the vampire, on its expulsion from its amphibious existence, is projected into a far more horrible life; and he resolved to save his once beloved Mircalla from this.

"He adopted the stratagem of a journey here, a pretended removal of her remains, and a real obliteration of her monument. When age had stolen upon him, and from the vale of years, he looked back on the scenes he was leaving, he considered, in a different spirit, what he had done, and a horror took possession of him. He made the tracings and notes which have guided me to the very spot, and drew up a confession of the deception that he had practiced. If he had intended any further action in this matter, death prevented him; and the hand of a remote descendant has, too late for many, directed the pursuit to the lair of the beast."

We talked a little more, and among other things he said was this:

"One sign of the vampire is the power of the hand. The slender hand of Mircalla closed like a vice of steel on the General's wrist when he raised the hatchet to strike. But its power is not confined to its grasp; it leaves a numbness in the limb it seizes, which is slowly, if ever, recovered from."

The following Spring my father took me a tour through Italy. We remained away for more than a year. It was long before the terror of recent events subsided; and to this hour the image of Carmilla returns to memory with ambiguous alternations—sometimes the playful, languid, beautiful girl; sometimes the writhing fiend I saw in the ruined church; and often from a reverie I have started, fancying I heard the light step of Carmilla at the drawing room door.

THE EVIL
GUEST

"When Lust hath conceived, it bringeth forth Sin: and Sin, when it is finished, bringeth forth Death."

About sixty years ago, and somewhat more than twenty miles from the ancient town of Chester, in a southward direction, there stood a large, and, even then, an old-fashioned mansion-house. It lay in the midst of a demesne of considerable extent, and richly wooded with venerable timber; but, apart from the somber majesty of these giant groups, and the varieties of the undulating ground on which they stood, there was little that could be deemed attractive in the place. A certain air of neglect and decay, and an indescribable gloom and melancholy, hung over it. In darkness, it seemed darker than any other tract; when the moonlight fell upon its glades and hollows, they looked spectral and awful, with a sort of churchyard loneliness; and even when the blush of the morning kissed its broad woodlands, there was a melancholy in the salute that saddened rather than cheered the heart of the beholder.

This antique, melancholy, and neglected place, we shall call, for distinctness sake, Gray Forest. It was then the property of the younger son of a nobleman, once celebrated for his ability and his daring, but who had long since passed to that land where human wisdom and courage avail naught. The representative of this noble house resided at the family mansion in Sussex, and the cadet, whose fortunes we mean to sketch in these pages, lived upon the narrow margin of an encumbered income, in a reserved and unsocial discontent, deep among the solemn shadows of the old woods of Gray Forest.

The Hon. Richard Marston was now somewhere between forty and fifty years of age—perhaps nearer the latter; he still, however, retained, in an eminent degree, the traits of manly beauty, not the less remarkable for its unquestionably haughty and passionate character. He had married a beautiful girl, of good family, but without much money, somewhere about eighteen years before; and two children, a son and a daughter, had been the fruit of this union. The boy, Harry Marston, was at this time at Cambridge; and his sister, scarcely fifteen, was at home with her parents, and under the training of an accomplished governess, who had been recommended to them by a noble relative of Mrs. Marston. She was a native of France, but thoroughly mistress of the English language, and, except for a foreign accent, which gave a certain prettiness to all she said, she spoke it as perfectly as any native Englishwoman. This young Frenchwoman was eminently handsome and attractive. Expressive, dark eyes, a clear olive complexion, small even teeth, and a beautifully-dimpling smile, more perhaps than a strictly classic regularity of features, were the secrets of her unquestionable influence, at first sight, upon the fancy of every man of taste who beheld her.

Mr. Marston's fortune, never very large, had been shattered by early dissipation. Naturally of a proud and somewhat exacting temper, he actively felt the mortifying consequences of his poverty. The want of what he felt ought to have been his position and influence in the county in which he resided, fretted and galled him; and he cherished a resentful and bitter sense of every slight, imaginary or real, to which the same fruitful source of annoyance and humiliation had exposed him. He held, therefore, but little intercourse with the surrounding gentry, and that little not of the pleasantest possible kind; for, not being himself in a condition to entertain, in that style which accorded with his own ideas of his station, he declined, as far as was compatible with good breeding, all the proffered hospitalities of the neighborhood; and, from his wild and neglected park, looked out upon the surrounding world in a spirit of moroseness and defiance, very unlike, indeed, to that of neighborly good-will.

In the midst, however, of many of the annoyances attendant upon crippled means, he enjoyed a few of those shadowy indications of hereditary importance, which are all the more dearly prized, as the substantial accessories of wealth have disappeared. The mansion in which he dwelt was, though old-fashioned, imposing in its aspect, and upon a scale unequivocally aristocratic; its walls were hung with ancestral portraits, and he managed to maintain about him a large and tolerably respectable staff of servants. In addition to these, he had his extensive demesne, his deer-park, and his unrivalled timber, wherewith to console himself; and, in the consciousness of these possessions, he found some imperfect assuagement of those bitter feelings of suppressed scorn and resentment, which a sense of lost station and slighted importance engendered. Mr. Marston's early habits had, unhappily, been of a kind to aggravate, rather than alleviate, the annoyances incidental to reduced means. He had been a gay man, a voluptuary, and a gambler. His vicious tastes had survived the means of their gratification. His love for his wife had been nothing more than one of those vehement and headstrong fancies, which, in self-indulgent men, sometimes result in marriage, and which seldom outlive the first few months of that life-long connection. Mrs. Marston was a gentle, noble-minded woman. After agonies or disappointment, which none ever suspected, she had at length learned to submit, in sad and gentle acquiescence, to her fate. Those feelings, which had been the charm of her young days, were gone, and, as she bitterly felt, forever. For them there was no recall they could not return; and, without complaint or reproach, she yielded to what she felt was inevitable. It was impossible to look at Mrs. Marston, and not to discern, at a glance, the ruin of a surpassingly beautiful woman; a good deal wasted, pale, and chastened with a deep, untold sorrow, but still possessing the outlines, both in face and form, of that noble beauty and matchless grace, which had made her, in happier days, the admired of all observers. But equally impossible was it to converse with her, for even a minute, without hearing, in the gentle and melancholy music of her voice, the sad echoes of those griefs to which her early beauty had been sacrificed, an undying sense of lost love, and happiness departed, never to come again.

One morning, Mr. Marston had walked, as was his custom when he expected the messenger who brought from the neighboring post office his letters, some way down the broad, straight avenue, with its double rows of lofty trees at each side, when he encountered the nimble emissary on his return. He took the letter-bag in silence. It contained but two letters—one addressed to "Mademoiselle de Barras, chez M. Marston," and the other to himself. He took them both, dismissed the messenger, and opening that addressed to himself, read as follows, while he slowly retraced his steps towards the house:—

Dear Richard,

I am a whimsical fellow, as you doubtless remember, and have lately grown, they tell me, rather hippish besides. I do not know to which infirmity I am to attribute a sudden fancy that urges me to pay you a visit, if you will admit me. To say truth, my dear Dick, I wish to see a little of your part of the world, and, I will confess it, en passant, to see a little of you too. I really wish to make acquaintance with your family; and though they tell me my health is very much shaken, I must say, in self-defense, I am not a troublesome inmate. I can perfectly take care of myself, and need no nursing or caudling whatever. Will you present this, my petition, to Mrs. Marston, and report her decision thereon to me. Seriously, I know that your house may be full, or some other contretemps may make it impracticable for me just now to invade you. If it be so, tell me, my dear Richard, frankly, as my movements are perfectly free, and my time all my own, so that I can arrange my visit to suit your convenience.
—Yours, &c.,
WYNSTON E. BERKLEY

P.S.—Direct to me at — Hotel, in Chester, as I shall probably be there by the time this reaches you.

"Ill-bred and pushing as ever," quoth Mr. Marston, angrily, as he thrust the unwelcome letter into his pocket. "This fellow, wallowing in wealth, without one nearer relative on earth than I, and associated more nearly still with me the—pshaw! not affection—the recollections of early and intimate companionship, leaves me unaided, for years of desertion and suffering, to the buffetings of the world, and the troubles or all but overwhelming pecuniary difficulties, and now, with the cool confidence of one entitled to respect and welcome, invites himself to my house. Coming here," he continued, after a gloomy pause, and still pacing slowly towards the house, "to collect amusing materials for next season's gossip-stories about the married Benedick—the bankrupt beau—the outcast tenant of a Cheshire wilderness"; and, as he said this, he looked at the neglected prospect before him with an eye almost of hatred. "Aye, to see the nakedness of the land is he coming, but he shall be disappointed. His money may buy him a cordial welcome at an inn, but curse me if it shall purchase him a reception here."

He again opened and glanced through the letter.

"Aye, purposely put in such a way that I can't decline it without affronting him," he continued doggedly. "Well, then, he has no one to blame but himself—affronted he shall be; I shall effectually put an end to this humorous excursion. Egad, it is rather hard if a man cannot keep his poverty to himself."

Sir Wynston Berkley was a baronet of large fortune—a selfish, fashionable man, and an inveterate bachelor. He and Marston had been schoolfellows, and the violent and implacable temper of the latter had as little impressed his companion with feelings of regard, as the frivolity and selfishness of the baronet had won the esteem of his relative. As boys, they had little in common upon which to rest the basis of a friendship, or even a mutual liking. Berkley was gay, cold, and satirical; his cousin—for cousins they were—was jealous, haughty, and relentless. Their negative disinclination to one another's society, not unnaturally engendered by uncongenial and unamiable dispositions, had for a time given place to actual hostility, while the two young men were at Oxford. In some intrigue, Marston discovered in his cousin a too-successful rival; the consequence was, a bitter and furious quarrel, which, but for the prompt and peremptory interference of friends, Marston would undoubtedly have pushed to a bloody issue. Time had, however, healed this rupture, and the young men came to regard one another with the same feelings, and eventually to re-establish the same sort of cold and indifferent intimacy which had subsisted between them before their angry collision.

Under these circumstances, whatever suspicion Marston might have felt on the receipt of the unexpected, and indeed accountable proposal, which had just reached him, he certainly had little reason to complain of any violation of early friendship in the neglect with which Sir Wynston had hitherto treated him. In deciding to decline his proposed visit, however, Marston had not consulted the impulses of spite or anger. He knew the baronet well; he knew that he cherished no good will towards him, and that in the project which he had thus unexpectedly broached, whatever indirect or selfish schemes might possibly be at the bottom of it, no friendly feeling had ever mingled. He was therefore resolved to avoid the trouble and the expense of a visit in all respects distasteful to him, and in a gentlemanlike way, but, at the same time, as the reader may suppose, with very little anxiety as to whether or not his gay correspondent should take offence at his reply, to decline, once for all, the proposed distinction.

With this resolution, he entered the spacious and somewhat dilapidated mansion which called him master; and entering a sitting room, appropriated to his daughter's use, he found her there, in company with her beautiful French governess. He kissed his child, and saluted her young preceptress with formal courtesy.

"Mademoiselle," said he, "I have got a letter for you; and, Rhoda," he continued, addressing his pretty daughter, "bring this to your mother, and say, I request her to read it."

He gave her the letter he himself had just received, and the girl tripped lightly away upon her mission.

Had he narrowly scrutinised the countenance of the fair Frenchwoman, as she glanced at the direction of that which he had just placed in her hand, he might have seen certain transient, but very unmistakable evidences of excitement and agitation. She quickly concealed the letter, however, and with a sigh, the momentary flush which it had called to her cheek subsided, and she was tranquil as usual.

Mr. Marston remained for some minutes—five, eight, or ten, we cannot say precisely—pretty much where he had stood on first entering the chamber, doubtless awaiting the return of his messenger, or the appearance of his wife. At length, however, he left the room himself to seek her; but, during his brief stay, his previous resolution had been removed. By what influence we cannot say; but removed completely it unquestionably was, and a final determination that Sir Wynston Berkley should become his guest had fixedly taken its place.

As Marston walked along the passages which led from this room, he encountered Mrs. Marston and his daughter.

"Well," said he, "you have read Wynston's letter?"

"Yes," she replied, returning it to him; "and what answer, Richard, do you purpose giving him?"

She was about to hazard a conjecture, but checked herself, remembering that even so faint an evidence of a disposition to advise might possibly be resented by her cold and imperious lord.

"I have considered it, and decided to receive him," he replied.

"Ah! I am afraid—that is, I hope—he may find our housekeeping such as he can enjoy," she said, with an involuntary expression of surprise; for she had scarcely had a doubt that her husband would have preferred evading the visit of his fine friend, under his gloomy circumstances.

"If our modest fare does not suit him," said Marston, with sullen bitterness, "he can depart as easily as he came. We, poor gentlemen, can but do our best. I have thought it over, and made up my mind."

"And how soon, my dear Richard, do you intend fixing his arrival?" she inquired, with the natural uneasiness of one upon whom, in an establishment whose pretensions considerably exceeded its resources, the perplexing cares of housekeeping devolved.

"Why, as soon as he pleases," replied he, "I suppose you can easily have his room prepared by tomorrow or next day. I shall write by this mail, and tell him to come down at once."

Having said this in a cold, decisive way, he turned and left her, as it seemed, not caring to be teased with further questions. He took his solitary way to a distant part of his wild park, where, far from the likelihood of disturbance or intrusion, he was often wont to amuse himself for the live-long day, in the sedentary sport of shooting rabbits. And there we leave him for the present, signifying to the distant inmates of his house the industrious pursuit of his unsocial occupation, by the dropping fire that sullenly, from hour to hour, echoed from the remote woods.

Mrs. Marston issued her orders; and having set on foot all the necessary preparations for so unwonted an event as a stranger's visit of some duration, she betook herself to her little boudoir—the scene of many an hour of patient but bitter suffering, unseen by human eye, and unknown, except to the just Searcher of hearts, to whom belongs mercy—and vengeance.

Mrs. Marston had but two friends to whom she had ever spoken upon the subject nearest her heart—the estrangement of her husband, a sorrow to which even time had failed to reconcile her. From her children this grief was carefully concealed. To them she never uttered the semblance of a complaint. Anything that could by possibility have reflected blame or dishonor upon their father, she would have perished rather than have allowed them so much as to suspect. The two friends who did understand her feelings, though in different degrees, were, one, a good and venerable clergyman, the Rev. Doctor Danvers, a frequent visitor and occasional guest at Gray Forest, where his simple manners and

unaffected benignity and tenderness of heart had won the love of all, with the exception of its master, and commanded even his respect. The second was no other than the young French governess, Mademoiselle de Barras, in whose ready sympathy and consolatory counsels she found no small happiness. The society of this young lady had indeed become, next to that of her daughter, her greatest comfort and pleasure.

Mademoiselle de Barras was of a noble though ruined French family, and a certain nameless elegance and dignity attested, spite of her fallen condition, the purity of her descent. She was accomplished—possessed of that fine perception and sensitiveness, and that ready power of self-adaptation to the peculiarities and moods of others, which we term tact—and was, moreover, gifted with a certain natural grace, and manners the most winning imaginable. In short, she was a fascinating companion; and when the melancholy circumstances of her own situation; and the sad history of her once rich and noble family, were taken into account, with her striking attractions of person and air, the combination of all these associations and impressions rendered her one of the most interesting persons that could well be imagined. The circumstances of Mademoiselle de Barras's history and descent seemed to warrant, on Mrs. Marston's part, a closer intimacy and confidence than usually subsists between parties mutually occupying such a relation.

Mrs. Marston had hardly established herself in this little apartment, when a light foot approached, a gentle tap was given at the door, and Mademoiselle de Barras entered.

"Ah, mademoiselle, so kind—such pretty flowers. Pray sit down," said the lady, with a sweet and grateful smile, as she took from the tapered fingers of the foreigner the little bouquet, which she had been at the pains to gather.

Mademoiselle sat down, and gently took the lady's hand and kissed it. A small matter will overflow a heart charged with sorrow—a chance word, a look, some little office of kindness—and so it was with mademoiselle's bouquet and gentle kiss. Mrs. Marston's heart was touched; her eyes filled with bright tears; she smiled gratefully upon her fair and humble companion, and as she smiled, her tears overflowed, and she wept in silence for some minutes.

"My poor mademoiselle," she said, at last, "you are so very, very kind."

Mademoiselle said nothing; she lowered her eyes, and pressed the poor lady's hand.

Apparently to interrupt an embarrassing silence, and to give a more cheerful tone to their little interview, the governess, in a gay tone, on a sudden said—

"And so, madame, we are to have a visitor, Miss Rhoda tells me—a baronet, is he not?"

"Yes, indeed, mademoiselle—Sir Wynston Berkley, a gay London gentleman, and a cousin of Mr. Marston's," she replied.

"Ha—a cousin!" exclaimed the young lady, with a little more surprise in her tone than seemed altogether called for—"a cousin? oh, then, that is the reason of his visit. Do, pray, madame, tell me all about him; I am so much afraid of strangers, and what you call men of the world. Oh, dear Mrs. Marston, I am not worthy to be here, and he will see all that in a moment; indeed, indeed, I am afraid. Pray tell me all about him."

She said this with a simplicity which made the elder lady smile, and while mademoiselle re-adjusted the tiny flowers which formed the bouquet she had just presented to her, Mrs. Marston good-naturedly recounted to her all she knew of Sir Wynston Berkley, which, in substance, amounted to no more than we have already stated. When she concluded, the young Frenchwoman continued for some time silent, still busy with her flowers. But, suddenly, she heaved a deep sigh, and shook her head.

"You seem disquieted, mademoiselle," said Mrs. Marston, in a tone of kindness.

"I am thinking, madame," she said, still looking upon the flowers which she was adjusting, and again sighing profoundly, "I am thinking of what you said to me a week ago; alas!"

"I do not remember what it was, my good mademoiselle—nothing, I am sure, that ought to grieve you—at least nothing that was intended to have that effect," replied the lady, in a tone of gentle encouragement.

"No, not intended, madame," said the young Frenchwoman, sorrowfully.

"Well, what was it? Perhaps you misunderstood; perhaps I can explain what I said," replied Mrs. Marston, affectionately.

"Ah, madame, you think—you think I am unlucky," answered the young lady, slowly and faintly.

"Unlucky! Dear mademoiselle, you surprise me," rejoined her companion.

"I mean—what I mean is this, madame; you date unhappiness—if not its beginning, at least its great aggravation and increase," she answered, dejectedly, "from the time of my coming here, madame; and though I know you are too good to dislike me on that account, yet I must, in your eyes, be ever connected with calamity, and look like an ominous thing."

"Dear mademoiselle, allow no such thought to enter your mind. You do me great wrong, indeed you do," said Mrs. Marston, laying her hand upon the young lady's, kindly.

There was a silence for a little time, and the elder lady resumed:—"I remember now what you allude to, dear mademoiselle—the increased estrangement, the widening separation which severs me from one unutterably dear to me—the first and bitter disappointment of my life, which seems to grow more hopelessly incurable day by day."

Mrs. Marston paused, and, after a brief silence, the governess said:—

"I am very superstitious myself, dear madame, and I thought I must have seemed to you an inauspicious inmate—in short, unlucky—as I have said; and the thought made me very unhappy—so unhappy, that I was going to leave you, madame—I may now tell you frankly—going away; but you have set my doubts at rest, and I am quite happy again."

"Dear mademoiselle," cried the lady, tenderly, and rising, as she spake, to kiss the cheek of her humble friend; "never—never speak of this again. God knows I have too few friends on earth, to spare the kindest and tenderest among them all. No, no. You little think what comfort I have found in your warm-hearted and ready sympathy, and how dearly I prize your affection, my poor mademoiselle."

The young Frenchwoman rose, with downcast eyes, and a dimpling, happy smile; and, as Mrs. Marston drew her affectionately toward her, and kissed her, she timidly returned the embrace of her kind patroness.

For a moment her graceful arms encircled her, and she whispered to her, "Dear madame, how happy—how very happy you make me."

Had Ithuriel touched with his spear the beautiful young woman, thus for a moment, as it seemed, lost in a trance of gratitude and love, would that angelic form have stood the test unscathed? A spectator, marking the scene, might have observed a strange gleam in her eyes—a strange expression in her face—an influence for a moment not angelic, like a shadow of some passing spirit, cross her visibly, as she leaned over the gentle lady's neck, and murmured, "Dear madame, how happy—how very happy you make me." Such a spectator, as he looked at that gentle lady, might have seen, for one dreamy moment, a lithe and painted serpent, coiled round and round, and hissing in her ear.

A few minutes more, and mademoiselle was in the solitude of her own apartment. She shut and bolted the door, and taking from her desk the letter which she had that morning received, threw herself into an armchair, and studied the document profoundly. Her actual revision and scrutiny of the letter itself was interrupted by long intervals of profound abstraction; and, after a full hour thus spent, she locked it carefully up again, and with a clear brow, and a gay smile, rejoined her pretty pupil for a walk.

We must now pass over an interval of a few days, and come at once to the arrival of Sir Wynston Berkley, which duly occurred upon the evening of the day appointed. The baronet descended from his chaise but a short time before the hour at which the little party, which formed the family at Gray Forest were wont to assemble for the social meal of supper. A few minutes devoted to the mysteries of the toilet, with the aid of an accomplished valet, enabled him to appear, as he conceived, without disadvantage at this domestic reunion.

Sir Wynston Berkley was a particularly gentleman-like person. He was rather tall, and elegantly made, with gay, easy manners, and something indefinably aristocratic in his face, which, however, was a little more worn than his years would have strictly accounted for. But Sir Wynston had been a roué, and, spite of the cleverest possible making up, the ravages of excess were very traceable in the lively beau of fifty. Perfectly well dressed, and with a manner that was ease and gaiety itself, he was at home from the moment he entered the room. Of course, anything like genuine cordiality was out of the question; but Mr. Marston embraced his relative with perfect good breeding, and the baronet appeared determined to like everybody, and be pleased with everything. He had not been five minutes in the parlor, chatting gaily with Mr. and Mrs. Marston and their pretty daughter, when Mademoiselle de Barras entered the room. As she moved towards Mrs. Marston, Sir Wynston rose, and, observing her with evident admiration, said in an undertone, inquiringly, to Marston, who was beside him—

"And this?"

"That is Mademoiselle de Barras, my daughter's governess, and Mrs. Marston's companion," said Marston, drily.

"Ha!" said Sir Wynston; "I thought you were but three at home just now, and I was right. Your son is at Cambridge; I heard so from our old friend, Jack Manbury. Jack has his boy there too. Egad, Dick, it seems but last week that you and I were there together."

"Yes," said Marston, looking gloomily into the fire, as if he saw, in its smoke and flicker, the phantoms of murdered time and opportunity; "but I hate looking back, Wynston. The past is to me but a medley of ill-luck and worse management."

"Why what an ungrateful dog you are!" returned Sir Wynston, gaily, turning his back upon the fire, and glancing round the spacious and handsome, though somewhat faded apartment. "I was on the point of congratulating you on the possession of the finest park and noblest demesne in Cheshire, when you begin to grumble. Egad, Dick, all I can say to your complaint is, that I don't pity you, and there are dozens who may honestly envy you—that is all."

In spite of this cheering assurance, Marston remained sullenly silent. Supper, however, had now been served, and the little party assumed their places at the table.

"I am sorry, Wynston, I have no sport of any kind to offer you here," said Marston, "except, indeed, some good trout-fishing, if you like it. I have three miles of excellent fishing at your command."

"My dear fellow, I am a mere cockney," rejoined Sir Wynston; "I am not a sportsman; I never tried it, and should not like to begin now. No, Dick, what I much prefer is, abundance of your fresh air, and the enjoyment of your scenery. When I was at Rouen three years ago—"

"Ha!—Rouen? Mademoiselle will feel an interest in that; it is her birth-place," interrupted Marston, glancing at the Frenchwoman.

"Yes—Rouen—ah—yes!" said mademoiselle, with very evident embarrassment.

Sir Wynston appeared for a moment a little disconcerted too, but rallied speedily, and pursued his detail of his doings at that fair town of Normandy.

Marston knew Sir Wynston well; and he rightly calculated that whatever effect his experience of the world might have had in intensifying his selfishness or hardening his heart, it certainly could have had none in improving a character originally worthless and unfeeling. He knew, moreover, that his wealthy cousin was gifted with a great deal of that small cunning which is available for masking the little scheming of frivolous and worldly men; and that Sir Wynston never took trouble of any kind without a sufficient purpose, having its center in his own personal gratification.

This visit greatly puzzled Marston; it gave him even a vague sense of uneasiness. Could there exist any flaw in his own title to the estate of Gray Forest? He had an unpleasant, doubtful sort of remembrance of some apprehensions of this kind, when he was but a child, having been whispered in the family. Could this really be so, and could the baronet have been led to make this unexpected visit merely for the purpose of personally examining into the condition or a property of which he was about to become the legal invader? The nature of this suspicion affords, at all events, a fair gauge of Marston's estimate of his cousin's character. And as he revolved these doubts from time to time, and as he thought of Mademoiselle de Barras's transient, but unaccountable embarrassment at the mention of Rouen by Sir Wynston—an embarrassment which the baronet himself appeared for a moment to reciprocate—undefined, glimmering suspicions of another kind flickered through the darkness of his mind. He was effectually puzzled; his surmises and conjectures baffled; and he more than half repented that he had acceded to his cousin's proposal, and admitted him as an inmate of his house.

Although Sir Wynston comported himself as if he were conscious of being the very most welcome visitor who could possibly have established himself at Gray Forest, he was, doubtless, fully aware of the real feelings with which he was regarded by his host. If he had in reality an object in prolonging his stay, and wished to make the postponement of his departure the direct interest of his entertainer, he unquestionably took effectual measures for that purpose.

The little party broke up every evening at about ten o'clock, and Sir Wynston retired to his chamber at the same hour. He found little difficulty in inducing Marston to amuse him there with a quiet game of piquet. In his own room, therefore, in the luxurious ease of dressing gown and slippers he sat at cards with his host, often until an hour or two past midnight. Sir Wynston was exorbitantly wealthy, and very reckless in expenditure. The stakes for which they played, although they gradually became in reality pretty heavy, were in his eyes a very unimportant consideration. Marston, on the other hand, was poor, and played with the eye of a lynx and the appetite of a shark. The ease and perfect good-humor with which Sir Wynston lost were not unimproved by his entertainer, who, as may readily be supposed, was not sorry to reap this golden harvest, provided without the slightest sacrifice, on his part, of pride or independence. If, indeed, he sometimes suspected that his guest was a little more anxious to lose than to win, he was also quite resolved not to perceive it, but calmly persisted in, night after night, giving

Sir Wynston, as he termed it, his revenge; or, in other words, treating him to a repetition of his losses. All this was very agreeable to Marston, who began to treat his visitor with, at all events, more external cordiality and distinction than at first.

An incident, however, occurred, which disturbed these amicable relations in an unexpected way. It becomes necessary here to mention that Mademoiselle de Barras's sleeping apartment opened from a long corridor. It was en suite with two dressing rooms, each opening also upon the corridor, but wholly unused and unfurnished. Some five or six other apartments also opened at either side, upon the same passage. These little local details being premised, it so happened that one day Marston, who had gone out with the intention of angling in the trout-stream which flowed through his park, though at a considerable distance from the house, having unexpectedly returned to procure some tackle which he had forgotten, was walking briskly through the corridor in question to his own apartment, when, to his surprise, the door of one of the deserted dressing-rooms, of which we have spoken, was cautiously pushed open, and Sir Wynston Berkley issued from it. Marston was almost beside him as he did so, and Sir Wynston made a motion as if about instinctively to draw back again, and at the same time the keen ear of his host distinctly caught the sound of rustling silks and a tiptoe tread hastily withdrawing from the deserted chamber. Sir Wynston looked nearly as much confused as a man of the world can look. Marston stopped short, and scanned his visitor for a moment with a very peculiar expression.

"You have caught me peeping, Dick. I am an inveterate explorer," said the baronet, with an effectual effort to shake off his embarrassment. "An open door in a fine old house is a temptation which—"

"That door is usually closed, and ought to be kept so," interrupted Marston, drily; "there is nothing whatever to be seen in the room but dust and cobwebs."

"Pardon me," said Sir Wynston, more easily, "you forget the view from the window."

"Aye, the view, to be sure; there is a good view from it," said Marston, with as much of his usual manner as he could resume so soon; and, at the same time, carelessly opening the door again, he walked in, accompanied by Sir Wynston, and both stood at the window together, looking out in silence upon a prospect which neither of them saw.

"Yes, I do think it is a good view," said Marston; and as he turned carelessly away, he darted a swift glance round the chamber. The door opening toward the French lady's apartment was closed, but not actually shut. This was enough; and as they left the room, Marston repeated his invitation to his guest to accompany him; but in a tone which showed that he scarcely followed the meaning of what he himself was saying.

He walked undecidedly toward his own room, then turned and went down stairs. In the hall he met his pretty child.

"Ha! Rhoda," said he, "you have not been out today?"

"No, papa; but it is so very fine, I think I shall go now."

"Yes; go, and mademoiselle can accompany you. Do you hear, Rhoda, mademoiselle goes with you, and you had better go at once."

A few minutes more, and Marston, from the parlor-window, beheld Rhoda and the elegant French girl walking together towards the woodlands. He watched them gloomily, himself unseen, until the crowding underwood concealed their receding figures. Then, with a sigh, he turned, and reascended the great staircase.

"I shall sift this mystery to the bottom," thought he. "I shall foil the conspirators, if so they be, with their own weapons; art with art; chicane with chicane; duplicity with duplicity."

He was now in the long passage, which we have just spoken of, and glancing back and before him, to ascertain that no chance eye discerned him, he boldly entered mademoiselle's chamber. Her writing desk lay upon the table. It was locked; and coolly taking it in his hands, Marston carried it into his own room, bolted his chamber-door, and taking two or three bunches of keys, he carefully tried nearly a dozen in succession, and when almost despairing of success, at last found one which fitted the lock, turned, and opened the desk.

Sustained throughout his dishonorable task by some strong and angry passion, the sight of the open escritoire checked and startled him for a moment. Violated privilege, invaded secrecy, base, perfidious espionage upbraided and stigmatized him, as the intricacies of the outraged sanctuary opened upon his intrusive gaze. He felt for a moment shocked and humbled. He was impelled to lock and replace the desk where he had originally found it, without having effected his meditated treason; but this hesitation was transient the fiery and reckless impulse which had urged him to the act returned to enforce its consummation. With a guilty eye and eager hands, he searched the contents of this tiny repository of the fair Norman's written secrets.

"Ha! the very thing," he muttered, as he detected the identical letter which he himself had handed to Mademoiselle de Barras but a few days before. "The handwriting struck me, ill-disguised; I thought I knew it; we shall see."

He had opened the letter; it contained but a few lines: he held his breath while he read it. First he grew pale, then a shadow came over his face, and then another, and another, darker and darker, shade upon shade, as if an exhalation from the pit was momentarily blackening the air about him. He said nothing; there was but one long, gentle sigh, and in his face a mortal sternness, as he folded the letter again, replaced it, and locked the desk.

Of course, when Mademoiselle de Barras returned from her accustomed walk, she found everything in her room, to all appearances, undisturbed, and just as when she left it. While this young lady was making her toilet for the evening, and while Sir Wynston Berkley was worrying himself with conjectures as to whether Marston's evil looks, when he encountered him that morning in the passage, existed only in his own fancy, or were, in good truth, very grim and significant realities, Marston himself was striding alone through the wildest and darkest solitudes of his park, haunted by his own unholy thoughts, and, it may be, by those other evil and unearthly influences which wander, as we know, "in desert places." Darkness overtook him, and the chill of night, in these lonely tracts. In his solitary walk, what fearful company had he been keeping! As the shades of night deepened round him, the sense of the neighborhood of ill, the consciousness of the foul fancies or which, where he was now treading, he had been for hours the sport, oppressed him with a vague and unknown terror; a certain horror of the thoughts which had been his comrades through the day, which he could not now shake off, and which haunted him with a ghastly and defiant pertinacity, scared, while they half-enraged him. He stalked swiftly homewards, like a guilty man pursued.

Marston was not perfectly satisfied, though very nearly, with the evidence now in his possession. The letter, the stolen perusal of which had so agitated him that day, bore no signature; but, independently of the handwriting, which seemed, spite of the constraint of an attempted disguise, to be familiar to his eye, there existed, in the matter of the letter, short as it was, certain internal evidences, which, although not actually conclusive, raised, in conjunction with all the other circumstances, a powerful presumption in aid of his suspicions. He resolved, however, to sift the matter further, and to bide his time. Meanwhile his manner must indicate no trace of his dark surmises and bitter thoughts. Deception, in its two great branches, simulation and dissimulation, was easy to him. His habitual reserve and gloom would divest any accidental and momentary disclosure of his inward trouble of everything suspicious or unaccountable, which would have characterized such displays and eccentricities in another man.

His rapid and reckless ramble, a kind of physical vent for the paroxysm which had so agitated him throughout the greater part of the day, had soiled and disordered his dress, and thus had helped to give to his whole appearance a certain air of haggard wildness, which, in the privacy of his chamber, he hastened carefully and entirely to remove.

At supper, Marston was apparently in unusually good spirits. Sir Wynston and he chatted gaily and fluently upon many subjects, grave and gay. Among them the inexhaustible topic of popular superstition happened to turn up, and especially the subject of strange prophecies of the fates and fortunes of individuals, singularly fulfilled in the events of their afterlife.

"By-the-by, Dick, this is rather a nervous topic for me to discuss," said Sir Wynston.

"How so?" asked his host.

"Why, don't you remember?" urged the baronet.

"No, I don't recollect what you allude to," replied Marston, in all sincerity.

"Why, don't you remember Eton?" pursued Sir Wynston.

"Yes, to be sure," said Marston.

"Well?" continued his visitor.

"Well, I really don't recollect the prophecy," replied Marston.

"What! do you forget the gypsy who predicted that you were to murder me, Dick—eh?"

"Ah-ha, ha!" laughed Marston, with a start.

"Don't you remember it now?" urged his companion.

"Ah, why yes, I believe I do," said Marston; "but another prophecy was running in my mind; a gypsy prediction, too. At Ascot, do you recollect the girl told me I was to be Lord Chancellor of England, and a duke besides?"

"Well, Dick," rejoined Sir Wynston, merrily, "if both are to be fulfilled, or neither, I trust you may never sit upon the woolsack of England."

The party soon after broke up: Sir Wynston and his host, as usual, to pass some hours at piquet; and Mrs. Marston, as was her wont, to, spend some time in her own boudoir, over notes and accounts, and the worrying details of housekeeping.

While thus engaged, she was disturbed by a respectful tap at her door, and an elderly servant, who had been for many years in the employment of Mr. Marston, presented himself.

"Well, Merton, do you want anything?" asked the lady.

"Yes, ma'am, please, I want to give warning; I wish to leave the service, ma'am;" replied he, respectfully, but doggedly.

"To leave us, Merton!" echoed his mistress, both surprised and sorry for the man had been long her servant, and had been much liked and trusted.

"Yes, ma'am," he repeated.

"And why do you wish to do so, Merton? Has anything occurred to make the place unpleasant to you?" urged the lady.

"No, ma'am—no, indeed," said he, earnestly, "I have nothing to complain of—nothing, indeed, ma'am."

"Perhaps, you think you can do better, if you leave us?" suggested his mistress.

"No, indeed, ma'am, I have no such thought," he said, and seemed on the point of bursting into tears; "but—but, somehow—ma'am, there is something come over me, lately, and I can't help, but think, if I stay here, ma'am—some—some—misfortune will happen us all— and that is the truth, ma'am."

"This is very foolish, Merton—a mere childish fancy," replied Mrs. Marston; "you like your place, and have no better prospect before you; and now, for a mere superstitious fancy, you propose giving it up, and leaving us. No, no, Merton, you had better think the matter over—and if you still, upon reflection, prefer going away, you can then speak to your master."

"Thank you ma'am—God bless you," said the man, withdrawing.

Mrs. Marston rang the bell for her maid, and retired to her room. "Has anything occurred lately," she asked, "to annoy Merton?"

"No, ma'am, I don't know of anything; but he is very changed, indeed, of late," replied the maid.

"He has not been quarreling?" inquired she.

"Oh, no, ma'am, he never quarrels; he is very quiet, and keeps to himself always; he thinks a wonderful deal of himself," replied the servant.

"But, you said that he is much changed—did you not?" continued the lady; for there was something strangely excited and unpleasant in the man's manner, in this little interview, which struck Mrs. Marston, and alarmed her curiosity. He had seemed like one charged with some horrible secret—intolerable, and which he yet dared not reveal.

"What," proceeded Mrs. Marston, "is the nature of the change of which you speak?"

"Why, ma'am, he is like one frightened, and in sorrow," she replied; "he will sit silent, and now and then shaking his head, as if he wanted to get rid of something that is teasing him, for an hour together."

"Poor man!" said she.

"And, then, when we are at meals, he will, all on a sudden, get up, and leave the table; and Jem Boulter, that sleeps in the next room to him, says, that, almost as often as he looks through the little window between the two rooms, no matter what hour in the night, he sees Mr. Merton on his knees by the bedside, praying or crying, he don't know which; but, any way, he is not happy—poor man!—and that is plain enough."

"It is very strange," said the lady, after a pause; "but, I think, and hope, after all, it will prove to have been no more than a little nervousness."

"Well, ma'am, I do hope it is not his conscience that is coming against him, now," said the maid.

"We have no reason to suspect anything of the kind," said Mrs. Marston, gravely, "quite the reverse; he has been always a particularly proper man."

"Oh, indeed," responded the attendant, "goodness forbid I should say or think anything against him; but I could not help telling you my mind, ma'am, meaning no harm."

"And, how long is it since you observed this sad change in poor Merton?" persisted the lady.

"Not, indeed, to say very long, ma'am," replied the girl; "somewhere about a week, or very little more—at least, as we remarked, ma'am."

Mrs. Marston pursued her inquiries no further that night. But, although she affected to treat the matter thus lightly, it had, somehow, taken a painful hold upon her imagination, and left in her mind those undefinable and ominous sensations, which, in certain mental temperaments, seem to foreshadow the approach of unknown misfortune.

For two or three days, everything went on smoothly, and pretty much as usual. At the end of this brief interval, however, the attention of Mrs. Marston was recalled to the subject of her servant's mysterious anxiety to leave, and give up his situation. Merton again stood before her, and repeated the intimation he had already given.

"Really, Merton, this is very odd," said the lady. "You like your situation, and yet you persist in desiring to leave it. What am I to think?"

"Oh, ma'am," said he, "I am unhappy; I am tormented, ma'am. I can't tell you, ma'am; I can't indeed ma'am!"

"If anything weighs upon your mind, Merton, I would advise you to consult our good clergyman, Dr. Danvers," urged the lady.

The servant hung his head, and mused for a time gloomily; and then said decisively—"No, ma'am; no use."

"And pray, Merton, how long is it since you first entertained this desire?" asked Mrs. Marston.

"Since Sir Wynston Berkley came, ma'am," answered he.

"Has Sir Wynston annoyed you in any way?" continued she.

"Far from it, ma'am," he replied; "he is a very kind gentleman."

"Well, his man, then; is he a respectable, inoffensive person?" she inquired.

"I never met one more so," said the man, promptly, and raising his head.

"What I wish to know is, whether your desire to go is connected with Sir Wynston and his servant?" said Mrs. Marston.

The man hesitated, and shifted his position uneasily.

"You need not answer, Merton, if you don't wish it," she said kindly.

"Why, ma'am, yes, it has something to say to them both," he replied, with some agitation.

"I really cannot understand this," said she.

Merton hesitated for some time, and appeared much troubled. "It was something, ma'am—something that Sir Wynston's man said to me; and there it is out," he said at last, with an effort.

"Well, Merton," said she, "I won't press you further; but I must say, that as this communication, whatever it may be, has caused you, unquestionably, very great uneasiness, it seems to me but probable that it affects the safety or the interests of some person—I cannot say of whom; and, if so, there can be no doubt that it is your duty to acquaint those who are so involved in the disclosure, with its purport."

"No, ma'am, there is nothing in what I heard that could touch anybody but myself. It was nothing but what others heard, without remarking it, or thinking about it. I can't tell you anymore, ma'am; but I am very unhappy, and uneasy in my mind."

As the man said this, he began to weep bitterly.

The idea that his mind was affected now seriously occurred to Mrs. Marston, and she resolved to convey her suspicions to her husband, and to leave him to deal with the case as to him should seem good.

"Don't agitate yourself so, Merton; I shall speak to your master upon what you have said; and you may rely upon it, that no surmise to the prejudice of your character has entered my mind," said Mrs. Marston, very kindly.

"Oh, ma'am, you are too good," sobbed the poor man, vehemently. "You don't know me, ma'am; I never knew myself till lately. I am a miserable man. I am frightened at myself, ma'am—frightened terribly. Christ knows, it would be well for me I was dead this minute."

"I am very sorry for your unhappiness, Merton," said Mrs. Marston; "and, especially, that I can do nothing to alleviate it; I can but speak, as I have said, to your master, and he will give you your discharge, and arrange whatever else remains to be done."

"God bless you, ma'am," said the servant, still much agitated, and left her.

Mr. Marston usually passed the early part of the day in active exercise, and she, supposing that he was, in all probability, at that moment far from home, went to "mademoiselle's" chamber, which was at the other end of the spacious house, to confer with her in the interval upon the strange application thus urged by poor Merton.

Just as she reached the door of Mademoiselle de Barras's chamber, she heard voices within exerted in evident excitement. She stopped in amazement. They were those of her husband and mademoiselle. Startled, confounded, and amazed, she pushed open the door, and entered. Her husband was sitting, one hand clutched upon the arm of the chair he occupied, and the other extended, and clenched, as it seemed, with the emphasis of rage, upon the desk that stood upon the table. His face was darkened with the stormiest passions, and his gaze was fixed upon the Frenchwoman, who was standing with a look half-guilty, half-imploring, at a little distance.

There was something, to Mrs. Marston, so utterly unexpected, and even so shocking, in this tableau, that she stood for some seconds pale and breathless, and gazing with a vacant stare of fear and horror from her husband to the French girl, and from her to her husband again. The three figures in this strange group remained fixed, silent, and aghast, for several seconds. Mrs. Marston endeavored to speak; but, though her lips moved, no sound escaped her; and, from very weakness, she sank, half-fainting, into a chair.

Marston rose, throwing, as he did so, a guilty and furious glance at the young Frenchwoman, and walked a step or two toward the door; he hesitated, however, and turned, just as mademoiselle, bursting into tears, threw her arms round Mrs. Marston's neck, and passionately exclaimed, "Protect me, madame, I implore, from the insults and suspicions of your husband."

Marston stood a little behind his wife, and he and the governess exchanged a glance of keen significance, as the latter sank, sobbing, like an injured child into its mother's embrace, upon the poor lady's tortured bosom.

"Madame, madame! he says—Mr. Marston says—I have presumed to give you advice, and to meddle, and to interfere; that I am endeavoring to make you despise his authority. Madame, speak for me. Say, madame, have I ever done so?—say, madame, am I the cause of bitterness and contumacy? Ah, mon Dieu! c'est trop—it is too much, madame. I shall go—I must go, madame. Why, ah! why, did I stay for this?"

As she thus spoke, mademoiselle again burst into a paroxysm of weeping, and again the same significant glance was interchanged.

"Go; yes, you shall go," said Marston, striding toward the window. "I will have no whispering or conspiring in my house: I have heard of your confidences and consultations. Mrs. Marston, I meant to have done this quietly," he continued, addressing his wife; "I meant to have given Mademoiselle de Barras my opinion and her dismissal without your assistance; but it seems you wish to interpose. You are sworn friends, and never fail one another, of course, at a pinch. I take it for granted that I owe your presence at our interview which I am resolved shall be, as respects mademoiselle, a final one, to a message from that intriguing young lady—eh?"

"I have had no message, Richard," said Mrs. Marston; "I don't know—do tell me, for God's sake, what is all this about?" And as the poor lady thus spoke, her overwrought feelings found vent in a violent flood of tears.

"Yes, madame, that is the question. I have asked him frequently what is all this anger, all these reproaches about; what have I done?" interposed mademoiselle, with indignant vehemence, standing erect, and viewing Marston with a flashing eye and a flushed cheek. "Yes, I am called conspirator, meddler, intrigant. Ah, madame, it is intolerable."

"But what have I done, Richard?" urged the poor lady, stunned and bewildered; "how have I offended you?"

"Yes, yes," continued the Frenchwoman, with angry volubility, "what has she done that you call contumacy and disrespect? Yes, dear madame, there is the question; and if he cannot answer, is it not most cruel to call me conspirator, and spy, and intrigant, because I talk to my dear madame, who is my only friend in this place?"

"Mademoiselle de Barras, I need no declamation from you; and, pardon me, Mrs. Marston, nor from you either," retorted he; "I have my information from one on whom I can rely; let that suffice. Of course you are both agreed in a story. I dare say you are ready to swear you never so much as canvassed my conduct, and my coldness and estrangement—eh? These are the words, are not they?"

"I have done you no wrong, sir; madame can tell you. I am no mischief-maker; no, I never was such a thing. Was I, madame?" persisted the governess—"bear witness for me?"

"I have told you my mind, Mademoiselle de Barras," interrupted Marston; "I will have no altercation, if you please. I think, Mrs. Marston, we have had enough of this; may I accompany you hence?"

So saying, he took the poor lady's passive hand, and led her from the room. Mademoiselle stood in the center of the apartment, alone, erect, with heaving breast and burning cheek—beautiful, thoughtful, guilty—the very type of the fallen angelic. There for a time, her heart all confusion, her mind darkened, we must leave her; various courses before her, and as yet without resolution to choose among them; a lost spirit, borne on the eddies of the storm; fearless and self-reliant, but with no star to guide her on her dark, malign, and forlorn way.

Mrs. Marston, in her own room, reviewed the agitating scene through which she had just been so unexpectedly carried. The tremendous suspicion which, at the first disclosure of the tableau we have described, smote the heart and brain of the poor lady with the stun of a thunderbolt, had been, indeed, subsequently disturbed, and afterwards contradicted; but the shock of her first impression remained still upon her mind and heart. She felt still through every nerve the vibrations of that maddening terror and despair which had overcome her senses for a moment. The surprise, the shock, the horror, outlived the obliterating influence of what followed. She was in this agitation when Mademoiselle de Barras entered her chamber, resolved with all her art to second and support the success of her prompt measures in the recent critical emergency. She had come, she said, to bid her dear madame farewell, for she was resolved to go. Her own room had been invaded, that insult and reproach might be heaped upon her; how utterly unmerited Mrs. Marston knew. She had been called by every foul name which applied to the spy and the maligner; she could not bear it. Some one had evidently been endeavoring to procure her removal, and had but too effectually succeeded. Mademoiselle was determined to go early the next morning; nothing should prevent or retard her departure; her resolution was taken. In this strain did mademoiselle run on, but in a subdued and melancholy tone, and weeping profusely.

The wild and ghastly suspicions which had for a moment flashed terribly upon the mind of Mrs. Marston, had faded away under the influences of reason and reflection, although, indeed, much painful excitement still remained, before Mademoiselle de Barras had visited her room. Marston's temper she knew but too well; it was violent, bitter, and impetuous; and though he cared little, if at all, for her, she had ever perceived that he was angrily jealous of the slightest intimacy or confidence by which any other than himself might establish an influence over her mind. That he had learned the subject of some of her most interesting conversations with mademoiselle she could not doubt, for he had violently upbraided that young lady in her presence with having discussed it, and here now was mademoiselle herself taking refuge with her from galling affront and unjust reproach, incensed, wounded, and weeping. The whole thing was consistent; all the circumstances bore plainly in the same direction; the evidence was conclusive; and Mrs. Marston's thoughts and feelings respecting her fair young confidante quickly found their old level, and flowed on tranquilly and sadly in their accustomed channel.

While Mademoiselle de Barras was thus, with the persevering industry of the spider, repairing the meshes which a chance breath had shattered, she would, perhaps, have been in her turn shocked and startled, could she have glanced into Marston's mind, and seen, in what was passing there, the real extent of her danger.

Marston was walking, as usual, alone, and in the most solitary region of his lonely park. One hand grasped his walking stick, not to lean upon it, but as if it were the handle of a battle-axe; the other was buried in his bosom; his dark face looked upon the ground, and he strode onward with a slow but energetic step, which had the air of deep resolution. He found himself at last in a little churchyard, lying far among the wild forest of his demesne, and in the midst of which, covered with ivy and tufted plants, now ruddy with autumnal tints, stood the ruined walls of a little chapel. In the dilapidated vault close by lay buried many of his ancestors, and under the little wavy hillocks of fern and nettles, slept many an humble villager. He sat down upon a worn tombstone in this lowly ruin, and with his eyes fixed upon the ground, he surrendered his spirit to the stormy and evil thoughts which he had invited. Long and motionless he sat there, while his foul fancies and schemes began to assume shape and order. The wind rushing through the ivy roused him for a moment, and as he raised his gloomy eye it alighted accidentally upon a skull, which some wanton hand had fixed in a crevice of the wall. He averted his glance quickly, but almost as quickly refixed his gaze upon the impassive symbol of death, with an expression glowering and contemptuous, and with an angry gesture struck it down among the weeds with his stick. He left the place, and wandered on through the woods.

"Men can't control the thoughts that flit across their minds," he muttered, as he went along, "anymore than they can direct the shadows of the clouds that sail above them. They come and pass, and leave no stain behind. What, then, of omens, and that wretched effigy of death? Stuff—pshaw! Murder, indeed! I'm incapable of murder. I have drawn my sword upon a man in fair duel; but murder! Out upon the thought, out upon it."

He stamped upon the ground with a pang at once of fury and horror. He walked on a little, stopped again, and folding his arms, leaned against an ancient tree.

"Mademoiselle de Barras, _vous êtes une traîtresse_, and you shall go. Yes, go you shall; you have deceived me, and we must part."

He said this with melancholy bitterness; and, after a pause, continued:

"I will have no other revenge. No; though, I dare say, she will care but little for this; very little, if at all."

"And then, as to the other person," he resumed, after a pause, "it is not the first time he has acted like a trickster. He has crossed me before, and I will choose an opportunity to tell him my mind. I won't mince matters with him either, and will not spare him one insulting syllable that he deserves. He wears a sword, and so do I; if he pleases, he may draw it; he shall have the opportunity; but, at all events, I will make it impossible for him to prolong his disgraceful visit at my house."

On reaching home and his own study, the servant, Merton, presented himself, and his master, too deeply excited to hear him then, appointed the next day for the purpose. There was no contending against Marston's peremptory will, and the man reluctantly withdrew. Here was, apparently, a matter of no imaginable moment; whether this menial should be discharged on that day, or on the morrow; and yet mighty things were involved in the alternative.

There was a deeper gloom than usual over the house. The servants seemed to know that something had gone wrong, and looked grave and mysterious. Marston was more than ever dark and moody. Mrs. Marston's dimmed and swollen eyes showed that she had been weeping. Mademoiselle absented herself from supper, on the plea of a bad headache. Rhoda saw that something, she knew not what, had occurred to agitate her elders, and was depressed and anxious. The old clergyman, whom we have already mentioned, had called, and stayed to supper. Dr. Danvers was a man of considerable learning, strong sense, and remarkable simplicity of character. His thoughtful blue eye, and well-marked countenance, were full of gentleness and benevolence, and elevated by a certain natural dignity, of which purity and goodness, without one debasing shade of self-esteem and arrogance, were the animating spirit. Mrs. Marston loved and respected this good minister of God; and many a time had sought and found, in his gentle and earnest counsels, and in the overflowing tenderness of his sympathy, much comfort and support in the progress of her sore and protracted earthly trial. Most especially at one critical period in her history had he endeared himself to her, by interposing, and successfully, to prevent a formal separation which (as ending forever the one hope that cheered her on, even in the front of despair) she would probably not long have survived.

With Mr. Marston, however, he was far from being a favorite. There was that in his lofty and simple purity which abashed and silently reproached the sensual, bitter, disappointed man of the world. The angry pride of the scornful man felt its own meanness in the grand presence of a simple and humble Christian minister. And the very fact that all his habits had led him to hold such a character in contempt, made him but the more unreasonably resent the involuntary homage which its exhibition in Dr. Danvers's person invariably extorted from him. He felt in this good man's presence under a kind of irritating restraint; that he was in the presence of one with whom he had, and could have, no sympathy whatever, and yet one whom he could not help both admiring and respecting; and in these conflicting feelings were involved certain gloomy and humbling inferences about himself, which he hated, and almost feared to contemplate.

It was well, however, for the indulgence of Sir Wynston's conversational propensities, that Dr. Danvers had happened to drop in; for Marston was doggedly silent and sullen, and Mrs. Marston was herself scarcely more disposed than he to maintain her part in a conversation; so that, had it not been for the opportune arrival of the good clergyman, the supper must have been dispatched with a very awkward and unsocial taciturnity.

Marston thought, and, perhaps, not erroneously, that Sir Wynston suspected something of the real state of affairs, and he was, therefore, incensed to perceive, as he thought, in his manner, very evident indications of his being in unusually good spirits. Thus disposed, the party sat down to supper.

"One of our number is missing," said Sir Wynston, affecting a slight surprise, which, perhaps, he did not feel.

"Mademoiselle de Barras—I trust she is well?" said Doctor Danvers, looking towards Marston.

"I suppose she is; I don't know," said Marston, drily.

"Why! how should he know," said the baronet, gaily, but with something almost imperceptibly sarcastic in his tone. "Our friend, Marston, is privileged to be as ungallant as he pleases, except where he has the happy privilege to owe allegiance; but I, a gay young bachelor of fifty, am naturally curious. I really do trust that our charming French friend is not unwell."

He addressed his inquiry to Mrs. Marston, who, with some slight confusion, replied:—

"No; nothing, at least, serious; merely a slight headache. I am sure she will be quite well enough to come down to breakfast."

"She is, indeed, a very charming and interesting young person," said Doctor Danvers. "There is a certain simplicity about her which argues a good and kind heart, and an open nature."

"Very true, indeed, doctor," observed Berkley, with the same faint, but, to Marston, exquisitely provoking approximation to sarcasm. "There is, as you say, a very charming simplicity. Don't you think so, Marston?"

Marston looked at him for a moment, but continued silent.

"Poor mademoiselle!—she is, indeed, a most affectionate creature," said Mrs. Marston, who felt called upon to say something.

"Come, Marston, will you contribute nothing to the general fund of approbation?" said Sir Wynston, who was gifted by nature with an amiable talent for teasing, which he was fond of exercising in a quiet way. "We have all, but you, said something handsome of our absent young friend."

"I never praise anybody, Wynston; not even you," said Marston, with an obvious sneer.

"Well, well, I must comfort myself with the belief that your silence covers a great deal of good-will, and, perhaps, a little admiration, too," answered his cousin, significantly.

"Comfort yourself in any honest way you will, my dear Wynston," retorted Marston, with a degree of asperity, which, to all but the baronet himself, was unaccountable. "You may be right, you may be wrong; on a subject so unimportant it matters very little which; you are at perfect liberty to practice delusions, if you will, upon yourself."

"By-the-bye, Mr. Marston, is not your son about to come down here?" asked Doctor Danvers, who perceived that the altercation was becoming, on Marston's part, somewhat testy, if not positively rude.

"Yes; I expect him in a few days," replied he, with a sudden gloom.

"You have not seen him, Sir Wynston?" asked the clergyman.

"I have that pleasure yet to come," said the baronet.

"A pleasure it is, I do assure you," said Doctor Danvers, heartily. "He is a handsome lad, with the heart of a hero—a fine, frank, generous lad, and as merry as a lark."

"Yes, yes," interrupted Marston; "he is well enough, and has done pretty well at Cambridge. Doctor Danvers, take some wine."

It was strange, but yet mournfully true, that the praises which the good Doctor Danvers thus bestowed upon his son were bitter to the soul of the unhappy Marston. They jarred upon his ear, and stung his heart; for his conscience converted them into so many latent insults and humiliations to himself.

"Your wine is very good, Marston. I think your clarets are many degrees better than any I can get," said Sir Wynston, sipping a glass of his favorite wine. "You country gentlemen are sad selfish dogs; and, with all your grumbling, manage to collect the best of whatever is worth having about you."

"We sometimes succeed in collecting a pleasant party," retorted Marston, with ironical courtesy, "though we do not always command the means of entertaining them quite as we would wish."

It was the habit of Doctor Danvers, without respect of persons or places, to propose, before taking his departure from whatever domestic party he chanced to be thrown among for the evening, to read some verses from that holy Book, on which his own hopes and peace were founded, and to offer up a prayer for all to the throne of grace. Marston, although he usually absented himself from such exercises, did not otherwise discourage them; but upon the present occasion, starting from his gloomy reverie, he himself was the first to remind the clergyman of his customary observance. Evil thoughts loomed upon the mind of Marston, like measureless black mists upon a cold, smooth sea. They rested, grew, and darkened there; and no heaven-sent breath came silently to steal them away. Under this dread shadow his mind lay waiting, like the deep, before the Spirit of God moved upon its waters, passive and awful. Why for the first time now did religion interest him? The unseen, intangible, was even now at work within him. A dreadful power shook his very heart and soul. There was some strange, ghastly wrestling going on in his own immortal spirit, a struggle that made him faint, which he had no power to determine. He looked upon the holy influence of the good man's prayer—a prayer in which he could not join—with a dull, superstitious hope that the words, inviting better influence, though uttered by another, and with other objects, would, like a spell, chase away the foul fiend that was busy with his soul. Marston sate, looking into the fire, with a countenance of stern gloom, upon which the wayward lights of the flickering hearth sported fitfully; while at a distant table Doctor Danvers sate down, and, taking his well-worn Bible from his pocket, turned over its leaves, and began, in gentle but impressive tones, to read.

Sir Wynston was much too well bred to evince the slightest disposition to aught but the most proper and profound attention. The faintest imaginable gleam of ridicule might, perhaps, have been discerned in his features, as he leaned back in his chair, and, closing his eyes, composed himself to at least an attitude of attention. No man could submit with more cheerfulness to an inevitable bore.

In these things, then, thou hast no concern; the judgment troubles thee not; thou hast no fear of death, Sir Wynston Berkley; yet there is a heart beating near thee, the mysteries of which, could they glide out and stand before thy face, would perchance appal thee, cold, easy man of the world. Aye, couldst thou but see with those cunning eyes of thine, but twelve brief hours into futurity, each syllable that falls from that good man's lips unheeded would peal through thy heart and brain like maddening thunder. Hearken, hearken, Sir Wynston Berkley, perchance these are the farewell words of thy better angel—the last pleadings of despised mercy!

The party broke up. Doctor Danvers took his leave, and rode homeward, down the broad avenue, between the gigantic ranks of elm that closed it in. The full moon was rising above the distant hills; the mists lay like sleeping lakes in the laps of the hollows; and the broad demesne looked tranquil and sad under this chastened and silvery glory. The good old clergyman thought, as he pursued his way, that here at least, in a spot so beautiful and sequestered, the stormy passions and fell contentions of the outer world could scarcely penetrate. Yet, in that calm secluded spot, and under the cold, pure light which fell so holily, what a hell was weltering and glaring!—what a spectacle was that moon to go down upon! As Sir Wynston was leaving the parlor for his own room, Marston accompanied him to the hall, and said—"I shan't play tonight, Sir Wynston."

"Ah, ha! very particularly engaged?" suggested the baronet, with a faint, mocking smile. "Well, my dear fellow, we must endeavor to make up for it tomorrow—eh?"

"I don't know that," said Marston, "and—in a word, there is no use, sir, in our masquerading with one another. Each knows the other; each understands the other. I wish to have a word or two with you in your room tonight, when we shan't be interrupted."

Marston spoke in a fierce and grating whisper, and his countenance, more even than his accents, betrayed the intensity of his bridled fury. Sir Wynston, however, smiled upon his cousin as if his voice had been melody, and his looks all sunshine.

"Very good, Marston, just as you please," he said; "only don't be later than one, as I shall be getting into bed about that hour."

"Perhaps, upon second thoughts, it is as well to defer what I have to say," said Marston, musingly. "Tomorrow will do as well; so, perhaps, Sir Wynston, I may not trouble you tonight."

"Just as suits you best, my dear Marston," replied the baronet, with a tranquil smile; "only don't come after the hour I have stipulated."

So saying, the baronet mounted the stairs, and made his way to his chamber. He was in excellent spirits, and in high good-humor with himself: the object of his visit to Gray Forest had been, as he now flattered himself, attained. He had conducted an affair requiring the profoundest mystery in its prosecution, and the nicest tactic in its management, almost to a triumphant issue. He had perfectly masked his design, and completely outwitted Marston; and to a person who piqued himself upon his clever diplomacy, and vaunted that he had never yet sustained a defeat in any object which he had seriously proposed to himself, such a combination of successes was for the moment quite intoxicating.

Sir Wynston not only enjoyed his own superiority with all the vanity of a selfish nature, but he no less enjoyed, with a keen and malicious relish, the intense mortification which, he was well assured, Marston must experience; and all the more acutely, because of the utter impossibility, circumstanced as he was, of his taking any steps to manifest his vexation, without compromising himself in a most unpleasant way.

Animated by these amiable feelings, Sir Wynston Berkley sate down, and wrote the following short letter, addressed to Mrs. Gray, Wynston Hall:—

"Mrs. Gray,

"On receipt of this have the sitting rooms and several bedrooms put in order, and thoroughly aired. Prepare for my use the suite of three rooms over the library and drawing room; and have the two great wardrobes, and the cabinet in the state bedroom, removed into the large dressing room which opens upon the bedroom I have named. Make everything as comfortable as possible. If anything is wanted in the way of furniture, drapery, ornament, &c., you need only write to John Skelton, Esq., Spring-garden, London, stating what is required, and he will order and send them down. You must be expeditious, as I shall probably go down to Wynston, with two or three friends, at the beginning of next month.
"WYNSTON BERKLEY
"P.S.—I have written to direct Arkins and two or three of the other servants to go down at once. Set them all to work immediately."

He then applied himself to another letter of considerably greater length, and from which, therefore, we shall only offer a few extracts. It was addressed to John Skelton, Esq., and began as follows.—

"My Dear Skelton,

"You are, doubtless, surprised at my long silence, but I have had nothing very particular to say. My visit to this

dull and uncomfortable place was (as you rightly surmise) not without its object—a little bit of wicked romance; the pretty demoiselle of Rouen, whom I mentioned to you more than once—la belle de Barras—was, in truth, the attraction that drew me hither; and I think (for, as yet, she affects hesitation), I shall have no further trouble with her. She is a fine creature, and you will admit, when you have seen her, well worth taking some trouble about. She is, however, a very knowing little minx, and evidently suspects me of being a sad, fickle dog—and, as I surmise, has some plans, moreover, respecting my morose cousin, Marston, a kind of wicked Penruddock, who has carried all his London tastes into his savage retreat, a paradise of bogs and bushes. There is, I am very confident, a liaison in that quarter. The young lady is evidently a good deal afraid of him, and insists upon such precautions in our interviews, that they have been very few, and far between, indeed. Today, there has been a fracas of some kind. I have no doubt that Marston, poor devil, is jealous. His situation is realty pitiably comic—with an intriguing mistress, a saintly wife, and a devil of a jealous temper of his own. I shall meet Mary on reaching town. Has Clavering (shabby dog!) paid his I.O.U. yet? Tell the little opera woman she had better be quiet. She ought to know me by this time; I shall do what is right, but won't submit to be bullied. If she is troublesome, snap your fingers at her, on my behalf, and leave her to her remedy. I have written to Gray, to get things at Wynston in order. She will draw upon you for what money she requires. Send down two or three of the servants, if they have not already gone. The place is very dusty and dingy, and needs a great deal of brushing and scouring. I shall see you in town very soon. By the way, *has the claret I ordered from the Dublin house arrived yet? It is consigned to you, and goes by the 'Lizard'; pay the freightage, and get Edwards to pack it; ten dozen or so may as well go down to Wynston, and send other wines in proportion. I leave details to you...."*

Some further directions upon other subjects followed; and having subscribed the dispatch, and addressed it to the gentlemanlike scoundrel who filled the onerous office of factotum to this prof ligate and exacting man of the world, Sir Wynston Berkley rang his bell, and gave the two letters into the hand of his man, with special directions to carry them himself in person, to the post office in the neighboring village, early next morning. These little matters completed, Sir Wynston stirred his fire, leaned back in his easy chair, and smiled blandly over the sunny prospect of his imaginary triumphs.

It here becomes necessary to describe, in a few words, some of the local relations of Sir Wynston's apartments. The bedchamber which he occupied opened from the long passage of which we have already spoken—and there were two other smaller apartments opening from it in train. In the further of these, which was entered from a lobby, communicating by a back stair with the kitchen and servants' apartments, lay Sir Wynston's valet, and the intermediate chamber was fitted up as a dressing room for the baronet himself. These circumstances it is necessary to mention, that what follows may be clearly intelligible.

While the baronet was penning these records of vicious schemes—dire waste of wealth and time—irrevocable time!—Marston paced his study in a very different frame of mind. There were a gloom and disorder in the room accordant with those of his own mind. Shelves of ancient tomes, darkened by time, and upon which the dust of years lay sleeping—dark oaken cabinets, filled with piles of deeds and papers, among which the nimble spiders were crawling—and, from the dusky walls, several stark, pale ancestors, looking down coldly from their tarnished frames. An hour, and another hour passed—and still Marston paced this melancholy chamber, a prey to his own fell passions and dark thoughts. He was not a superstitious man, but, in the visions which haunted him, perhaps, was something which made him unusually excitable—for, he experienced a chill of absolute horror, as, standing at the farther end of the room, with his face turned towards the entrance, he beheld the door noiselessly and slowly pushed open, by a pale, thin hand, and a figure dressed in a loose white robe, glide softly in. He stood for some seconds gazing upon this apparition, as it moved hesitatingly towards him from the dusky extremity of the large apartment, before he perceived that the form was that of Mrs. Marston.

"Hey, ha!—Mrs. Marston—what on earth has called you hither?" he asked, sternly. "You ought to have been at rest an hour ago; get to your chamber, and leave me, I have business to attend to."

"Now, dear Richard, you must forgive me," she said, drawing near, and looking up into his haggard face with a sweet and touching look of timidity and love; "I could not rest until I saw you again; your looks have been all this night so unlike yourself; so strange and terrible, that I am afraid some great misfortune threatens you, which you fear to tell me of."

"My looks! Why, curse it, must I give an account of my looks?" replied Marston, at once disconcerted and wrathful. "Misfortune! What misfortune can befall us more? No, there is nothing, nothing, I say, but your own foolish fancy; go to your room—go to sleep—my looks, indeed; pshaw!"

"I came to tell you, dear Richard, that I will do, in all respects, just as you desire. If you continue to wish it, I will part with poor mademoiselle; though, indeed, Richard, I shall miss her more than you can imagine; and all your suspicions have wronged her deeply," said Mrs. Marston. Her husband darted a sudden flashing glance of suspicious scrutiny upon her face; but its expression was frank, earnest, noble. He was disarmed; he hung his head gloomily upon his breast, and was silent for a time. She came nearer, and laid her hand upon his arm. He looked darkly into her upturned eyes, and a feeling which had not touched his heart for many a day—an emotion of pity, transient, indeed, but vivid, revisited him. He took her hand in his, and said, in gentler terms than she had heard him use for a long time—

"No, indeed, Gertrude, you have deceived yourself; no misfortune has happened, and if I am gloomy, the source of all my troubles is within. Leave me, Gertrude, for the present. As to the other matter, the departure of Mademoiselle de Barras, we can talk of that tomorrow—now I cannot; so let us part. Go to your room; good night."

She was withdrawing, and he added, in a subdued tone—"Gertrude, I am very glad you came—very glad. Pray for me tonight."

He had followed her a few steps toward the door, and now stopped short, turned about, and walked dejectedly back again—

"I am right glad she came," he muttered, as soon as he was once more alone. "Wynston is provoking and fiery, too. Were I, in my present mood, to seek a tête-à-tête with him, who knows what might come of it? Blood; my own heart whispers—blood! I'll not trust myself."

He strode to the study door, locked it, and taking out the key, shut it in the drawer of one of the cabinets.

"Now it will need more than accident or impulse to lead me to him. I cannot go, at least, without reflection, without premeditation. Avaunt, fiend. I have baffled you."

He stood in the center of the room, cowering and scowling as he said this, and looked round with a glance half-defiant, half-fearful, as if he expected to see some dreadful form in the dusky recesses of the desolate chamber. He sat himself by the smouldering fire, in somber and agitated rumination. He was restless; he rose again, unbuckled his sword, which he had not loosed since evening, and threw it hastily into a corner. He looked at his watch, it was half-past twelve; he glanced at the door, and thence at the cabinet in which he had placed the key; then he turned hastily, and sate down again. He leaned his elbows on his knees, and his chin upon his clenched hand; still he was restless and excited. Once more he arose, and paced up and down. He consulted his watch again; it was now but a quarter to one.

Sir Wynston's man having received the letters, and his master's permission to retire to rest, got into his bed, and was soon beginning to dose. We have already mentioned that his and Sir Wynston's apartments were separated by a small dressing room, so that any ordinary noise or conversation could be heard but imperfectly from one to the other. The servant, however, was startled by a sound of something falling on the floor of his master's apartment, and broken to pieces by the violence of the shock. He sate up in his bed, listened, and heard some sentences spoken vehemently, and gabbled very fast. He thought he distinguished the words "wretch" and "God"; and there was something so strange in the tone in which they were spoken, that the man got up and stole noiselessly through the dressing room, and listened at the door.

He heard him, as he thought, walking in his slippers through the room, and making his customary arrangements previously to getting into bed. He knew that his master had a habit of speaking when alone, and concluded that the accidental breakage of some glass or chimney-ornament had elicited the volley of words he had heard. Well knowing that, except at the usual hours, or in obedience to Sir Wynston's bell, nothing more displeased his master than his presuming to enter his sleeping-apartment while he was there, the servant quietly retreated, and, perfectly satisfied that all was right, composed himself to slumber, and was soon beginning to dose again.

The adventures of the night, however, were not yet over. Waking, as men sometimes do, without any ascertainable cause; without a start or an uneasy sensation; without even a disturbance of the attitude of repose, he opened his eyes and beheld Merton, the servant of whom we have spoken, standing at a little distance from his bed. The moonlight fell in a clear flood upon this figure: the man was ghastly pale; there was a blotch of blood on his face; his hands were clasped upon something which they nearly concealed; and his eyes, fixed on the servant who had just awakened, shone in the cold light with a wild and lifeless glitter. This specter drew close to the side of the bed, and stood for a few moments there with a look of agony and menace, which startled the newly-awakened man, who rose upright, and said—

"Mr. Merton, Mr. Merton—in God's name, what is the matter?"

Merton recoiled at the sound of his voice; and, as he did so, dropped something on the floor, which rolled away to a distance; and he stood gazing silently and horribly upon his interrogator.

"Mr. Merton, I say, what is it?" urged the man. "Are you hurt? Your face is bloody."

Merton raised his hand to his face mechanically, and Sir Wynston's man observed that it, too, was covered with blood.

"Why, man," he said, vehemently, "and actually freezing with horror you are all bloody; hands and face; all over blood."

"My hand is cut to the bone," said Merton, in a harsh whisper; and speaking to himself, rather than addressing the servant—"I wish it was my neck; I wish to God I bled to death."

"You have hurt your hand, Mr. Merton," repeated the man, scarce knowing what he said.

"Aye," whispered Merton, wildly drawing toward the bedside again; "who told you I hurt my hand? It is cut to the bone, sure enough."

He stooped for a moment over the bed, and then cowered down toward the floor to search for what he had dropped.

"Why, Mr. Merton, what brings you here at this hour?" urged the man, after a pause of a few seconds. "It is drawing toward morning."

"Aye, aye," said Merton, doubtfully, and starting upright again, while he concealed in his bosom what he had been in search of. "Near morning, is it? Night and morning, it is all one to me. I believe I am going mad, by—"

"But what do you want? What did you come here for at this hour?" persisted the man.

"What! Aye, that is it; why, his boots and spurs, to be sure. I forgot them. His—his—Sir Wynston's boots and spurs; I forgot to take them, I say," said Merton, looking toward the dressing room, as if about to enter it.

"Don't mind them tonight, I say, don't go in there," said the man, peremptorily, and getting out upon the floor. "I say, Mr. Merton, this is no hour to be going about searching in the dark for boots and spurs. You'll waken the master. I can't have it, I say; go down, and let it be for tonight."

Thus speaking, in a resolute and somewhat angry under-key, the valet stood between Merton and the entrance of the dressing-room; and, signing with his hand toward the other door of the apartment, continued—

"Go down, I say, Mr. Merton, go down; you may as well quietly, for, I tell you plainly, you shall neither go a step further, nor stay here a moment longer."

The man drew his shoulders up, and made a sort of shivering moan, and clasping his hands together, shook them, as it seemed, in great agony. He then turned abruptly, and hurried from the room by the door leading to the kitchen.

"By my faith," said the servant, "I am glad he is gone. The poor chap is turning crazy, as sure as I am a living man. I'll not have him prowling about here anymore, however; that I am resolved on."

In pursuance of this determination, by no means an imprudent one, as it seemed, he fastened the door communicating with the lower apartments upon the inside. He had hardly done this, when he heard a step traversing the stable-yard, which lay under the window of his apartment. He looked out, and saw Merton walking hurriedly across, and into a stable at the farther end.

Feeling no very particular curiosity about his movements, the man hurried back to his bed. Merton's eccentric conduct of late had become so generally remarked and discussed among the servants, that Sir Wynston's man was by no means surprised at the oddity of the visit he had just had; nor, after the first few moments of doubt, before the appearance of blood had been accounted for, had he entertained any suspicions whatever connected with the man's unexpected presence in the room. Merton was in the habit of coming up every night to take down Sir Wynston's boots, whenever the baronet had ridden in the course of the day; and this attention had been civilly undertaken as a proof of good-will toward the valet, whose duty this somewhat soiling and ungentlemanlike process would otherwise have been. So far, the nature of the visit was explained; and the remembrance of the friendly feeling and good offices which had been mutually interchanged, as well as of the inoffensive habits for which Merton had earned a character for himself, speedily calmed the uneasiness, for a moment amounting to actual alarm, with which the servant had regarded his appearance.

We must now pass on to the morrow, and ask the reader's attention for a few moments to a different scene.

In contact with Gray Forest upon the northern side, and divided by a common boundary, lay a demesne, in many respects presenting a very striking contrast to its grander neighbor. It was a comparatively modern place. It could not boast the towering timber which enriched and overshadowed the vast and varied expanse of its aristocratic rival; but, if it was inferior in the advantages of antiquity, and, perhaps, also in some of those of nature, its superiority in other respects was striking, and important. Gray Forest was not more remarkable for its wild and neglected condition, than was Newton Park for the care and elegance with which it was kept. No one could observe the contrast, without, at the same time, divining its cause. The proprietor of the one was a man of wealth, fully commensurate with the extent and pretensions of the residence he had chosen; the owner of the other was a man of broken fortunes.

Under a green shade, which nearly met above, a very young man, scarcely one-and-twenty, of a frank and sensible, rather than a strictly handsome countenance, was walking, followed by half a dozen dogs of as many breeds and sizes. This young man was George Mervyn, the only son of the present proprietor of the place. As be approached the great gate, the clank of a horses' hoofs in quick motion upon the sequestered road which ran outside it, reached him; and hardly had he heard these sounds, when a young gentleman rode briskly by, directing his look into the demesne as he passed. He had no sooner seen him, than wheeling his horse about, he rode up to the iron gate, and dismounting, threw it open, and let his horse in.

"Ha! Charles Marston, I protest!" said the young man, quickening his pace to meet his friend. "Marston, my dear fellow," he called aloud, "how glad I am to see you."

There was another entrance into Newton Park, opening from the same road, about half a mile further on; and Charles Marston made his way lie through this. Thus the young people walked on, talking of a hundred things as they proceeded, in the mirth of their hearts.

Between the fathers of the two young men, who thus walked so affectionately together, there subsisted unhappily no friendly feelings. There had been several slight disagreements between them, touching their proprietary rights, and one of these had ripened into a formal and somewhat expensive litigation, respecting a certain right of fishing claimed by each. This legal encounter had terminated in the defeat of Marston. Mervyn, however, promptly wrote to his opponent, offering him the free use of the waters for which they had thus sharply contested, and received a curt and scarcely civil reply, declining the proposed courtesy. This exhibition of resentment on Marston's part had been followed by some rather angry collisions, where chance or duty happened to throw them together. It is but justice to say that, upon all such occasions, Marston was the aggressor. But Mervyn was a somewhat testy old gentleman, and had a certain pride of his own, which was not to be trifled with. Thus, though near neighbors, the parents of the young friends were more than strangers to each other. On Mervyn's side, however, this estrangement was unalloyed with bitterness, and simply of that kind which the great moralist would have referred to "defensive pride." It did not include any member of Marston's family, and Charles, as often as he desired it, which was, in truth, as often as his visits could escape the special notice of his father, was a welcome guest at Newton Park.

These details respecting the mutual relation in which the two families stood, it was necessary to state, for the purpose of making what follows perfectly clear. The young people had now reached the further gate, at which they were to part. Charles Marston, with a heart beating happily in the anticipation of many a pleasant meeting, bid him farewell for the present, and in a few minutes more was riding up the broad, straight avenue, towards the gloomy mansion which closed in the hazy and somber perspective. As he moved onward, he passed a laborer, with whose face, from his childhood, he had been familiar.

"How do you do, Tom?" he cried.

"At your service, sir," replied the man, uncovering, "and welcome home, sir."

There was something dark and anxious in the man's looks, which ill-accorded with the welcome he spoke, and which suggested some undefined alarm.

"The master, and mistress, and Miss Rhoda—are all well?" he asked eagerly.

"All well, sir, thank God," replied the man.

Young Marston spurred on, filled with vague apprehensions, and observing the man still leaning upon his spade, and watching his progress with the same gloomy and curious eye.

At the hall-door he met with one of the servants, booted and spurred.

"Well, Daly," he said, as he dismounted, "how are all at home?"

This man, like the former, met his smile with a troubled countenance, and stammered—

"All, sir—that is, the master, and mistress, and Miss Rhoda—quite well, sir; but—"

"Well, well," said Charles, eagerly, "speak on—what is it?"

"Bad work, sir," replied the man, lowering his voice. "I am going off this minute for—"

"For what?" urged the young gentleman.

"Why, sir, for the coroner," replied he.

"The coroner—the coroner! Why, good God, what has happened?" cried Charles, aghast with horror.

"Sir Wynston," commenced the man, and hesitated.

"Well?" pursued Charles, pale and breathless.

"Sir Wynston—he—it is he," said the man.

"He? Sir Wynston? Is he dead, or who is?—Who is dead?" demanded the young man, almost fiercely.

"Sir Wynston, sir; it is he that is dead. There is bad work, sir—very bad, I'm afraid," replied the man.

Charles did not wait to inquire further, but, with a feeling of mingled horror and curiosity, entered the house.

He hurried up the stairs, and entered his mother's sitting room. She was there, perfectly alone, and so deadly pale, that she scarcely looked like a living being. In an instant they were locked in one another's arms.

"Mother—my dear mother, you are ill," said the young man, anxiously.

"Oh, no, no, dear Charles, but frightened, horrified;" and as she said this, the poor lady burst into tears.

"What is this horrible affair? Something about Sir Wynston. He is dead, I know, but is it—is it suicide?" he asked.

"Oh, no, not suicide," said Mrs. Marston, greatly agitated.

"Good God! Then he is murdered," whispered the young man, growing very pale.

"Yes, Charles—horrible—dreadful! I can scarcely believe it," replied she, shuddering while she wept.

"Where is my father?" inquired the young man, after a pause.

"Why, why, Charles, darling—why do you ask for him?" she said, wildly, grasping him by the arm, as she looked into his face with a terrified expression.

"Why—why, he could tell me the particulars of this horrible tragedy," answered he, meeting her agonized look with one of alarm and surprise, "as far as they have been as yet collected. How is he, mother—is he well?"

"Oh, yes, quite well, thank God," she answered, more collectedly—"quite well, but, of course, greatly, dreadfully shocked."

"I will go to him, mother; I will see him," said he, turning towards the door.

"He has been, wretchedly depressed and excited for some days," said Mrs. Marston, dejectedly, "and this dreadful occurrence will, I fear, affect him most deplorably."

The young man kissed her tenderly and affectionately, and hurried down to the library, where his father usually sat when he desired to be alone, or was engaged in business. He opened the door softly. His father was standing at one of the windows, his face haggard as from a night's watching, unkempt and unshorn, and with his hands thrust into his pockets. At the sound of the revolving door he started, and seeing his son, first recoiled a little, with a strange, doubtful expression, and then rallying, walked quickly towards him with a smile, which had in it something still more painful.

"Charles, I am glad to see you," he said, shaking him with an agitated pressure by both hands, "Charles, this is a great calamity, and what makes it still worse, is that the murderer has escaped; it looks badly, you know."

He fixed his gaze for a few moments upon his son, turned abruptly, and walked a little way into the room then, in a disconcerted manner, he added, hastily turning back—

"Not that it signifies to us, of course—but I would fain have justice satisfied."

"And who is the wretch—the murderer?" inquired Charles.

"Who? Why, everyone knows!—that scoundrel, Merton," answered Marston, in an irritated tone—"Merton murdered him in his bed, and fled last night; he is gone—escaped—and I suspect Sir Wynston's man of being an accessory."

"Which was Sir Wynston's bedroom?" asked the young man.

"The room that old Lady Mostyn had—the room with the portrait of Grace Hamilton in it."

"I know—I know," said the young man, much excited. "I should wish to see it."

"Stay," said Marston; "the door from the passage is bolted on the inside, and I have locked the other; here is the key, if you choose to go, but you must bring Hughes with you, and do not disturb anything; leave all as it is; the jury ought to see, and examine for themselves."

Charles took the key, and, accompanied by the awestruck servant, he made his way by the back stairs to the door opening from the dressing-room, which, as we have said, intervened between the valet's chamber and Sir Wynston's. After a momentary hesitation, Charles turned the key in the door, and stood.

"In the dark chamber of white death."

The shutters lay partly open, as the valet had left them some hours before, on making the astounding discovery, which the partially admitted light revealed. The corpse lay in the silk-embroidered dressing gown, and other habiliments, which Sir Wynston had worn, while taking his ease in his chamber, on the preceding night. The coverlet was partially dragged over it. The mouth was gaping, and filled with clotted blood; a wide gash was also visible in the neck, under the ear; and there was a thickening pool of blood at the bedside, and quantities of blood, doubtless from other wounds, had saturated the bedclothes under the body. There lay Sir Wynston, stiffened in the attitude in which the struggle of death had left him, with his stern, stony face, and dim, terrible gaze turned up.

Charles looked breathlessly for more than a minute upon this mute and unchanging spectacle, and then silently suffered the curtain to fall back again, and stepped, with the light tread of awe, again to the door. There he turned back, and pausing for a minute, said, in a whisper, to the attendant—

"And Merton did this?"

"Troth, I'm afeard he did, sir," answered the man, gloomily.

"And has made his escape?" continued Charles.

"Yes, sir; he stole away in the night-time," replied the servant, "after the murder was done" (and he glanced fearfully toward the bed); "God knows where he's gone."

"The villain!" muttered Charles; "but what was his motive? why did he do all this—what does it mean?"

"I don't know exactly, sir, but he was very queer for a week and more before it," replied the man; "there was something bad over him for a long time."

"It is a terrible thing," said Charles, with a profound sigh; "a terrible and shocking occurrence."

He hesitated again at the door, but his feelings had sustained a terrible revulsion at sight of the corpse, and he was no longer disposed to prosecute his purposed examination of the chamber and its contents; with a view to conjecturing the probable circumstances of the murder.

"Observe, Hughes, that I have moved nothing in the chamber from the place it occupied when we entered," he said to the servant, as they withdrew.

He locked the door, and as he passed through the hall, on his return, he encountered his father, and, restoring the key, said—

"I could not stay there; I am almost sorry I have seen it; I am overpowered; what a determined, ferocious murder it was; the place is all in a pool of gore; he must have received many wounds."

"I can't say; the particulars will be elicited soon enough; those details are for the inquest; as for me, I hate such spectacles," said Marston, gloomily; "go now, and see your sister; you will find her there."

He pointed to the small room where we have first seen her and her fair governess; Charles obeyed the direction, and Marston proceeded himself to his wife's sitting room.

The young man, dispirited and horrified by the awful spectacle he had just contemplated, hurried to the little study occupied by his sister, Marston himself ascended, as we have said, the great staircase leading to his wife's private sitting room.

"Mrs. Marston," he said, entering, "this is a hateful occurrence, a dreadful thing to have taken place here; I don't mean to affect grief which I don't feel; but the thing is very shocking, and particularly so, as having occurred under my roof; but that cannot now be helped. I have resolved to spare no exertions, and no influence, to bring the assassin to justice; and a coroner's jury will, within a few hours, sift the evidence which we have succeeded in collecting. But my purpose in seeking you now is, to recur to the conversation we yesterday had, respecting a member of this establishment."

"Mademoiselle de Barras?" suggested the lady.

"Yes, Mademoiselle de Barras," echoed Marston; "I wish to say, that, having reconsidered the circumstances affecting her, I am absolutely resolved that she shall not continue to be an inmate of this house."

He paused, and Mrs. Marston said—

"Well, Richard, I am sorry, very sorry for it; but your decision shall never be disputed by me."

"Of course," said Marston, drily; "and, therefore, the sooner you acquaint her with it, and let her know that she must go, the better."

Having said this, he left her, and went to his own chamber, where he proceeded to make his toilet with elaborate propriety, in preparation for the scene which was about to take place under his roof.

Mrs. Marston, meanwhile, suffered from a horrible uncertainty. She never harbored, it is true, one doubt as to her husband's perfect innocence of the ghastly crime which filled their house with fear and gloom; but at the same time that she thoroughly and indignantly scouted the possibility of his, under any circumstances, being accessory to such a crime, she experienced a nervous and agonizing anxiety lest anyone else should possibly suspect him, however obliquely and faintly, of any participation whatever in the foul deed. This vague fear tortured her; it had taken possession of her mind; and it was the more acutely painful, because it was of a kind which precluded the possibility of her dispelling it, as morbid fears so often are dispelled, by taking counsel upon its suggestions with a friend.

The day wore on, and strange faces began to fill the great parlor. The coroner, accompanied by a physician, had arrived. Several of the gentry in the immediate vicinity had been summoned as jurors, and now began to arrive in succession. Marston, in a handsome and sober suit, received these visitors with a stately and melancholy courtesy, befitting the occasion. Mervyn and his son had both been summoned, and, of course, were in attendance. There being now a sufficient number to form a jury, they were sworn, and immediately proceeded to the chamber where the body of the murdered man was lying.

Marston accompanied them, and with a pale and stern countenance, and in a clear and subdued tone, called their attention successively to every particular detail which he conceived important to be noted. Having thus employed some minutes, the jury again returned to the parlor, and the examination of the witnesses commenced.

Marston, at his own request, was first sworn and examined. He deposed merely to the circumstance of his parting, on the night previous, with Sir Wynston, and to the state in which he had seen the room and the body in the morning. He mentioned also the fact, that on hearing the alarm in the morning, he had hastened from his own chamber to Sir Wynston's, and found, on trying to enter, that the door opening upon the passage was secured on the inside. This circumstance showed that the murderer must have made his egress at least through the valet's chamber, and by the back-stairs. Marston's evidence went no further.

The next witness sworn was Edward Smith, the servant of the late Sir Wynston Berkley. His evidence was a narrative of the occurrences we have already stated. He described the sounds which he had overheard from his master's room, the subsequent appearance of Merton, and the conversation which had passed between them. He then proceeded to mention, that it was his master's custom to have himself called at seven o'clock, at which hour he usually took some medicine, which it was the valet's duty to bring to him; after which he either settled again to rest, or rose in a short time, if unable to sleep. Having measured and prepared the dose in the dressing room, the servant went on to say, he had knocked at his master's door, and receiving no answer, had entered the room, and partly unclosed the shutters. He perceived the blood on the carpet, and on opening the curtains, saw his master lying with his mouth and eyes open, perfectly dead, and weltering in gore. He had stretched out his hand, and seized that of the dead man, which was quite stiff and cold; then, losing heart, he had run to the door communicating with the passage, but found it locked, and turned to the other entrance, and ran down the back-stairs, crying "murder." Mr. Hughes, the butler, and James Carney, another servant, came immediately, and they all three went back into the room. The key was in the outer door, upon the inside, but they did not unlock it until they had viewed the body. There was a great pool of blood in the bed, and in it was lying a red-handled case knife, which was produced, and identified by the witness. Just then they heard Mr. Marston calling for admission, and they opened the door with some difficulty, for the lock was rusty. Mr. Marston had ordered them to leave the things as they were, and had used very stern language to the witness. They had then left the room, securing both doors.

This witness underwent a severe and searching examination, but his evidence was clear and consistent.

In conclusion, Marston produced a dagger, which was stained with blood, and asked the man whether he recognized it.

Smith at once stated this to have been the property of his late master, who, when traveling, carried it, together with his pistols, along with him. Since his arrival at Gray Forest, it had lain upon the chimney-piece in his bedroom, where he believed it to have been upon the previous night.

James Carney, one of Marston's servants, was next sworn and examined. He had, he said, observed a strange and unaccountable agitation and depression in Merton's manner for some days past; he had also been several times disturbed at night by his talking aloud to himself, and walking to and fro in his room. Their bedrooms were separated by a thin partition, in which was a window, through which Carney had, on the night of the murder, observed a light in Merton's room, and, on looking in, had seen him dressing hastily. He also saw him twice take up, and again lay down, the red-hafted knife which had been found in the bed of the murdered man. He knew it by the handle being broken near the end. He had no suspicion of Merton having any mischievous intentions, and lay down again to rest. He afterwards heard him pass out of his room, and go slowly up the back-stairs leading to the upper story. Shortly after this he had fallen asleep, and did not hear or see him return. He then described, as Smith had already done, the scene which presented itself in the morning, on his accompanying him into Sir Wynston's bedchamber.

The next witness examined was a little Irish boy, who described himself as "a poor scholar." His testimony was somewhat singular. He deposed that he had come to the house on the preceding evening, and had been given some supper, and was afterwards permitted to sleep among the hay in one of the lofts. He had, however, discovered what he considered a snugger berth. This was an unused stable, in the further end of which lay a quantity of hay. Among this he had lain down, and gone to sleep. He was, however, awakened in the course of the night by the entrance of a man, whom he saw with perfect distinctness in the moonlight, and his description of his dress and appearance tallied exactly with those of Merton. This man occupied himself for sometime in washing his hands and face in a stable bucket, which happened to stand by the door; and, during the whole of this process, he continued to moan and mutter, like one in woeful perturbation. He said, distinctly, twice or thrice, "by ——, I am done for;" and every now and then he muttered, "and nothing for it, after all." When he had done washing his hands, he took something from his coat-pocket, and looked at it, shaking his head; at this time he was standing with his back turned toward the boy, so that he could not see what this object might be. The man, however, put it into his breast, and then began to search hurriedly, as it seemed, for some hiding place for it. After looking at the pavement, and poking at the chinks of the wall, he suddenly went to the window, and forced up the stone which formed the sill. Under this he threw the object which the boy had seen him examine with so much perplexity, and then he readjusted the stone, and removed the evidences of its having been recently stirred. The boy was a little frightened, but very curious about all that he saw; and when the man left the stable in which he lay, he got up, and following to the door, peeped after him. He saw him putting on an outside-coat and hat, near the yard gate; and then, with great caution, unbolt the wicket, constantly looking back towards the house, and so let himself out. The boy was uneasy, and sat in the hay, wide-awake, until morning. He then told the servants what he had seen, and one of the men having raised the stone, which he had not strength to lift, they found the dagger, which Smith had identified as belonging to his master. This weapon was stained with blood; and some hair, which was found to correspond in color with Sir Wynston's, was sticking in the crevice between the blade and the handle.

"It appears very strange that one man should have employed two distinct instruments of this kind," observed Mervyn, after a pause. A silence followed.

"Yes, strange; it does seem strange," said Marston, clearing his voice.

"Yet, it is clear," said another of the jury, "that the same hand did employ them. It is proved that the knife was in Merton's possession just as he left his chamber; and proved, also, that the dagger was secreted by him after he quitted the house,"

"Yes," said Marston, with a grisly sort of smile, and glancing sarcastically at Mervyn, while he addressed the last speaker—"I thank you for recalling my attention to the facts. It certainly is not a very pleasant suggestion, that there still remains within my household an undetected murderer."

Mervyn ruminated for a time, and said he should wish to put a few more questions to Smith and Carney. They were accordingly recalled, and examined in great detail, with a view to ascertain whether any indication of the presence of a second person having visited the chamber with Merton was discoverable. Nothing, however, appeared, except that the valet mentioned the noise and the exclamations which he had indistinctly heard.

"You did not mention that before, sir," said Marston, sharply.

"I did not think of it, sir," replied the man, "the gentlemen were asking me so many questions; but I told you, sir, about it in the morning."

"Oh, ah—yes, yes—I believe you did," said Marston; "but you then said that Sir Wynston often talked when he was alone; eh, sir?"

"Yes, sir, and so he used, which was the reason I did not go into the room when I heard it," replied the man.

"How long afterwards was it when you saw Merton in your own room?" asked Mervyn.

"I could not say, sir," answered Smith; "I was soon asleep, and can't say how long I slept before he came."

"Was it an hour?" pursued Mervyn.

"I can't say," said the man, doubtfully.

"Was it five hours?" asked Marston.

"No, Sir; I am sure it was not five."

"Could you swear it was more than half-an-hour?" persisted Marston.

"No, I could not swear that," answered he. "I am afraid, Mr. Mervyn; you have found a mare's nest," said Marston, contemptuously.

"I have done my duty, sir," retorted Mervyn, cynically; "which plainly requires that I shall have no doubt, which the evidence of the witness can clear up, unsifted and unsatisfied. I happened to think it of some moment to ascertain, if possible, whether more persons than one were engaged in this atrocious murder. You don't seem to think the question so important a one; different men, sir, take different views."

"Views, sir, in matters of this sort, especially where they tend to multiply suspicions, and to implicate others, ought to be supported by something more substantial than mere fancies," retorted Marston.

"I don't know what you call fancies," replied Mervyn, testily; "but here are two deadly weapons, a knife and a dagger, each, it would seem, employed in doing this murder; if you see nothing odd in that, I can't enable you to do so."

"Well, sir," said Marston, grimly, "the whole thing is, as you term it, odd; and I can see no object in your picking out this particular singularity for long-winded criticism, except to cast scandal upon my household, by leaving a hideous and vague imputation floating among the members of it. Sir, sir, this is a foul way," he cried, sternly, "to gratify a paltry spite."

"Mr. Marston," said Mervyn, rising, and thrusting his hands into his pockets, while he confronted him to the full as sternly, "the country knows in which of our hearts the spite, if any there be between us, is harbored. I owe you no friendship, but, sir, I cherish no malice, either; and against the worst enemy I have on earth I am incapable of perverting an opportunity like this, and inflicting pain, under the pretence of discharging a duty."

Marston was on the point of retorting, but the coroner interposed, and besought them to confine their attention strictly to the solemn inquiry which they were summoned together to prosecute.

There remained still to be examined the surgeon who had accompanied the coroner, for the purpose of reporting upon the extent and nature of the injuries discoverable upon the person of the deceased. He, accordingly, deposed, that having examined the body, he found no less than three deep wounds, inflicted with some sharp instrument; two of them had actually penetrated the heart, and were, of course, supposed to cause instant death. Besides these, there were two contusions, one upon the back of the head, the other upon the forehead, with a slight abrasion of the eyebrow. There was a large lock of hair torn out by the roots at the front of the head, and the palm and fingers of the right hand were cut. This evidence having been taken, the jury once more repaired to the chamber where the body lay, and proceeded with much minuteness to examine the room, with a view to ascertain, if possible, more particularly the exact circumstances of the murder.

The result of this elaborate scrutiny was as follows: —The deceased, they conjectured, had fallen asleep in his easy chair, and, while he was unconscious, the murderer had stolen into the room, and, before attacking his victim, had secured the bedroom-door upon the inside. This was argued from the non-discovery of blood upon the handle, or any other part of the door. It was supposed that he had then approached Sir Wynston, with the view either of robbing, or of

GLENN CHADBOURNE

murdering him while he slept, and that the deceased had awakened just after he had reached him; that a brief and desperate struggle had ensued, in which the assailant had struck his victim with his fist upon the forehead, and having stunned him, had hurriedly clutched him by the hair, and stabbed him with the dagger, which lay close by upon the chimneypiece, forcing his head violently against the back of the chair. This part of the conjecture was supported by the circumstance of there being discovered a lock of hair upon the ground at the spot, and a good deal of blood. The carpet, too, was tumbled, and a water-decanter, which had stood upon the table close by, was lying in fragments upon the floor. It was supposed that the murderer had then dragged the half-lifeless body to the bed, where, having substituted the knife, which he had probably brought to the room in the same pocket from which the boy afterwards saw him take the dagger, he dispatched him; and either hearing some alarm—perhaps the movement of the valet in the adjoining room, or from some other cause—he dropped the knife in the bed, and was not able to find it again. The wounds upon the hand of the dead man indicated his having caught and struggled to hold the blade of the weapon with which he was assailed. The impression of a bloody hand thrust under the bolster, where it was Sir Wynston's habit to place his purse and watch, when making his arrangements for the night, supplied the motive of this otherwise unaccountable atrocity.

After some brief consultation, the jury agreed upon a verdict of willful murder against John Merton, a finding of which the coroner expressed his entire approbation.

Marston, as a justice of the peace, had informations, embodying the principal part of the evidence given before the coroner, sworn against Merton, and transmitted a copy of them to the Home Office. A reward for the apprehension of the culprit was forthwith offered, but for some months without effect.

Marston had, in the interval, written to several of Sir Wynston's many relations, announcing the catastrophe, and requesting that steps might immediately be taken to have the body removed. Meanwhile undertakers were busy in the chamber of death. The corpse was enclosed in lead, and that again in cedar, and a great oak shell, covered with crimson cloth and goldheaded nails, and with a gilt plate, recording the age, title, &c. &c., of the deceased, was screwed down firmly over all.

Nearly a fortnight elapsed before any reply to Marston's letters was received. A short epistle at last arrived from Lord H——, the late Sir Wynston's uncle, deeply regretting the "sad and inexplicable occurrence," and adding, that the will, which, on receipt of the "distressing intelligence," was immediately opened and read, contained no direction whatever respecting the sepulture of the deceased, which had therefore better be completed as modestly and expeditiously as possible, in the neighborhood; and, in conclusion, he directed that the accounts of the undertakers, &c., employed upon the melancholy occasion, might be sent in to Mr. Skelton, who had kindly undertaken to leave London without any delay, for the purpose of completing these last arrangements, and who would, in any matter of business connected with the deceased, represent him, Lord H——, as executor of the late baronet.

This letter was followed, in a day or two, by the arrival of Skelton, a well-dressed, languid, impertinent London tuft-hunter, a good deal faded, with a somewhat sallow and puffy face, charged with a pleasant combination at once of meanness, insolence, and sensuality—just such a person as Sir Wynston's parasite might have been expected to prove.

However well disposed to impress the natives with high notions of his extraordinary refinement and importance, he very soon discovered that, in Marston, he had stumbled upon a man of the world, and one thoroughly versed in the ways and characters of London life. After some ineffectual attempts, therefore, to overawe and astonish his host, Mr. Skelton became aware of the fruitlessness of the effort, and condescended to abate somewhat of his pretensions. Marston could not avoid inviting this person to pass the night at his house, an invitation which was accepted, of course; and next morning, after a late breakfast, Mr. Skelton observed, with a yawn—"And now, about this body—poor Berkley!—what do you propose to do with him?"

"I have no proposition to make," said Marston, drily. "It is no affair of mine, except that the body may be removed without more delay. I have no suggestion to offer."

"H——'s notion was to have him buried as near the spot as may be," said Skelton.

Marston nodded.

"There is a kind of vault, is not there, in the demesne, a family burial-place?" inquired the visitor.

"Yes, sir," replied Marston, curtly.

"Well?" drawled Skelton.

"Well, sir, what then?" responded Marston.

"Why, as the wish of the parties is to have him buried—poor fellow!—as quietly as possible, I think he might just as well be laid there as anywhere else!"

"Had I desired it, Mr. Skelton, I should myself have made the offer," said Marston, abruptly.

"Then you don't wish it?" said Skelton.

"No, sir; certainly not—most peremptorily not," answered Marston, with more sharpness than, in his early days, he would have thought quite consistent with politeness.

"Perhaps," replied Skelton, for want of something better to say, and with a callous sort of levity; "perhaps you hold the idea—some people do—that murdered men can't rest in their graves until their murderers have expiated their guilt?"

Marston made no reply, but shot two or three lurid glances from under his brow at the speaker.

"Well, then, at all events," continued Skelton, indolently resuming his theme, "if you decline your assistance, may I, at least, hope for your advice? Knowing nothing of this country, I would ask you whither you would recommend me to have the body conveyed?"

"I don't care to advise in the matter," said Marston; "but if I were directing, I should have the remains buried in Chester. It is not more than twenty miles from this; and if, at any future time, his family should desire to remove the body, it could be effected more easily from thence. But you can decide."

"Egad! I believe you are right," said Skelton, glad to be relieved of the trouble of thinking about the matter; "and I shall take your advice."

In accordance with this declaration the body was, within four-and-twenty hours, removed to Chester, and buried there, Mr. Skelton attending on behalf of Sir Wynston's numerous and afflicted friends and relatives.

There are certain heartaches for which time brings no healing; nay, which grow but the sorer and fiercer as days and years roll on of this kind, perhaps, were the stern and bitter feelings which now darkened the face of Marston with an almost perpetual gloom. His habits became even more unsocial than before. The society of his son he no longer seemed to enjoy. Long and solitary rambles in his wild and extensive demesne consumed the listless hours or his waking existence; and when the weather prevented this, he shut himself up, upon pretence of business, in his study.

He had not, since the occasion we have already mentioned, referred to the intended departure of Mademoiselle de Barras. Truth to say, his feelings with respect to that young lady were of a conflicting and mysterious kind; and as often as his dark thoughts wandered to her (which, indeed, was frequently enough), his muttered exclamation seemed to imply some painful and horrible suspicions respecting her.

"Yes," he would mutter, "I thought I heard your light foot upon the lobby, on that accursed night. Fancy! Well, it may have been, but assuredly a strange fancy. I cannot comprehend that woman. She baffles my scrutiny. I have looked into her face with an eye she might well understand, were it indeed as I sometimes suspect, and she has been calm and unmoved. I have watched and studied her; still—doubt, doubt, hideous doubt!—is she what she seems, or—a tigress?"

Mrs. Marston, on the other hand, procrastinated from day to day the painful task of announcing to Mademoiselle de Barras the stern message with which she had been charged by her husband. And thus several weeks had passed, and she began to think that his silence upon the subject, notwithstanding his seeing the young French lady at breakfast every morning, amounted to a kind of tacit intimation that the sentence of banishment was not to be carried into immediate execution, but to be kept suspended over the unconscious offender.

It was now six or eight weeks since the hearse carrying away the remains of the ill-fated Sir Wynston Berkley had driven down the dusky avenue; the autumn was deepening into winter, and as Marston gloomily trod the woods of Gray Forest, the withered leaves whirled drearily along his pathway, and the gusts that swayed the mighty branches above him were rude and ungenial. It was a bleak and somber day, and as he broke into a long and picturesque vista, deep among the most sequestered woods, he suddenly saw before him, and scarcely twenty paces from the spot on which he stood, an apparition, which for some moments absolutely froze him to the earth.

Travel-soiled, tattered, pale, and wasted, John Merton, the murderer, stood before him. He did not exhibit the smallest disposition to turn about and make his escape. On the contrary, he remained perfectly motionless, looking upon his former master with a wild and sorrowful gaze. Marston twice or thrice essayed to speak; his face was white as death, and had he beheld the specter of the murdered baronet himself, he could not have met the sight with a countenance of ghastlier horror.

"Take me, sir" said Merton, doggedly.

Still Marston did not stir.

"Arrest me, sir, in God's name! here I am," he repeated, dropping his arms by his side; "I'll go with you wherever you tell me."

"Murderer!" cried Marston, with a sudden burst of furious horror, "murderer—assassin—miscreant—take that!"

And, as he spoke, he discharged one of the pistols he always carried about him full at the wretched man. The shot did not take effect, and Merton made no other gesture but to clasp his hands together, with an agonized pressure, while his head sunk upon his breast.

"Shoot me; shoot me," he said hoarsely; "kill me like a dog: better for me to be dead than what I am."

The report of Marston's pistol had, however, reached another ear; and its ringing echoes had hardly ceased to vibrate among the trees, when a stern shout was heard not fifty yards away, and, breathless and amazed, Charles Marston sprang to the place. His father looked from Merton to him, and from him again to Merton, with a guilty and stupefied scowl, still holding the smoking pistol in his hand.

"What—how! Good God—Merton!" ejaculated Charles.

"Aye, sir, Merton; ready to go to gaol, or wherever you will," said the man, recklessly.

"A murderer; a madman; don't believe him," muttered Marston, scarce audibly, with lips as white as wax.

"Do you surrender yourself, Merton?" demanded the young man, sternly, advancing toward him.

"Yes, sir; I desire nothing more; God knows I wish to die," responded he, despairingly, and advancing slowly to meet Charles.

"Come, then," said young Marston, seizing him by the collar, "come quietly to the house. Guilty and unhappy man, you are now my prisoner, and, depend upon it, I shall not let you go."

"I don't want to go, I tell you, sir. I have traveled fifteen miles today, to come here and give myself up to the master."

"Accursed madman." said Marston unconsciously, gazing at the prisoner; and then suddenly rousing himself, he said, "Well, miscreant, you wish to die, and, by ——, you are in a fair way to have your wish."

"So best," said the man, doggedly. "I don't want to live; I wish I was in my grave; I wish I was dead a year ago."

Some fifteen minutes afterwards, Merton, accompanied by Marston and his son Charles, entered the hall of the mansion which, not ten weeks before, he had quitted under circumstances so guilty and terrible. When they reached the house, Merton seemed much agitated, and wept bitterly on seeing two or three of his former fellow servants, who looked on him in silence as they passed, with a gloomy and fearful curiosity. These, too, were succeeded by others, peeping and whispering, and upon one pretence or another crossing and re-crossing the hall, and stealing hurried glances at the criminal. Merton sate with his face buried in his hands, sobbing, and taking no note of the humiliating scrutiny of which he was the subject. Meanwhile Marston, pale and agitated, made out his committal, and having sworn in several of his laborers and servants as special constables, dispatched the prisoner in their charge to the county gaol, where, under lock and key, we leave him in safe custody for the present.

After this event Marston became excited and restless. He scarcely ate or slept, and his health seemed now as much scattered as his spirits had been before. One day he glided into the room in which, as we have said, it was Mrs. Marston's habit frequently to sit alone.

His wife was there, and, as he entered, she uttered an exclamation of doubtful joy and surprise. He sate down near her in silence, and for some time looked gloomily on the ground. She did not care to question him, and anxiously waited until he should open the conversation. At length he raised his eyes, and, looking full at her, asked abruptly—"Well, what about mademoiselle?"

Mrs. Marston was embarrassed, and hesitated.

"I told you what I wished with respect to that young lady some time ago, and commissioned you to acquaint her with my pleasure; and yet I find her still here, and apparently as much established as ever."

Again Mrs. Marston hesitated. She scarcely knew how to confess to him that she had not conveyed his message.

"Don't suppose, Gertrude, that I wish to find fault. I merely wanted to know whether you had told Mademoiselle de Barras that we were agreed as to the necessity or expediency, or what you please, of dispensing henceforward with her services, I perceive by your manner that you have not done so. I have no doubt your motive was a kind one, but my decision remains unaltered; and I now assure you again that I wish you to speak to her; I wish you explicitly to let her know my wishes and yours."

"Not mine, Richard," she answered faintly.

"Well, mine, then," he replied, roughly; "we shan't quarrel about that."

"And when—how soon—do you wish me to speak to her on this, to both of us, most painful subject?" asked she, with a sigh.

"Today—this hour—this minute, if you can; in short the sooner the better," he replied, rising. "I see no reason for holding it back any longer. I am sorry my wishes were not complied with immediately. Pray, let there be no further hesitation or delay. I shall expect to learn this evening that all is arranged."

Marston having thus spoken, left her abruptly, went down to his study with a swift step, shut himself in, and throwing himself into a great chair, gave a loose to his agitation, which was extreme.

Meanwhile Mrs. Marston had sent for Mademoiselle de Barras, anxious to get through her painful task as speedily as possible. The fair French girl quickly presented herself.

"Sit down, mademoiselle," said Mrs. Marston, taking her hand kindly, and drawing her to the prie-dieu chair beside herself.

Mademoiselle de Barras sate down, and, as she did so, read the countenance of her patroness with one rapid glance of her flashing eyes. These eyes, however, when Mrs. Marston looked at her the next moment, were sunk softly and sadly upon the floor. There was a heightened color, however, in her cheek, and a quicker heaving of her bosom, which indicated the excitement of an anticipated and painful disclosure. The outward contrast of the two women, whose hands were so lovingly locked together, was almost as striking as the moral contrast of their hearts. The one, so chastened, sad, and gentle; the other, so capable of pride and passion; so darkly excitable, and yet so mysteriously beautiful. The one, like a Niobe seen in the softest moonshine; the other, a Venus, lighted in the glare of distant conflagration.

"Mademoiselle, dear mademoiselle, I am so much grieved at what I have to say, that I hardly know how to speak to you," said poor Mrs. Marston, pressing her hand; "but Mr. Marston has twice desired me to tell you, what you will hear with far less pain than it costs me to say it."

Mademoiselle de Barras stole another flashing glance at her companion, but did not speak.

"Mr. Marston still persists, mademoiselle, in desiring that we shall part."

"Est-il possible?" cried the Frenchwoman, with a genuine start.

"Indeed, mademoiselle, you may well be surprised," said Mrs. Marston, encountering her full and dilated gaze, which, however, dropped again in a moment to the ground. "You may, indeed, naturally be surprised and shocked at this, to me, most severe decision."

"When did he speak last of it?" said she, rapidly.

"But a few moments since," answered Mrs. Marston.

"Ha," said mademoiselle, and remained silent and motionless for more than a minute.

"Madame," she cried at last, mournfully, "I suppose, then, I must go; but it tears my heart to leave you and dear Miss Rhoda. I would be very happy if, before departing, you would permit me, dear madame, once more to assure Mr. Marston of my innocence, and, in his presence, to call heaven to witness how unjust are all his suspicions."

"Do so, mademoiselle, and I will add my earnest assurances again; though, heaven knows," she said, despondingly, "I anticipate little success; but it is well to leave no chance untried."

Marston was sitting, as we have said, in his library. His agitation had given place to a listless gloom, and he leaned back in his chair, his head supported by his hand, and undisturbed, except by the occasional fall of the embers upon the hearth. There was a knock at the chamber door. His back was towards it, and, without turning or moving, he called to the applicant to enter. The door opened—closed again: a light tread was audible—a tall shadow darkened the wall: Marston looked round, and Mademoiselle de Barras was standing before him. Without knowing how or why, he rose, and stood gazing upon her in silence.

"Mademoiselle de Barras!" he said, at last, in a tone of cold surprise.

"Yes, poor Mademoiselle de Barras," replied the sweet voice of the young Frenchwoman, while her lips hardly moved as the melancholy tones passed them.

"Well, mademoiselle, what do you desire?" he asked, in the same cold accents, and averting his eyes.

"Ah, monsieur, do you ask?—can you pretend to be ignorant? Have you not sent me a message, a cruel, cruel message?"

She spoke so low and gently, that a person at the other end of the room could hardly have heard her words.

"Yes, Mademoiselle de Barras, I did send you a message," he replied, doggedly. "A cruel one you will scarcely presume to call it, when you reflect upon your own conduct, and the circumstances which have provoked the measures I have taken."

"What have I done, Monsieur?—what circumstances do you mean?" asked she, plaintively.

"What have you done! A pretty question, truly. Ha, ha!" he repeated, bitterly, and then added, with suppressed vehemence, "ask your own heart, mademoiselle."

"I have asked, I do ask, and my heart answers— nothing," she replied, raising her fine melancholy eyes for a moment to his face.

"It lies, then," he retorted, with a fierce scoff.

"Monsieur, before heaven I swear, you wrong me foully," she said, earnestly, clasping her hands together.

"Did ever woman say she was accused rightly, mademoiselle?" retorted Marston, with a sneer.

"I don't know—I don't care. I only know that I am innocent," continued she, piteously. "I call heaven to witness you have wronged me."

"Wronged you!—why, after all, with what have I charged you?" said he, scoffingly; "but let that pass. I have formed my opinions, arrived at my conclusions. If I have not named them broadly, you at least seem to understand their nature thoroughly. I know the world. I am no novice in the arts of women, mademoiselle. Reserve your vows and attestations for schoolboys and simpletons; they are sadly thrown away upon me."

Marston paced to and fro, with his hands thrust into his pockets, as he thus spoke.

"Then you don't, or rather you will not believe what I tell you?" said she, imploringly. "No," he answered, drily and slowly, as he passed her. "I don't, and I won't (as you say) believe one word of it; so, pray spare yourself further trouble about the matter."

She raised her head, and darted after him a glance that seemed absolutely to blaze, and at the same time smote her little hand fast clenched upon her breast. The words, however, that trembled on her pale lips were not uttered; her eyes were again cast down, and her fingers played with the little locket that hung round her neck.

"I must make, before I go," she said, with a deep sigh and a melancholy voice, "one confidence—one last confidence: judge me by it. You cannot choose but believe me now: it is a secret, and it must even here be whispered, whispered, whispered!"

As she spoke, the color fled from her face, and her tones became so strange and resolute, that Marston turned short upon his heel, and stopped before her. She looked in his face; he frowned, but lowered his eyes. She drew nearer, laid her hand upon his shoulder, and whispered for a few moments in his ear. He raised his face suddenly: its features were sharp and fixed; its hue was changed; it was livid and moveless, like a face cut in gray stone. He staggered back a little and a little more, and then a little more, and fell backward. Fortunately, the chair in which he had been sitting received him, and he lay there insensible as a corpse. When at last his eyes opened, there was no gleam of triumph, no shade of anger, nothing perceptible of guilt or menace, in the young woman's countenance. The flush had returned to her cheeks; her dimpled chin had sunk upon her full white throat; sorrow, shame, and pride seemed struggling in her handsome facet and she stood before him like a beautiful penitent, who has just made a strange and humbling shrift to her father confessor.

Next day, Marston was mounting his horse for a solitary ride through his park, when Doctor Danvers rode abruptly into the courtyard from the back entrance. Marston touched his hat, and said—

"I don't stand on forms with you, doctor, and you, I know, will waive ceremony with me. You will find Mrs. Marston at home."

"Nay, my dear sir," interrupted the clergyman, sitting firm in his saddle, "my business lies with you today."

"The devil it does!" said Marston, with discontented surprise.

"Truly it does, sir," repeated he, with a look of gentle reproof, for the profanity of Marston's ejaculation, far more than the rudeness of his manner, offended him; "and I grieve that your surprise should have somewhat carried you away—"

"Well, then, Doctor Danvers," interrupted Marston, drily, and without heeding his concluding remark, "if you really have business with me, it is, at all events, of no very pressing kind, and may be as well told after supper as now. So, pray, go into the house and rest yourself: we can talk together in the evening."

"My horse is not tired," said the clergyman, patting his steed's neck; "and if you do not object, I will ride by your side for a short time, and as we go, I can say out what I have to tell."

"Well, well, be it so," said Marston, with suppressed impatience, and without more ceremony, he rode slowly along the avenue, and turned off upon the soft sward in the direction of the wildest portion of his wooded demesne, the clergyman keeping close beside him. They proceeded some little way at a walk before Doctor Danvers spoke.

"I have been twice or thrice with that unhappy man," at length he said.

"What unhappy man? Unhappiness is no distinguishing singularity, is it?" said Marston, sharply.

"No, truly, you have well said," replied Doctor Danvers. "True it is that man is born unto trouble as the sparks fly upward. I speak, however, of your servant, Merton—a most unhappy wretch."

"Ha! you have been with him, you say?" replied Marston, with evident interest and anxiety.

"Yes, several times, and conversed with him long and gravely," continued the clergyman.

"Humph! I thought that had been the chaplain's business, not yours, my good friend," observed Marston.

"He has been unwell," replied Dr. Danvers; "and thus, for a day or two, I took his duty, and this poor man, Merton, having known something of me, preferred seeing me rather than a stranger; and so, at the chaplain's desire and his, I continued my visits."

"Well, and you have taught him to pray and sing psalms, I suppose; and what has come of it all?" demanded Marston, testily.

"He does pray, indeed, poor man! and I trust his prayers are heard with mercy at the throne of grace," said his companion, in his earnestness disregarding the sneering tone of his companion. "He is full or compunction, and admits his guilt."

"Ho! that is well—well for himself—well for his soul, at least; you are sure of it; he confesses; confesses his guilt?"

Marston put his question so rapidly and excitedly, that the clergyman looked with a slight expression of surprise; and recovering himself, he added, in an unconcerned tone—

"Well, well—it was just as well he did so; the evidence is too clear for doubt or mystification; he knew he had no chance, and has taken the seemliest course; and, doubtless, the best for his hopes hereafter."

"I did not question him upon the subject," said Doctor Danvers; "I even declined to hear him speak upon it at first; but he told me he was resolved to offer no defense, and that he saw the finger of God in the rate which had overtaken him."

"He will plead guilty, then, I suppose?" suggested Marston, watching the countenance or his companion with an anxious and somewhat sinister eye.

"His words seem to imply so much," answered he; "and having thus frankly owned his guilt, and avowed his resolution to let the law take its due course in his case, without obstruction or evasion, I urged him to complete the grand work he had begun, and to confess to you, or to some other magistrate fully, and in detail, every circumstance connected with the perpetration of the dreadful deed."

Marston knit his brows, and rode on for some minutes in silence. At length he said, abruptly—

"In this, it seems to me, sir, you a little exceeded your commission."

"How so, my dear sir?" asked the clergyman.

"Why, sir," answered Marston, "the man may possibly change his mind before the day of trial, and it is the hangman's office, not yours, my good sir, to fasten the halter about his neck. You will pardon my freedom; but, were this deposition made as you suggest, it would undoubtedly hang him."

"God forbid, Mr. Marston," rejoined Danvers, "that I should induce the unhappy man to forfeit his last chances of escape, and to shut the door of human mercy against himself, but on this he seems already resolved; he says so; he has solemnly declared his resolution to me; and even against my warning, again and again reiterated the same declaration."

"That I should have thought quite enough, were I in your place, without inviting a detailed description of the whole process by which this detestable butchery was consummated. What more than the simple knowledge of the man's guilt does any mortal desire; guilty, or not guilty, is the plain question which the law asks, and no more; take my advice, sir, as a poor Protestant layman, and leave the acts of the confessional and inquisition to Popish priests."

"Nay, Mr. Marston, you greatly misconceive me; as matters stand, there exists among the coroner's jury, and thus among the public, some faint and unfounded suspicion of the possibility of Merton's having had an accessory or accomplice in the perpetration of this foul murder."

"It is a lie, sir—a malignant, d——d lie—the jury believe no such thing, nor the public neither," said Marston, starting in his saddle, and speaking in a voice of thunder; "you have been crammed with lies, sir; malicious, unmeaning, vindictive lies; lies invented to asperse my family, and torture my feelings; suggested in my presence by that scoundrel Mervyn, and scouted by the common sense of the jury."

"I do assure you," replied Doctor Danvers, in a voice which seemed scarcely audible, after the stunning and passionate explosion of Marston's wrath, "I did not imagine that you could feel thus sorely upon the point; nay, I thought that you yourself were not without such painful doubts."

"Again, I tell you, sir," said Marston, in a tone somewhat calmer, but no less stern, "such doubts as you describe have no existence; your unsuspecting ear has been alarmed by a vindictive wretch, an old scoundrel who has scarce a passion left but spite towards me; few such there are, thank God; few such villains as would, from a man's very calamities, distil poison to kill the peace and character of his family."

"I am sorry, Mr. Marston," said the clergyman, "you have formed so ill an opinion of a neighbor, and I am very sure that Mr. Mervyn meant you no ill in frankly expressing whatever doubts still rested on his mind, after the evidence was taken."

"He did—the scoundrel!" said Marston, furiously striking his hand, in which his whip was clutched, upon his thigh; "he did mean to wound and torture me; and with the same object he persists in circulating what he calls his doubts. Meant me no ill, forsooth! why, my great God, sir, could any man be so stupid as not to perceive that the suggestion of such suspicions—absurd, contradictory, incredible as they were—was precisely the thing to exasperate feelings sufficiently troubled already, and not content with raising the question, where it was scouted, as I said, as soon as named, the vindictive slanderer proceeds to propagate and publish his pretended surmises—d——n him."

"Mr. Marston, you will pardon me when I say that, as a Christian minister, I cannot suffer a spirit so ill as that you manifest, and language so unseemly as that you have just uttered, to pass unreproved," said Danvers, solemnly. "If you will cherish those bitter and unchristian feelings, at least for the brief space that I am with you, command your fierce, unbecoming words."

Marston was about to make a sneering retort, but restrained himself, and turned his head away.

"The wretched man himself appears now very anxious to make some further disclosures," resumed

Doctor Danvers, after a pause, "and I recommended him to make them to you, Mr. Marston, as the most natural depository of such a statement."

"Well, Mr. Danvers, to cut the matter short, as it appears that a confession of some sort is to be made, be it so. I will attend and receive it. The judges will not be here for eight or ten weeks to come, so there is no great hurry about it. I shall ride down to the town, and see him in the jail some time in the next week."

With this assurance Marston parted from the old clergyman, and rode on alone through the furze and fern of his wild and somber park.

After supper that evening Marston found himself alone in the parlor with his wife. Mrs. Marston availed herself of the opportunity to redeem her pledge to Mademoiselle de Barras. She was not aware of the strange interview which had taken place between him and the lady for whom she pleaded. The result of her renewed entreaties perhaps the reader has anticipated. Marston listened, doubted, listened, hesitated again, put questions, pondered the answers; debated the matter inwardly, and at last gruffly consented to give the young lady another trial, and permit her to remain some time longer. Poor Mrs. Marston, little suspecting the dreadful future, overwhelmed her husband with gratitude for granting to her entreaties (as he had predetermined to do) this fatal boon. Not caring to protract this scene— either from a disinclination to listen to expressions of affection, which had long lost their charm for him, and had become even positively distasteful, or perhaps from some instinctive recoil from the warm expression of gratitude from lips which, were the truth revealed, might justly have trembled with execration and reproach—he abruptly left the room, and Mrs. Marston, full of her good news, hastened, in the kindness of her heart, to communicate the fancied result of her advocacy to Mademoiselle de Barras.

It was about a week after this, that Marston was one evening surprised in his study by the receipt of the following letter from Dr. Danvers:—

"My Dear Sir,

"You will be shocked to hear that Merton is most dangerously ill, and at this moment in imminent peril. He is thoroughly conscious of his situation, and himself regards it as a merciful interposition of Providence to spare him the disgrace and terror of the dreadful fate, which he anticipated. The unhappy man has twice repeated his anxious desire, this day, to state some facts connected with the murder of the late Sir Wynston Berkley, which, he says, it is of the utmost moment that you should hear. He says that he could not leave the world in peace without having made this disclosure, which he especially desires to make to yourself, and entreats that you will come to receive his communication as early as you can in the morning. This is indeed needful, as the physician says that he is fast sinking. I offer no apology for adding my earnest solicitations to those of the dying man; and am, dear sir, your very obedient servant,
"J. Danvers"

"He regards it as a merciful interposition of Providence," muttered Marston, as he closed the letter, with a sneer. "Well, some men have odd notions of mercy and providence, to be sure; but if it pleases him, certainly I shall not complain for one."

Marston was all this evening in better spirits than he had enjoyed for months, or even years. A mountain seemed to have been lifted from his heart. He joined in the conversation during and after supper, listened with apparent interest, talked with animation, and even laughed and jested. It is needless to say all this flowed not from the healthy cheer of a heart at ease, but from the excited and almost feverish sense of sudden relief.

Next morning, Marston rode into the old-fashioned town, at the further end of which the dingy and grated front of the jail looked warningly out upon the rustic passengers. He passed the sentries and made his inquiries of the official at the hatch. He was relieved from the necessity of pushing these into detail, however, by the appearance of the physician, who at that moment passed from the interior of the prison.

"Dr. Danvers told me he expected to see you here this morning," said the medical man, after the customary salutation had been interchanged. "Your call, I believe, is connected with the prisoner, John Merton?"

"Yes, sir, so it is," said Marston. "Is he in a condition, pray, to make a statement of considerable length?"

"Far from it, Mr. Marston; he has but a few hours to live," answered the physician, "and is now insensible; but I believe he last night saw Dr. Danvers, and told him whatever was weighing upon his mind."

"Ha!—And can you say where Dr. Danvers now is?" inquired Marston, anxiously and hurriedly. "Not here, is he?"

"No; but I saw him, as I came here, not ten minutes since, ride into the town. It is market-day, and you will probably find him somewhere in the high street for an hour or two to come," answered he.

Marston thanked him, and, lost in abstraction, rode down to the little inn, entered a sitting room, and wrote a hurried line to Dr. Danvers, entreating his attendance there, as a place where they might converse less interruptedly than in the street; and committing this note to the waiter, with the injunction to deliver it at once, and an intimation of where Dr. Danvers was probably to be found, he awaited, with intense and agitating anxiety, the arrival of the clergyman.

It was not for nearly ten minutes, however, which his impatience magnified into an eternity, that the well-known voice of Dr. Danvers reached him from the little hall. It was in vain that Marston strove to curb his violent agitation: his heart swelled as if it would smother him; he felt, as it were, the chill of death pervade his frame, and he could scarcely see the door through which he momentarily expected the entrance of the clergyman.

A few minutes more, and Dr. Danvers entered the little apartment.

"My dear sir," said he, gravely and earnestly, as he grasped the cold hand of Marston, "I am rejoiced to see you. I have matters of great moment and the strangest mystery to lay before you."

"I dare say—I was sure—that is, I suspected so much," answered Marston, breathing fast, and looking very pale. "I heard at the prison that the murderer, Merton, was fast dying, and now is in an unconscious state; and from the physician, that you had seen him, at his urgent entreaty, last night. My mind misgives me, sir, I fear I know not what. I long, yet dread, to hear the wretched man's confession. For God's sake tell me, does it implicate anybody else in the guilt?"

"No; no one specifically; but it has thrown a hideous additional mystery over the occurrence. Listen to me, my dear sir, and the whole narrative, as he stated it to me, shall be related now to you," said Dr. Danvers.

Marston had closed the door carefully, and they sate down together at the further end of the apartment. Marston, breathless and ghastly pale; his lips compressed—his brows knit—and his dark, dilated gaze fixed immovably upon the speaker. Dr. Danvers, on the other hand, tranquil and solemn, and with, perhaps, some shade of awe overcasting the habitual sweetness of his countenance.

"His confession was a strange one," renewed Dr. Danvers, shaking his head gravely. "He said that the first idea of the crime was suggested by Sir Wynston's man accidentally mentioning, a few days after their arrival, that his master slept with his bank-notes, to the amount of some hundreds of pounds, in a pocketbook under his pillow. He declared that as the man mentioned this circumstance, something muttered the infernal suggestion in his ear, and from that moment he was the slave of that one idea; it was ever present with him. He contended against it in vain; he dreaded and abhorred it; but still it possessed him; he felt his power of resistance yielding. This horrible stranger which had stolen into his heart, waxed in power and importunity, and tormented him day and night. He resolved to fly from the house. He gave notice to you and Mrs. Marston of his intended departure; but accident protracted his stay until that fatal night which sealed his doom. The influence which had mastered him forced him to rise from his bed, and take the knife—the discovery of which afterwards helped to convict him—and led him to Sir Wynston's chamber; he entered; it was a moonlight night."

Here the clergyman, glancing round the room, lowered his voice, and advanced his lips so near to Marston, that their heads nearly touched. In this tone and attitude he continued his narrative for a few minutes. At the end of this brief space, Marston rose up slowly, and with a movement backward, every feature strung with horror, and saying, in a long whisper, the one word, "yes," which seemed like the hiss of a snake before he makes his last deadly spring. Both were silent for a time. At last Marston broke out with hoarse vehemence.

"Dreadful—horrible—oh, God! God!—My God! How frightful!"

And throwing himself into a chair, he clasped his hands across his eyes and forehead, while the sweat of agony literally poured down his pale face.

"Truly it is so," said the clergyman, scarcely above his breath; and, after a long interval—"horrible indeed!"

"Well," said Marston, rising suddenly to his feet, wiping the dews of horror from his face, and looking wildly round, like one newly awoke from a nightmare, "I must make the most of this momentous and startling disclosure. I shall spare no pains to come at the truth," said he, energetically. "Meanwhile, my dear sir, for the sake of justice and of mercy, observe secrecy. Leave me to sift this matter; give no note anywhere that we suspect. Observe this reserve and security, and with it detection will follow. Breathe but one word, and you arm the guilty with double caution, and turn licentious gossip loose upon the fame of an innocent and troubled family. Once more I entreat—I expect—I implore silence—silence, at least, for the present—silence!"

"I quite agree with you, my dear Mr. Marston," answered Dr. Danvers. "I have not divulged one syllable of that poor wretch's confession, save to yourself alone. You, as a magistrate, a relative of the murdered gentleman, and the head of that establishment among whom the guilt rests, are invested with an interest in detecting, and powers of sifting the truth in this matter, such as none other possesses. I clearly see, with you, too, the inexpediency and folly of talking, for talking's sake, of this affair. I mean to keep my counsel, and shall most assuredly, irrespectively even of your request—which should, however, of course, have weight with me— maintain a strict and cautious silence upon this subject."

Some little time longer they remained together, and Marston, buried in strange thoughts, took his leave, and rode slowly back to Gray Forest.

Months passed away—a year, and more—and though no new character appeared upon the stage, the relations which had subsisted among the old ones became, in some respects, very materially altered. A gradual and disagreeable change came over Mademoiselle de Barras's manner; her affectionate attentions to Mrs. Marston became less and less frequent; nor was the change merely confined to this growing coldness; there was something of a positive and still more unpleasant kind in the alteration we have noted. There was a certain independence and carelessness, conveyed in a hundred intangible but significant little incidents and looks—a something which, without being open to formal rebuke or remonstrance, yet bordered, in effect, upon impertinence, and even insolence. This indescribable and provoking self-assertion, implied in glances, tones, emphasis, and general bearing, surprised Mrs. Marston far more than it irritated her. As often as she experienced one of these studied slights or insinuated impertinences, she revolved in her own mind all the incidents of their past intercourse, in the vain endeavor to recollect some one among them which could possibly account for the offensive change so manifest in the conduct of the young Frenchwoman.

Mrs. Marston, although she sometimes rebuked these artful affronts by a grave look, a cold tone, or a distant manner, yet had too much dignity to engage in a petty warfare of annoyance, and had, in reality, no substantial and well-defined ground of complaint against her, such as would have warranted her either in taking the young lady herself to task, or in bringing her conduct under the censure of Marston.

One evening, it happened that Mrs. Marston and Mademoiselle de Barras had been left alone together. After the supper-party had dispersed, they had been for a long time silent. Mrs. Marston resolved to improve the Tate-à-Tate, for the purpose of eliciting from mademoiselle an explanation of her strange behavior.

"Mademoiselle," said she, "I have lately observed a very marked change in your conduct to me."

"Indeed!" said the Frenchwoman.

"Yes, mademoiselle; you must be yourself perfectly aware of that change; it is a studied and intentional one," continued Mrs. Marston, in a gentle but dignified tone. "Although I have felt some doubt as to whether it were advisable, so long as you observe toward me the forms of external respect, and punctually discharge the duties you have undertaken, to open any discussion whatever upon the subject; yet I have thought it better to give you a fair opportunity of explaining frankly, should you desire to do so, the feelings and impressions under which you are acting."

"Ah, you are very obliging, madame," said she, coolly.

"It is quite clear, mademoiselle, that you have either misunderstood me, or that you are dissatisfied with your situation among us: your conduct cannot otherwise be accounted for," said Mrs. Marston, gravely.

"My conduct—_ma foi!_ what conduct?" retorted the handsome Frenchwoman, confidently, and with a disdainful glance.

"If you question the fact, mademoiselle," said the elder lady, "it is enough. Your ungracious manner and ungentle looks, I presume, arise from what appears to you a sufficient and well-defined cause, of which, however, I know nothing."

"I really was not aware," said Mademoiselle de Barras, with a supercilious smile, "that my looks and my manner were subjected to so strict a criticism, or that it was my duty to regulate both according to so nice and difficult a standard."

"Well, mademoiselle," continued Mrs. Marston, "it is plain that whatever may be the cause of your dissatisfaction, you are resolved against confiding it to me. I only wish to know frankly from your own lips, whether you have formed a wish to leave this situation. If so, I entreat you to declare it freely."

"You are very obliging, indeed, madame," said the pretty foreigner, drily, "but I have no such wish, at least at present."

"Very well, mademoiselle," replied Mrs. Marston, with gentle dignity; "I regret your want of candor, on your own account. You would, I am sure, be much happier, were you to deal frankly with me."

"May I now have your permission, madame, to retire to my room?" asked the French girl, rising, and making a low courtesy—"that is, if madame has nothing further to censure."

"Certainly, mademoiselle; I have nothing further to say," replied the elder lady.

The Frenchwoman made another and a deeper courtesy, and withdrew. Mrs. Marston, however, heard, as she was designed to do, the young lady tittering and whispering to herself, as she lighted her candle in the hall. This scene mortified and grieved poor Mrs. Marston inexpressibly. She was little, if at all, accessible to emotions of anger and certainly, none such mingled in the feelings with which she regarded Mademoiselle de Barras. But she had found in this girl a companion, and even a confidante in her melancholy solitude; she had believed her affectionate, sympathetic, tender, and the disappointment was as bitter as unimagined.

The annoyances which she was fated to receive from Mademoiselle de Barras were destined, however, to grow in number and in magnitude. The Frenchwoman sometimes took a fancy, for some unrevealed purpose, to talk a good deal to Mrs. Marston, and on such occasions would persist, notwithstanding that lady's marked reserve and discouragement, in chatting away, as if she were conscious that her conversation was the most welcome entertainment possible to her really unwilling auditor. No one of their interviews did she ever suffer to close without in some way or other suggesting or insinuating something mysterious and untold to the prejudice of Mr. Marston. Those vague and intangible hints, the meaning of which, for an instant legible and terrific, seemed in another moment to dissolve and disappear, tortured

Mrs. Marston like the intrusion of a specter; and this, along with the portentous change, rather felt than visible, in mademoiselle's conduct toward her, invested the beautiful Frenchwoman, in the eyes of her former friend and patroness, with an indefinable character that was not only repulsive but formidable.

Mrs. Marston's feelings with respect to this person were still further disturbed by the half-conveyed hints and innuendoes of her own maid, who never lost an opportunity of insinuating her intense dislike of the Frenchwoman, and appeared perpetually to be upon the very verge of making some explicit charges, or some shocking revelations, respecting her, which, however, she as invariably evaded; and even when Mrs. Marston once or twice insisted upon her explaining her meaning distinctly, she eluded her mistress's desire, and left her still in the same uneasy uncertainty.

Marston, on his part, however much his conduct might tend to confirm suspicion, certainly did nothing to dissipate the painful and undefined apprehension respecting himself, which Mademoiselle de Barras, with such malign and mysterious industry, labored to raise. His spirits and temper were liable to strange fluctuations. In the midst of that excited gaiety, to which, until lately, he had been so long a stranger, would sometimes intervene paroxysms of the blackest despair, all the ghastlier for the contrast, and with a suddenness so abrupt and overwhelming, that one might have fancied him crossed by the shadow of some terrific apparition. Sometimes for a whole day, or even more, he would withdraw himself from the society of his family, and, in morose and moody solitude, take his meals alone in his library, and steal out unattended to wander among the thickets and glades of his park. Sometimes, again, he would sit for hours in the room which had been Sir Wynston's, and, with a kind of horrible resolution, often loiter there till after nightfall. In such hours, the servants would listen with curious awe, as they heard his step, pacing to and fro, in that deserted and inauspicious chamber, while his voice, in broken sentences, was also imperfectly audible, as if maintaining a muttered dialogue. These eccentric practices gradually invested him, in the eyes of his domestics, with a certain preternatural mystery, which enhanced the fear with which they habitually regarded him, and was subsequently confirmed by his giving orders to have the furniture taken out of the ominous suite of rooms, and the doors nailed up and secured. He gave no reason for this odd and abrupt measure, and gossip of course reported that the direction had originated in his having encountered the specter of the murdered baronet, in one of these strange and unseasonable visits to the scene of the fearful catastrophe.

In addition to all this, Marston's conduct towards his wife became strangely capricious. He avoided her society more than ever; and when he did happen to exchange a few words with her, they were sometimes harsh and violent, and at others remorsefully gentle and sad, and this without any changes of conduct upon her part to warrant the wayward uncertainty of his treatment. Under all these circumstances, Mrs. Marston's unhappiness and uneasiness greatly increased. Mademoiselle de Barras, too, upon several late occasions, had begun to assume a tone of authority and dictation, which justly offended the mistress of the establishment. Meanwhile Charles Marston had returned to Cambridge; and Rhoda, no longer enjoying happy walks with her brother, pursued her light and easy studies with Mademoiselle de Barras, and devoted her leisure hours to the loved society of her mother.

One day Mrs. Marston, sitting in her room with Rhoda, had happened to call her own maid, to take down and carefully dust some richly bound volumes which filled a bookcase in the little chamber.

"You have been crying, Willett," said Mrs. Marston, observing that the young woman's eyes were red and swollen.

"Indeed, and I was, ma'am," she replied, reluctantly, "and I could not help it, so I could not."

"Why, what has happened to vex you? Has anyone ill-treated you?" said Mrs. Marston, who had an esteem for the poor girl. "Come, come, you must not fret about it; only tell me what has vexed you."

"Oh! Ma'am, no one has ill-used me, ma'am; but I can't but be vexed sometimes, ma'am, and fretted to see how things is going on. I have one wish, just one wish, ma'am, and if I got that, I'd ask no more," said the girl.

"And what is it?" asked Mrs. Marston; "what do you wish for? Speak plainly, Willett; what is it?"

"Ah! Ma'am, if I said it, maybe you might not be pleased. Don't ask me, ma'am," said the girl dusting the books very hard, and tossing them down again with angry emphasis. "I don't desire anybody's harm, God knows; but, for all that, I wish what I wish, and that is the truth."

"Why, Willett, I really cannot account for your strange habit of lately hinting, and insinuating, and always speaking riddles, and refusing to explain your meaning. What do you mean? Speak plainly. If there are any dishonest practices going on, it is your duty to say so distinctly."

"Oh! Ma'am, it is just a wish I have. I wish—; but it's no matter. If I could once see the house clear of that Frenchwoman—"

"If you mean Mademoiselle de Barras, she is a lady," interrupted Mrs. Marston.

"Well, ma'am, I beg pardon," continued the woman; "lady or no lady, it is all one to me; for I am very sure, ma'am, she'll never leave the house till there is something bad comes about; and—and—. I can't bring myself to talk to you about her, ma'am. I can't say what I want to tell you: but—but—. Oh, ma'am, for God's sake, try and get her out, any way, no matter how; try and get rid of her."

As she said this, the poor girl burst into a passionate agony of tears, and Mrs. Marston and Rhoda looked on in silent amazement, while she for some minutes continued to sob and weep.

The party were suddenly recalled from their various reveries by a knock at the chamber-door. It opened, and the subject of the girl's deprecatory entreaty entered. There was something unusually excited and assured in Mademoiselle de Barras's air and countenance; perhaps she had a suspicion that she had been the topic of their conversation. At all events, she looked round upon them with a smile, in which there was something supercilious, and even defiant; and, without waiting to be invited, sate herself down, with a haughty air.

"I was about to ask you to sit down, mademoiselle, but you have anticipated me," said Mrs. Marston, gravely. "You have something to say to me, I suppose; I am quite at leisure, so pray let me hear it now."

"Thank you, thank you, madame," replied she, with a sharp, and even scornful glance; "I ought to have asked your permission to sit; I forgot; but you have condescended to give it without my doing so; that was very kind, very kind, indeed."

"But I wish to know, mademoiselle, whether you have anything very particular to say to me?" said Mrs. Marston.

"You wish to know!—and why, pray madame?" asked Mademoiselle de Barras, sharply.

"Because, unless it is something very urgent, I should prefer your talking to me some other time; as, at present, I desire to be alone with my daughter."

"Oh, ho! I ought to ask pardon again," said mademoiselle, with the same glance, and the same smile. "I find I am de trop—quite in the way. Hélas! I am very unfortunate today."

Mademoiselle de Barras made not the slightest movement, and it was evident that she was resolved to prolong her stay, in sheer defiance of Mrs. Marston's wishes.

"Mademoiselle, I conclude from your silence that you have nothing very pressing to say, and, therefore, must request that you will have the goodness to leave me for the present," said Mrs. Marston, who felt that the spirit of the French girl's conduct was too apparent not to have been understood by Rhoda and the servant, and that it was of a kind, for example sake, impossible to be submitted to, or tolerated.

Mademoiselle de Barras darted a fiery and insolent glance at Mrs. Marston, and was, doubtless, upon the point of precipitating the open quarrel which was impending, by setting her authority at defiance; but she checked herself, and changed her line of operations.

"We are not alone madame," she said, with a heightened color, and a slight toss of the head. "I was about to speak of Mr. Marston. I had something, not much, I confess, to say; but before servants I shan't speak; nor, indeed, now at all. So, madame, as you desire it, I shall no further interrupt you. Come, Miss Rhoda, come to the music-room, if you please, and finish your practice for today."

"You forget, mademoiselle, that I wish to have my daughter with me at present," said Mrs. Marston.

"I am very sorry, madame," said the French lady, with the same heightened color and unpleasant smile, and her finely-penciled brows just discernibly knit, so as to give a novel and menacing expression to her beautiful face—"I am very sorry, madame, but she must, so long as I remain accountable for her education, complete her allotted exercises at the appointed hours; and nothing shall, I assure you, with my consent, interfere with these duties. Come, Miss Rhoda, precede me, if you please, to the music-room. Come, come."

"Stay where you are, Rhoda," said Mrs. Marston, firmly and gently, and betraying no symptom of excitement, except in a slight tremor of her voice, and a faint flush upon her cheek—"Stay where you are, my dear child. I am your mother, and, next to your father, have the first claim upon your obedience. Mademoiselle," she continued, addressing the Frenchwoman, calmly but firmly, "my daughter will remain here for some time longer, and you will have the goodness to withdraw. I insist upon it, Mademoiselle de Barras."

"I will not leave the room, I assure you, madame, without my pupil," retorted mademoiselle, with resolute insolence. "Your husband, madame, has invested me with this authority, and she shall obey me. Miss Rhoda, I say again, go down to the music-room."

"Remain where you are, Rhoda," said Mrs. Marston again. "Mademoiselle; you have long been acting as if your object were to provoke me to part with you. I find it impossible any longer to overlook this grossly disrespectful conduct; conduct of which I had, indeed, believed you absolutely incapable. Willett," she continued, addressing the maid, who was evidently bursting with rage at the scene she had just witnessed, "your master is, I believe, in the library; go down, and tell him that I entreat him to come here immediately."

The maid started on her mission with angry alacrity, darting a venomous glance at the handsome Frenchwoman as she passed.

Mademoiselle de Barras, meanwhile, sate, listless and defiant, in her chair, and tapping her little foot with angry excitement upon the floor. Rhoda sate close by her mother, holding her hand fast, and looking frightened, perplexed, and as if she were on the point of weeping. Mrs. Marston, though flushed and excited, yet maintained her dignified and grave demeanor. And thus, in silence, did they all three await the arrival of the arbiter to whom Mrs. Marston had so promptly appealed.

A few minutes more, and Marston entered the room. Mademoiselle's expression changed as he did so to one of dejected and sorrowful submission; and, as Marston's eye lighted upon her, his brow darkened and his face grew pale.

"Well, well—what is it?—What is all this?" he said, glancing with a troubled eye from one to the other. "Speak, someone. Mrs. Marston, you sent for me; what is it?"

"I want to know, Mr. Marston, from your own lips," said the lady, in reply, "whether Rhoda is to obey me or Mademoiselle de Barras?"

"Bah!—A question of women's prerogative," said Marston, with muttered vehemence.

"Of a wife's and a mother's prerogative, Richard," said Mrs. Marston, with gentle emphasis. "A very simple question, and one I should have thought needing no deliberation to decide it."

"Well, child," sad he, turning to Rhoda, with angry irony, "pray what is all this fuss about? You are a very ill used young lady, I dare aver. Pray what cruelties does Mademoiselle de Barras propose inflicting upon you, that you need to appeal thus to your mother for protection?"

"You quite mistake me, Richard," interposed Mrs. Marston; "Rhoda is perfectly passive in the matter. I simply wish to learn from you, in mademoiselle's presence, whether I or she is to command my daughter?"

"Command!" said Marston, evading the direct appeal; "and pray what is all this commanding about?— What do you want the girl to do?"

"I wish her to remain here with me for a little time, and mademoiselle, knowing this, desires her instantly to go to the music-room, and leave me. That is all," said Mrs. Marston.

"And pray, is there nothing to make her going to the music-room advisable or necessary? Has she no music to learn, or studies to pursue? Pshaw! Mrs. Marston, what needs all this noise about nothing? Go, miss," he added, sharply and peremptorily, addressing Rhoda, "go this moment to the music-room."

The girl glided from the room, and mademoiselle, as she followed, shot a glance at Mrs. Marston which wounded and humbled her in the dust.

"Oh! Richard, Richard, if you knew all, you would not have subjected me to this indignity," she said; and throwing her arms about his neck, she wept, for the first time for many a long year, upon his breast.

Marston was embarrassed and agitated. He disengaged her arms from his neck, and placed her gently in a chair. She sobbed on for some time in silence—a silence which Marston himself did not essay to break. He walked to the door, apparently with the intention of leaving her. He hesitated however, and returned; took a hurried turn through the room; hesitated again; sat down; then returned to the door, not to depart, but to close it carefully, and walked gloomily to the window, whence he looked forth, buried in agitating and absorbing thoughts.

"Richard, to you this seems a trifling thing; but, indeed it is not so," said Mrs. Marston, sadly.

"You are very right, Gertrude," he said, quickly, and almost with a start; "it is very far from a trifling thing; it is very important."

"You don't blame me, Richard?" said she.

"I blame nobody," said he.

"Indeed, I never meant to offend you, Richard," she urged.

"Of course not; no, no; I never said so," he interrupted, sarcastically; "what could you gain by that?"

"Oh! Richard, better feelings have governed me," she said, in a melancholy and reproachful tone.

"Well, well, I suppose so," he said; and after an interval, he added abstractedly, "This cannot, however, go on; no, no—it cannot. Sooner or later it must have come; better at once—better now."

"What do you mean, Richard?" she said, greatly alarmed, she knew not why. "What are you resolving upon? Dear Richard, in mercy tell me. I implore of you, tell me."

"Why, Gertrude, you seem to me to fancy that, because I don't talk about what is passing, that I don't see it either. Now this is quite a mistake," said Marston, calmly and resolutely—"I have long observed your growing dislike of Mademoiselle de Barras. I have thought it over; this fracas of today has determined me; it is decisive. I suppose you now wish her to go, as earnestly as you once wished her to stay. You need not answer. I know it. I neither ask nor care to whose fault I am to attribute these changed feelings—female caprice accounts sufficiently for it; but whatever the cause, the effect is undeniable; and the only way to deal satisfactorily with it is, to dismiss mademoiselle at once. You need take no part in the matter; I take it upon myself. Tomorrow morning she shall have left this house. I have said it, and am perfectly resolved."

As he thus spoke, as if to avoid the possibility of any further discussion, he turned abruptly from her, and left the room.

The extreme agitation which she had just undergone combined with her physical delicacy to bring on an hysterical attack; and poor Mrs. Marston, with an aching head and a heavy heart, lay down upon her bed. She had swallowed an opiate, and before ten o'clock upon that night, an eventful one as it proved, she had sunk into a profound slumber.

Some hours after this, she became in a confused way conscious of her husband's presence in the room. He was walking, with an agitated mien, up and down the chamber, and casting from time to time looks of great trouble toward the bed where she lay. Though the presence of her husband was a strange and long unwonted occurrence there, at such an hour, and though she felt the strangeness of the visit, the power of the opiate overwhelmed her so, that she could only see this apparition gliding slowly back and forward before her, with the passive wonder and curiosity with which one awaits the issue of an interesting dream.

For a time she lay once more in an uneasy sleep; but still, throughout even this, she was conscious of his presence; and when, a little while after, she again saw him, he was not walking to and fro before the foot of the bed, but sitting beside her, with one hand laid upon the pillow on which her head was resting, the other supporting his chin. He was looking steadfastly upon her, with a changed face, an expression of bitter sorrow, compunction, and tenderness. There was not one trace of sternness; all was softened. The look was what she fancied he might have turned upon her had she lain there dead, ere yet the love of their early and ill-fated union had grown cold in his heart. There was something in it which reminded her of days and feelings gone, never to return. And while she looked in his face with a sweet and mournful fascination, tears unconsciously wet the pillow on which her poor head was resting. Unable to speak, unable to move, she heard him say—"It was not your fault, Gertrude—it was not yours, nor mine. There is a destiny in these things too strong for us. Past is past— what is done, is done forever; and even were it all to do over again, what power have I to mend it? No, no; how could I contend against the combined power of passions, circumstances, influences—in a word, of fate? You have been good and patient, while I—; but no matter. Your lot, Gertrude, is a happier one than mine."

Mrs. Marston heard him and saw him, but she had not the power, nor even the will, herself to speak or move. He appeared before her passive sense like the phantasm of a dream. He stood up at the bedside, and looked on her steadfastly, with the same melancholy expression. For a moment he stooped over her, as if about to kiss her face, but checked himself, stood erect again at the bedside, then suddenly turned; the curtain fell back into its place, and she saw him no more.

With a strange mixture of sweet and bitter feelings this vision rested upon the memory of Mrs. Marston, until, gradually, deep slumber again overcame her senses, and the incident and all its attendant circumstances faded into oblivion.

It was past eight o'clock when Mrs. Marston awoke next morning. The sun was shining richly and cheerily in at the windows; and as the remembrance of Marston's visit to her chamber, and the unwonted manifestations of tenderness and compunction which accompanied it, returned, she felt something like hope and happiness, to which she had long been a stranger, flutter her heart. The pleasing reverie to which she was yielding was, however, interrupted. The sound of stifled sobbing in the room reached her ear, and, pushing back the bed-curtains, and leaning forward to look, she saw her maid, Willett, sitting with her back to the wall, crying bitterly, and striving, as it seemed, to stifle her sobs with her apron, which was wrapped about her face.

"Willet, Willett, is it you who are sobbing? What is the matter with you, child?" said Mrs. Marston, anxiously.

The girl checked herself, dried her eyes hastily, and walking briskly to a little distance, as if engaged in arranging the chamber, she said, with an affectation of carelessness—

"Oh, ma'am, it is nothing; nothing at all, indeed, ma'am."

Mrs. Marston remained silent for a time, while all her vague apprehensions returned. Meantime the girl continued to shove the chairs hither and thither, and to arrange and disarrange everything in the room with a fidgety industry, intended to cover her agitation. A few minutes, however, served to weary her of this, for she abruptly stopped, stood by the bedside, and, looking at her mistress, burst into tears.

"Good God! What is it?" said Mrs. Marston, shocked and even terrified, while new alarms displaced her old ones. "Is Miss Rhoda—can it be—is she—is my darling well?"

"Oh, yes, ma'am," answered the maid, "very well, ma'am; she is up, and out walking and knows nothing of all this."

"All what?" urged Mrs. Marston. "Tell me, tell me, Willett, what has happened. What is it? Speak, child; say what it is?"

"Oh, ma'am! Oh my poor dear mistress!" continued the girl, and stopped, almost stifled with sobs.

"Willett, you must speak; you must say what is the matter. I implore of you—desire you!" urged the distracted lady. Still the girl, having made one or two ineffectual efforts to speak, continued to sob.

"Willett, you will drive me mad. For mercy's sake, for God's sake, speak—tell me what it is!" cried the unhappy lady.

"Oh, ma'am, it is—it is about the master," sobbed the girl.

"Why he can't—he has not—oh, merciful God! He has not hurt himself." she almost screamed.

"No, ma'am, no; not himself; no, no, but—" and again she hesitated.

"But what? Speak out, Willett; dear Willett have mercy on me, and speak out," cried her wretched mistress.

"Oh, ma'am, don't be fretted; don't take it to heart, ma'am," said the maid, clasping her hands together in anguish.

"Anything, anything, Willett; only speak at once," she answered.

"Well, ma'am, it is soon said—it is easy told. The master, ma'am—the master is gone with the Frenchwoman; they went in the traveling coach last night, ma'am; he is gone away with her, ma'am; that is all."

Mrs. Marston looked at the girl with a gaze of stupefied, stony terror; not a muscle of her face moved; not one heaving respiration showed that she was living. Motionless, with this fearful look fixed upon the girl, and her thin hands stretched towards her, she remained, second after second. At last her outstretched hands began to tremble more and more violently; and as if for the first time the knowledge of his calamity had reached her, with a cry, as though body and soul were parting, she fell back motionless in her bed.

Several hours had passed before Mrs. Marston was restored to consciousness. To this state of utter insensibility, one of silent, terrified stupor succeeded; and it was not until she saw her daughter Rhoda standing at her bedside, weeping, that she found voice and recollection to speak.

"My child; my darling, my poor child," she cried, sobbing piteously, as she drew her to her heart and looked in her face alternately—"my darling, my darling child!"

Rhoda could only weep, and return her poor mother's caresses in silence. Too young and inexperienced to understand the full extent and nature of this direful calamity, the strange occurrence, the general and apparent consternation of the whole household, and the spectacle of her mother's agony, had filled her with fear, perplexity, and anguish. Scared and stunned with a vague sense of danger, like a young bird that, for the first time, cowers under a thunderstorm, she nestled in her mother's bosom; there, with a sense of protection, and of boundless love and tenderness, she lay frightened, wondering, and weeping.

Two or three days passed, and Dr. Danvers came and sate for several hours with poor Mrs. Marston. To comfort and console were, of course, out of his power. The nature of the bereavement, far more terrible than death—its recent occurrence—the distracting consciousness of all its complicated consequences—rendered this a hopeless task. She bowed herself under the blow with the submission of a broken heart. The hope to which she had clung for years had vanished; the worst that ever her imagination feared had come in earnest.

One idea was now constantly present in her mind. She felt a sad, but immovable assurance, that she should not live long, and the thought, "what will become of my darling when I am gone; who will guard and love my child when I am in my grave; to whom is she to look for tenderness and protection then?" perpetually haunted her, and superadded the pangs of a still wilder despair to the desolation of a broken heart.

It was not for more than a week after this event, that one day Willett, with a certain air of anxious mystery, entered the silent and darkened chamber where Mrs. Marston lay. She had a letter in her hand; the seal and handwriting were Mr. Marston's. It was long before the injured wife was able to open it; when she did so, the following sentences met her eye:—

"Gertrude,

"You can be ignorant neither of the nature nor of the consequences of the decisive step I have taken: I do not seek to excuse it. For the censure of the world, its meddling and mouthing hypocrisy, I care absolutely nothing; I have long set it at defiance. And you yourself, Gertrude, when you deliberately reconsider the circumstances of estrangement and coldness under which, though beneath the same roof, we have lived for years, without either sympathy or confidence, can scarcely, if at all, regret the rupture of a tie which had long ceased to be anything better than an irksome and galling formality. I do not desire to attribute to you the smallest blame. There was an incompatibility, not of temper but of feelings, which made us strangers though calling one another man and wife. Upon this fact I rest my own justification; our living together under these circumstances was, I dare say, equally undesired by us both. It was, in fact, but a deference to the formal hypocrisy of the world. At all events, the irrevocable act which separates us forever is done, and I have now

merely to state so much of my intentions as may relate in anywise to your future arrangements. I have written to your cousin, and former guardian, Mr. Latimer, telling him how matters stand between us. You, I told him, shall have, without opposition from me, the whole of your own fortune to your own separate use, together with whatever shall be mutually agreed upon as reasonable, from my income, for your support and that of my daughter. It will be necessary to complete your arrangements with expedition, as I purpose returning to Gray Forest in about three weeks; and as, of course, a meeting between you and those by whom I shall be accompanied is wholly out of the question, you will see the expediency of losing no time in adjusting everything for yours and my daughter's departure. In the details, of course, I shall not interfere. I think I have made myself clearly intelligible, and would recommend your communicating at once with Mr. Latimer, with a view to completing temporary arrangements, until your final plans shall have been decided upon.
"RICHARD MARSTON"

The reader can easily conceive the feelings with which this letter was perused. We shall not attempt to describe them; nor shall we weary his patience by a detail of all the circumstances attending Mrs. Marston's departure. Suffice it to mention that, in less than a fortnight after the receipt of the letter which we have just copied, she had forever left the mansion of Gray Forest.

In a small house, in a sequestered part of the rich county of Warwick, the residence of Mrs. Marston and her daughter was for the present fixed. And there, for a time, the heart-broken and desolate lady enjoyed, at

least, the privilege of an immunity from the intrusions
of all external trouble. But the blow, under which the
feeble remains of her health and strength were gradually
to sink, had struck too surely home; and, from month
to month—almost from week to week—the progress of
decay was perceptible.

Meanwhile, though grieved and humbled, and
longing to comfort his unhappy mother Charles
Marston, for the present absolutely dependant upon his
father, had no choice but to remain at Cambridge, and
to pursue his studies there.

At Gray Forest Marston and the partner of his guilt
continued to live. The old servants were all gradually
dismissed, and new ones hired by Mademoiselle de
Barras. There they dwelt, shunned by everybody, in
a stricter and more desolate seclusion than ever. The
novelty of the unrestraint and licence of their new mode
of life speedily passed away, and with it the excited and
guilty sense of relief which had for a time produced a
false and hollow gaiety. The sense of security prompted
in mademoiselle a hundred indulgences which, in
her former precarious position, she would not have
dreamed of. Outbreaks of temper, sharp and sometimes
violent, began to manifest themselves on her part, and
renewed disappointment and blacker remorse to darken
the soul of Marston himself. Often, in the dead of the
night, the servants would overhear their bitter and fierce
altercations ringing through the melancholy mansion,
and often the reckless use of terrible and mysterious
epithets of crime. Their quarrels increased in violence
and in frequency, and, before two years had passed,
feelings of bitterness, hatred, and dread, alone seemed to
subsist between them. Yet upon Marston she continued

to exercise a powerful and mysterious influence. There was a dogged, apathetic submission on his part, and a growing insolence on hers, constantly more and more strikingly visible. Neglect, disorder, and decay, too, were more than ever apparent in the dreary air of the place.

Doctor Danvers, save by rumor and conjecture, knew nothing of Marston and his abandoned companion. He had, more than once, felt a strong disposition to visit Gray Forest, and expostulate, face to face, with its guilty proprietor. This idea, however, he had, upon consideration, dismissed; not on account of any shrinking from the possible repulses and affronts to which the attempt might subject him, but from a thorough conviction that the endeavor would be utterly fruitless for good, while it might, very obviously, expose him to painful misinterpretation and suspicion, and leave it to be imagined that he had been influenced, if by no meaner motive, at least by the promptings of a coarse curiosity.

Meanwhile he maintained a correspondence with Mrs. Marston, and had even once or twice since her departure visited her. Latterly, however, this correspondence had been a good deal interrupted, and its intervals had been supplied occasionally by Rhoda, whose letters, although she herself appeared unconscious of the mournful event the approach of which they too plainly indicated, were painful records of the rapid progress of mortal decay.

He had just received one of those ominous letters, at the little post office in the town we have already mentioned, and, full of the melancholy news, it contained, Dr. Danvers was returning slowly towards his home. As he rode into a lonely road, traversing an undulating tract of some three miles in length, the singularity, it may be, of his costume attracted the eye of another passenger, who was, as it turned out, no other than Marston himself. For two or three miles of this desolate road, their ways happened to lie together. Marston's first impulse was to avoid the clergyman; his second, which he obeyed, was to join company, and ride along with him, at all events, for so long as would show that he shrank from no encounter which fortune or accident presented. There was a spirit of bitter defiance in this, which cost him a painful effort.

"How do you do, Parson Danvers?" said Marston, touching his hat with the handle of his whip.

Danvers thought he had seldom seen a man so changed in so short a time. His face had grown sallow and wasted, and his figure slightly stooped, with an appearance almost of feebleness.

"Mr. Marston," said the clergyman, gravely, and almost sternly, though with some embarrassment, "it is a long time since you and I have seen one another, and many and painful events have passed in the interval. I scarce know upon what terms we meet. I am prompted to speak to you, and in a tone, perhaps, which you will hardly brook; and yet, if we keep company, as it seems likely we may, I cannot, and I ought not, to be silent."

"Well, Mr. Danvers, I accept the condition—speak what you will," said Marston, with a gloomy promptitude. "If you exceed your privilege, and grow uncivil, I need but use my spurs, and leave you behind me preaching to the winds."

"Ah! Mr. Marston," said Dr. Danvers, almost sadly, after a considerable pause, "when I saw you close beside me, my heart was troubled within me."

"You looked on me as something from the nether world, and expected to see the cloven hoof," said Marston, bitterly, and raising his booted foot a little as he spoke; "but, after all, I am but a vulgar sinner of flesh and blood, without enough of the preternatural about me to frighten an old nurse, much less to agitate a pillar of the Church."

"Mr. Marston, you talk sarcastically, but you feel that recent circumstances, as well as old recollections, might well disturb and trouble me at sight of you," answered Dr. Danvers.

"Well—yes—perhaps it is so," said Marston, hastily and sullenly, and became silent for a while.

"My heart is full, Mr. Marston; charged with grief, when I think of the sad history of those with whom, in my mind, you must ever be associated," said Doctor Danvers.

"Aye, to be sure," said Marston, with stern impatience; "but, then, you have much to console you. You have got your comforts and your respectability; all the dearer, too, from the contrast of other people's misfortunes and degradations; then you have your religion moreover—"

"Yes," interrupted Danvers, earnestly, and hastening to avoid a sneer upon this subject; "God be blessed, I am an humble follower of his gracious Son, our Redeemer; and though, I trust, I should bear with patient submission whatever chastisement in his wisdom and goodness he might see fit to inflict upon me, yet I do praise and bless him for the mercy which has hitherto spared me, and I do feel that mercy all the more profoundly, from the afflictions and troubles with which I daily see others overtaken."

"And in the matter of piety and decorum, doubtless, you bless God also," said Marston, sarcastically, "that you are not as other men are, nor even as this publican."

"Nay, Mr. Marston; God forbid I should harden my sinful heart with the wicked pride of the Pharisee. Evil and corrupt am I already over much. Too well I know the vileness of my heart, to make myself righteous in my own eyes," replied Dr. Danvers, humbly. "But, sinner as I am, I am yet a messenger of God, whose mission is one of authority to his fellow-sinners; and woe is me if I speak not the truth at all seasons, and in all places where my words may be profitably heard."

"Well, Doctor Danvers, it seems you think it your duty to speak to me, of course, respecting my conduct and my spiritual state. I shall save you the pain and trouble of opening the subject; I shall state the case for you in two words," said Marston, almost fiercely. "I have put away my wife without just cause, and am living in sin with another woman. Come, what have you to say on this theme? Speak out. Deal with me as roughly as you will, I will hear it, and answer you again."

"Alas, Mr. Marston! And do not these things trouble you?" exclaimed Dr. Danvers, earnestly. "Do they not weigh heavy upon your conscience? Ah, sir, do you not remember that, slowly and surely, you are drawing towards the hour of death, and the Day of Judgment?"

"The hour or death! Yes, I know it is coming, and I await it with indifference. But, for the Day of Judgment, with its books and trumpets! My dear doctor, pray don't expect to frighten me with that."

Marston spoke with an angry scorn, which had the effect of interrupting the conversation for some moments.

They rode on, side by side, for a long time, without speaking. At length, however, Marston unexpectedly broke the silence—

"Doctor Danvers," said he, "you asked me some time ago if I feared the hour of death, and the Day of Judgment. I answered you truly, I do not fear them; nay death, I think, I could meet with a happier and a quieter heart than any other chance that can befall me; but there are other fears; fears that do trouble me much."

Doctor Danvers looked inquiringly at him; but neither spoke for a time.

"You have not seen the catastrophe of the tragedy yet," said Marston, with a stern, stony look, made more horrible by a forced smile and something like a shudder. "I wish I could tell you—you, Doctor Danvers—for you are honorable and gentle-hearted. I wish I durst tell you what I fear; the only, only thing I really do fear. No mortal knows it but myself, and I see it coming upon me with slow, but unconquerable power. Oh, God— dreadful Spirit—spare me!"

Again they were silent, and again Marston resumed—

"Doctor Danvers, don't mistake me," he said, turning sharply, and fixing his eyes with a strange expression upon his companion. "I dread nothing human; I fear neither death, nor disgrace, nor eternity; I have no secrets to keep—no exposures to apprehend; but I dread—I dread—"

He paused, scowled darkly, as if stung with pain, turned away, muttering to himself, and gradually became much excited.

"I can't tell you now, sir, and I won't," he said, abruptly and fiercely, and with a countenance darkened with a wild and appalling rage that was wholly unaccountable. "I see you searching me with your eyes. Suspect what you will, sir, you shan't inveigle me into admissions. Aye, pry—whisper—stare—question, conjecture, sir—I suppose I must endure the world's impertinence, but d——n me if I gratify it."

It would not be easy to describe Dr. Danvers' astonishment at this unaccountable explosion of fury. He was resolved, however, to bear his companion's violence with temper.

They rode on slowly for fully ten minutes in utter silence, except that Marston occasionally muttered to himself, as it seemed, in excited abstraction. Danvers had at first felt naturally offended at the violent and insulting tone in which he had been so unexpectedly and unprovokedly addressed; but this feeling of irritation was but transient, and some fearful suspicions as to Marston's sanity flitted through his mind. In a calmer and more dogged tone, his companion now addressed him:—

"There is little profit you see, doctor, in worrying me about your religion," said Marston. "it is but sowing the wind, and reaping the whirlwind; and, to say the truth, the longer you pursue it, the less I am in the mood to listen. If ever you are cursed and persecuted as I have been, you will understand how little tolerant of gratuitous vexations and contradictions a man may become. We have squabbled over religion long enough, and each holds his own faith still. Continue to sun yourself in your happy delusions, and leave me untroubled to tread the way of my own dark and cheerless destiny."

Thus saying, he made a sullen gesture of farewell, and spurring his horse, crossed the broken fence at the roadside, and so, at a listless pace, through gaps and by farm-roads, penetrated towards his melancholy and guilty home.

Two years had now passed since the decisive event which had forever separated Marston from her who had loved him so devotedly and so fatally; two years to him of disappointment, abasement, and secret rage; two years to her of gentle and heart-broken submission to the chastening hand of heaven. At the end of this time she died. Marston read the letter that announced the event with a stern look, and silently, but the shock he felt was terrific. No man is so self-abandoned to despair and degradation, that at some casual moment thoughts of amendment—some gleams of hope, however faint and transient, from the distant future—will not visit him. With Marston, those thoughts had somehow ever been associated with vague ideas of a reconciliation with the being whom he had forsaken—good and pure, and looking at her from the darkness and distance of his own fallen state, almost angelic as she seemed. But she was now dead; he could make her no atonement; she could never smile forgiveness upon him. This long-familiar image—the last that had reflected for him one ray of the lost peace and love of happier times—had vanished, and henceforward there was before him nothing but storm and fear.

Marston's embarrassed fortunes made it to him an object to resume the portion of his income heretofore devoted to the separate maintenance of his wife and daughter. In order to effect this it became, of course, necessary to recall his daughter, Rhoda, and fix her residence once more at Gray Forest. No more dreadful penalty could have been inflicted upon the poor girl—no more agonizing ordeal than that she was thus doomed to undergo. She had idolized her mother, and now adored her memory. She knew that Mademoiselle de Barras had betrayed and indirectly murdered the parent she had so devotedly loved; she knew that that woman had been the curse, the fate of her family, and she regarded her naturally with feelings of mingled terror and abhorrence, the intensity of which was indescribable.

The few scattered friends and relatives, whose sympathies had been moved by the melancholy fate of poor Mrs. Marston, were unanimously agreed that the intended removal of the young and innocent daughter to the polluted mansion of sin and shame, was too intolerably revolting to be permitted. But each of these virtuous individuals unhappily thought it the duty of the others to interpose; and with a running commentary of wonder and reprobation, and much virtuous criticism, events were suffered uninterruptedly to take their sinister and melancholy course.

It was about two months after the death of Mrs. Marston, and on a bleak and ominous night at the wintry end of autumn, that poor Rhoda, in deep mourning, and pale with grief and agitation, descended from a chaise at the well-known door of the mansion of Gray Forest. Whether from consideration for her feelings, or, as was more probable, from pure indifference, Rhoda was conducted, on her arrival, direct to her own chamber, and it was not until the next morning that she saw her father. He entered her room unexpectedly, he was very pale, and as she thought, greatly altered, but he seemed perfectly collected, and free from agitation. The marked and even shocking change in his appearance, and perhaps even the trifling though painful circumstance that he wore no mourning for the beloved being who was gone, caused her, after a moment's mute gazing in his face, to burst into an irrepressible flood of tears. Marston waited stoically until the paroxysm had subsided, and then taking her hand, with a look in which a dogged sternness was contending with something like shame, he said:—

"There, there; you can weep when I am gone. I shan't say very much to you at present, Rhoda, and only wish you to attend to me for one minute. Listen, Rhoda; the lady whom you have been in the habit (here he slightly averted his eyes) of calling Mademoiselle de Barras, is no longer so; she is married; she is my wife, and consequently you will treat her with the respect due to"—he would have said "a mother," but could not, and supplied the phrase by adding, "to that relation."

Rhoda was unable to speak, but almost unconsciously bowed her head in token of attention and submission, and her father pressed her hand more kindly, as he continued:—

"I have always found you a dutiful and obedient child, Rhoda, and expected no other conduct from you. Mrs. Marston will treat you with proper kindness and consideration, and desires me to say that you can, whenever you please, keep strictly to yourself, and need not, unless you feel so disposed, attend the regular meals of the family. This privilege may suit your present depressed spirits, and you must not scruple to use it."

After a few words more, Marston withdrew, leaving his daughter to her reflections, and bleak and bitter enough they were.

Some weeks passed away, and perhaps we shall best consult our readers' ease by substituting for the formal precision of narrative, a few extracts from the letters which Rhoda wrote to her brother, still at Cambridge. These will convey her own impressions respecting the scenes and personages among whom she was now to move.

"The house and place are much neglected, and the former in some parts suffered almost to go to decay. The windows broken in the last storm, nearly eight months ago, they tell me, are still unmended, and the roof, too, unrepaired. The pretty garden, near the well, among the lime trees, that our darling mother was so fond of, is all but obliterated with weeds and grass, and since my first visit I have not had heart to go near it again. All the old servants are gone; new faces everywhere.

"I have been obliged several times, through fear of offending my father, to join the party in the drawing room. You may conceive what I felt at seeing mademoiselle in the place once filled by our dear mamma, I was so choked with sorrow, bitterness, and indignation, and my heart so palpitated, that I could not speak, and I believe they thought I was going to faint. Mademoiselle looked very angry, but my father pretending to show me, heaven knows what, from the window, led me to it, and the air revived me a little. Mademoiselle (for I cannot call her by her new name) is altered a good deal—more, however, in the character than in the contour of her face and figure. Certainly, however, she has grown a good deal fuller, and her color is higher; and whether it is fancy or not, I cannot say, but certainly to me it seems that the expression of her face has acquired something habitually lowering and malicious, and which, I know not how, inspires me with an undefinable dread. She has, however, been tolerably civil to me, but seems contemptuous and rude to my father, and I am afraid he is very wretched, I have seen them exchange such looks, and overheard such intemperate and even appalling altercations between them, as indicate something worse and deeper than ordinary ill-will. This makes me additionally wretched, especially as I cannot help thinking that some mysterious cause enables her to frighten and tyrannise over my poor father. I sometimes think he absolutely detests her; yet, though fiery altercations ensue, he ultimately submits to this bad and cruel woman. Oh, my dear Charles, you have no idea of the shocking, or rather the terrifying, reproaches I have heard interchanged between them, as I accidently passed the room where they were sitting—such terms as have sent me to my room, feeling as if I were in a horrid dream, and made me cry and tremble for hours after I got there.... I see my father very seldom, and when I do, he takes but little notice of me.... Poor Willett, you know, returned with me. She accompanies me in my walks, and is constantly dropping hints about mademoiselle, from which I know not what to gather....

"I often fear that my father has some secret and mortal ailment. He generally looks ill, and sometimes quite wretchedly. He came twice lately to my room, I think to speak to me on some matter of importance; but he said only a sentence or two, and even these broken and incoherent. He seemed unable to command spirits for the interview; and, indeed, he grew so agitated and strange, that I was alarmed, and felt greatly relieved when he left me....

"I do not, you see, disguise my feelings, dear Charles; I do not conceal from you the melancholy and anguish of my present situation. How intensely I long for your promised arrival. I have not a creature to whom I can say one word in confidence, except poor Willett; who, though very good-natured, and really dear to me, is yet far from being a companion. I sometimes think my intense anxiety to see you here is almost selfish; for I know you will feel as acutely as I do, the terrible change observable everywhere. But I cannot help longing for your return, dear Charles, and counting the days and the very hours till you arrive....

"Be cautious, in writing to me, not to say anything which you would not wish mademoiselle to see; for Willett tells me that she knows that she often examines, and even intercepts the letters that arrive; and, though Willett may be mistaken, and I hope she is, yet it is better that you should be upon your guard. Ever since I heard this, I have brought my letters to the post office myself, instead of leaving them with the rest upon the hall table; and you know it is a long walk for me....

"I go to church every Sunday, and take Willett along with me. No one from this seems to think of doing so but ourselves. I see the Mervyns there. Mrs. Mervyn is particularly kind; and I know that she wishes to offer me an asylum at Newton Park; and you cannot think with how much tenderness and delicacy she conveys the wish. But I dare not hint the subject to my father; and, earnestly as I desire it, I could not but feel that I should go there, not to visit, but to reside. And so even in this, in many respects, delightful project, is mingled the bitter apprehension of dependence—something so humiliating, that, kindly and delicately as the offer is made, I could not bring myself to embrace it. I have a great deal to say to you, and long to see you."...

These extracts will enable the reader to form a tolerably accurate idea of the general state of affairs at Gray Forest. Some particulars must, however, be added.

Marston continued to be the same gloomy and joyless being as heretofore. Sometimes moody and apathetic, sometimes wayward and even savage, but never for a moment at ease, never social—an isolated, disdainful, ruined man.

One day as Rhoda sate and read under the shade of some closely-interwoven evergreens, in a lonely and sheltered part of the neglected pleasure-grounds, with her honest maid Willett in attendance, she was surprised by the sudden appearance of her father, who stood unexpectedly before her. Though his attitude for some time was fixed, his countenance was troubled with anxiety and pain, and his sunken eyes rested upon her with a fiery and fretted gaze. He seemed lost in thought for a while, and then, touching Willett sharply on the shoulder, said abruptly.

"Go; I shall call you when you are wanted. Walk down that alley." And, as he spoke, he indicated with his walking-cane the course he desired her to take.

When the maid was sufficiently distant to be quite out of hearing, Marston sate down beside Rhoda upon the bench, and took her hand in silence. His grasp was cold, and alternately relaxed and contracted with an agitated uncertainty, while his eyes were fixed upon the ground, and he seemed meditating how to open the conversation. At last, as if suddenly awaking from a fearful reverie, he said—"You correspond with Charles?"

"Yes, sir," she replied, with the respectful formality prescribed by the usages of the time, "we correspond regularly."

"Aye, aye; and, pray, when did you last hear from him?" he continued.

"About a month since, sir," she replied.

"Ha—and—and—was there nothing strange—nothing—nothing mysterious and menacing in his letter? Come, come, you know what I speak of." He stopped abruptly, and stared in her face with an agitated gaze.

"No, indeed, sir; there was not anything of the kind," she replied.

"I have been greatly shocked, I may say incensed," said Marston excitedly, "by a passage in his last letter to me. Not that it says anything specific; but—but it amazes me—it enrages me."

He again checked himself, and Rhoda, much surprised, and even shocked, said, stammeringly—

"I am sure, sir, that dear Charles would not intentionally say or do anything that could offend you."

"Ah, as to that, I believe so, too. But it is not with him I am indignant; no, no. Poor Charles! I believe he is, as you say, disposed to conduct himself as a son ought to do, respectfully and obediently. Yes, yes, Charles is very well; but I fear he is leading a bad life, notwithstanding—a very bad life. He is becoming subject to influences which never visit or torment the good; believe me, he is."

Marston shook his head, and muttered to himself, with a look of almost craven anxiety, and then whispered to his daughter—

"Just read this, and then tell me is it not so. Read it, read it, and pronounce."

As he thus spoke, he placed in her hand the letter of which he had spoken, and with the passage to which he invited her attention folded down. It was to the following effect:—

"I cannot tell you how shocked I have been by a piece of scandal, as I must believe it, conveyed to me in an anonymous letter, and which is of so very delicate a nature, that without your special command I should hesitate to pain you by its recital. I trust it may be utterly false. Indeed I assume it to be so. It is enough to say that it is of a very distressing nature, and affects the lady (Mademoiselle de Barras) whom you have recently honored with your hand."

"Now you see," cried Marston, with a shuddering fierceness, as she returned the letter with a blanched cheek and trembling hand—"now you see it all. Are you stupid?—the stamp of the cloven hoof—eh?"

Rhoda, unable to gather his meaning, but, at the same time, with a heart full and trembling very much, stammered a few frightened words, and became silent.

"It is he, I tell you, that does it all; and if Charles were not living an evil life, he could not have spread his nets for him," said Marston, vehemently. "He can't go near anything good; but, like a scoundrel, he knows where to find a congenial nature; and when he does, he has skill enough to practice upon it. I know him well, and his arts and his smiles; aye, and his scowls and his grins, too. He goes, like his master, up and down, and to and fro upon the earth, for ceaseless mischief. There is not a friend of mine he can get hold of, but he whispered in his ear some damned slander of me. He is drawing them all into a common understanding against me; and he takes an actual pleasure in telling me how the thing goes on—how, one after the other, he has converted my friends into conspirators and libelers, to blast my character, and take my life, and now the monster essays to lure my children into the hellish confederation."

"Who is he, father, who is he?" faltered Rhoda.

"You never saw him," retorted Marston, sternly.

"No, no; you can't have seen him, and you probably never will; but if he does come here again, don't listen to him. He is half-fiend and half-idiot, and no good comes of his mouthing and muttering. Avoid him, I warn you, avoid him. Let me see: how shall I describe him? Let me see. You remember—you remember Berkley—Sir Wynston Berkley. Well, he greatly resembles that dead villain: he has all the same grins, and shrugs, and monkey airs, and his face and figure are like. But he is a grimed, ragged, wasted piece of sin, little better than a beggar—a shrunken, malignant libel on the human shape. Avoid him, I tell you, avoid him: he is steeped in lies and poison, like the very serpent that betrayed us. Beware of him, I say, for if he once gains your ear, he will delude you, spite of all your vigilance; he will make you his accomplice, and thenceforth, inevitably, there is nothing but mortal and implacable hatred between us!"

Frightened at this wild language, Rhoda did not answer, but looked up in his face in silence. A fearful transformation was there—a scowl so livid and maniacal, that her very senses seemed leaving her with terror. Perhaps the sudden alteration observable in her countenance, as this spectacle so unexpectedly encountered her, recalled him to himself; for he added, hurriedly, and in a tone of gentler meaning—

"Rhoda, Rhoda, watch and pray. My daughter, my child! keep your heart pure, and nothing bad can approach you for ill. No, no; you are good, and the good need not fear!"

Suddenly Marston burst into tears, as he ended this sentence, and wept long and convulsively. She did not dare to speak, or even to move; but after a while he ceased, appeared uneasy, half ashamed and half angry;

and looking with a horrified and bewildered glance into her face, he said—

"Rhoda, child, what—what have I said? My God! what have I been saying? Did I—do I look ill? Oh, Rhoda, Rhoda, may you never feel this!"

He turned away from her without awaiting her answer, and walked away with the appearance of intense agitation, as if to leave her. He turned again, however, and with a face pallid and sunken as death, approached her slowly—

"Rhoda," said he, "don't tell what I have said to anyone—don't, I conjure you, even to Charles. I speak too much at random, and say more than I mean—a foolish, rambling habit: so do not repeat one word of it, not one word to any living mortal. You and I, Rhoda, must have our little secrets."

He ended with an attempt at a smile, so obviously painful and fear-stricken that as he walked hurriedly away, the astounded girl burst into a bitter flood of tears. What was, what could be, the meaning of the shocking scene she had then been forced to witness? She dared not answer the question. Yet one ghastly doubt haunted her like her shadow—a suspicion that the malignant and hideous light of madness was already glaring upon his mind. As, leaning upon the arm of her astonished attendant, she retracted her steps, the trees, the flowers, the familiar hall-door, the echoing passages—every object that met her eye—seemed strange and unsubstantial, and she gliding on among them in a horrid dream.

Time passed on: there was no renewal of the painful scene which dwelt so sensibly in the affrighted imagination of Rhoda. Marston's manner was changed towards her; he seemed shy, cowed, and uneasy in her presence, and thenceforth she saw less than ever of him. Meanwhile the time approached which was to witness the long expected, and, by Rhoda, the intensely prayed for arrival of her brother.

Some four or five days before this event, Mr. Marston, having, as he said, some business in Chester, and further designing to meet his son there, took his departure from Gray Forest, leaving poor Rhoda to the guardianship of her guilty stepmother; and although she had seen so little of her father, yet the very consciousness of his presence had given her a certain confidence and sense of security, which vanished at the moment of his departure. Fear-stricken and wretched as he had been, his removal, nevertheless, seemed to her to render the lonely and inauspicious mansion still more desolate and ominous than before.

She had, with a vague and instinctive antipathy, avoided all contact and intercourse with Mrs. Marston, or as, for distinctness sake, we shall continue to call her, "Mademoiselle," since her return: and she on her part had appeared to acquiesce with a sort of scornful nonchalance, in the tacit understanding that she and her former pupil should see and hear as little as might be of one another.

Meanwhile poor Willett, with her good-natured honesty and her inexhaustible gossip, endeavored to amuse and reassure her young mistress, and sometimes even with some partial success.

We must now follow Mr. Marston in his solitary expedition to Chester. When he took his place in the stagecoach he had the whole interior of the vehicle to himself, and thus continued to be its solitary occupant for several miles. The coach, however, was eventually hailed, brought to, and the door being opened, Dr. Danvers got in, and took his place opposite to the passenger already established there. The worthy man was so busied in directing the disposition of his luggage from the window, and in arranging the sundry small parcels with which he was charged, that he did not recognize his companion until they were in motion. When he did so it was with no very pleasurable feeling; and it is probable that Marston, too, would have gladly escaped the coincidence which thus reduced them once more to the temporary necessity of a Tate-à-Tate. Embarrassing as each felt the situation to be, there was, however, no avoiding it, and, after a recognition and a few forced attempts at conversation, they became, by mutual consent, silent and uncommunicative.

The journey, though in point of space a mere trifle, was, in those slowcoach days, a matter of fully five hours' duration; and before it was completed the sun had set, and darkness began to close. Whether it was that the descending twilight dispelled the painful constraint under which Marston had seemed to labor, or that some more purely spiritual and genial influence had gradually dissipated the repulsion and distrust with which, at first, he had shrunk from a renewal of intercourse with Dr. Danvers, he suddenly accosted him thus.

"Dr. Danvers, I have been fifty times on the point of speaking to you—confidentially of course—while sitting here opposite to you, what I believe I could scarcely bring myself to hint to any other man living; yet I must tell it, and soon, too, or I fear it will have told itself."

Dr. Danvers intimated his readiness to hear and advise, if desired; and Marston resumed abruptly, after a pause—

"Pray, Doctor Danvers, have you heard any stories of an odd kind; any surmises—I don't mean of a moral sort, for those I hold very cheap—to my prejudice? Indeed I should hardly say to my prejudice; I mean—I ought to say—in short, have you heard people remark upon any fancied eccentricities, or that sort of thing, about me?"

He put the question with obvious difficulty, and at last seemed to overcome his own reluctance with a sort of angry and excited self-contempt and impatience. Doctor Danvers was a little puzzled by the interrogatory, and admitted, in reply, that he did not comprehend its drift.

"Doctor Danvers," he resumed, sternly and dejectedly, "I told you, in the chance interview we had some months ago, that I was haunted by a certain fear. I did not define it, nor do I think you suspect its nature. It is a fear of nothing mortal, but of the immortal tenant of this body. My mind; sir, is beginning to play me tricks; my guide mocks and terrifies me."

There was a perceptible tinge of horror in the look of astonishment with which Dr. Danvers listened.

"You are a gentleman, sir, and a Christian clergyman; what I have said and shall say is confided to your honor; to be held sacred as the confession of misery, and hidden from the coarse gaze of the world. I have become subject to a hideous delusion. It comes at intervals. I do not think any mortal suspects it, except, maybe, my daughter Rhoda. It comes and disappears, and comes again. I kept my pleasant secret for a long time, but at last I let it slip, and committed myself fortunately, to but one person, and that my daughter; and, even so, I hardly think she understood me. I recollected myself before I had disclosed the grotesque and infernal chimera that haunts me."

Marston paused. He was stooped forward, and looking upon the floor of the vehicle, so that his companion could not see his countenance. A silence ensued, which was interrupted by Marston, who once more resumed.

"Sir," said he, "I know not why, but I have longed, intensely longed, for some trustworthy ear into which to pour this horrid secret; why I repeat, I cannot tell, for I expect no sympathy, and hate compassion. It is, I suppose, the restless nature of the devil that is in me; but, be it what it may, I will speak to you, but to you only, for the present, at least, to you alone."

Doctor Danvers again assured him that he might repose the most entire confidence in his secrecy.

"The human mind, I take it, must have either comfort in the past or hope in the future," he continued, "otherwise it is in danger. To me, sir, the past is intolerably repulsive; one boundless, barren, and hideous Golgotha of dead hopes and murdered opportunities; the future, still blacker and more furious, peopled with dreadful features of horror and menace, and losing itself in utter darkness. Sir, I do not exaggerate. Between such a past and such a future I stand upon this miserable present; and the only comfort I still am capable of feeling is, that no human being pities me; that I stand aloof from the insults of compassion and the hypocrisies of sympathetic morality; and that I can safely defy all the respectable scoundrels in Christendom to enhance, by one feather's weight, the load which I myself have accumulated, and which I myself hourly and unaided sustain."

Doctor Danvers here introduced a word or two in the direction of their former conversation.

"No, sir, there is no comfort from that quarter either," said Marston, bitterly; "you but cast your seeds, as the parable terms your teaching, upon the barren sea, in wasting them on me. My fate, be it what it may, is as irrevocably fixed, as though I were dead and judged a hundred years ago.

"This cursed dream," he resumed abruptly, "that everyday enslaves me more and more, has reference to that—that occurrence about Wynston Berkley—he is the hero of the hellish illusion. At certain times, sir, it seems to me as if he, though dead, were still invested with a sort of spurious life; going about unrecognized, except by me, in squalor and contempt, and whispering away my fame and life; laboring with the malignant industry of a fiend to involve me in the meshes of that special perdition from which alone I shrink, and to which this emissary of hell seems to have predestined me. Sir, this is a monstrous and hideous extravagance, a delusion, but, after all, no more than a trick of the imagination; the reason, the judgment, is untouched. I cannot choose but see all the damned phantasmagoria, but I do not believe it real, and this is the difference between my case and—and—madness!"

They were now entering the suburbs of Chester, and Doctor Danvers, pained and shocked beyond measure by this unlooked-for disclosure, and not knowing what remark or comfort to offer, relieved his temporary embarrassment by looking from the window, as though attracted by the flash of the lamps, among which the vehicle was now moving. Marston, however, laid his hand upon his arm, and thus recalled him, for a moment, to a forced attention.

"It must seem strange to you, Doctor, that I should trust this cursed secret to your keeping," he said; "and, truth to say, it seems so to myself. I cannot account for the impulse, the irresistible power of which has forced me to disclose the hateful mystery to you, but the fact is this, beginning like a speck, this one idea has gradually darkened and dilated, until it has filled my entire mind. The solitary consciousness of the gigantic mastery it has established there had grown intolerable; I must have told it. The sense of solitude under this aggressive and tremendous delusion was agony, hourly death to my soul. That is the secret of my talkativeness; my sole excuse for plaguing you with the dreams of a wretched hypochondriac."

Doctor Danvers assured him that no apologies were needed, and was only restrained from adding the expression of that pity which he really felt, by the rear of irritating a temper so full of bitterness, pride and defiance. A few minutes more, and the coach having reached its destination, they bid one another farewell, and parted.

At that time there resided in a decent mansion about a mile from the town of Chester, a dapper little gentleman, whom we shall call Doctor Parkes. This gentleman was the proprietor and sole professional manager of a private asylum for the insane and enjoyed a high reputation, and a proportionate amount of business, in his melancholy calling. It was about the second day after the conversation we have just sketched, that this little gentleman, having visited, according to his custom, all his domestic patients, was about to take his accustomed walk in his somewhat restricted pleasure grounds, when his servant announced a visitor.

"A gentleman," he repeated; "you have seen him before-eh?"

"No, sir," replied the man; "he is in the study, sir."

"Ha! a professional call. Well, we shall see."

So saying, the little gentleman summoned his gravest look, and hastened to the chamber of audience.

On entering he found a man dressed well, but gravely, having in his air and manner something of high breeding. In countenance striking, dark-featured, and stern, furrowed with the lines of pain or thought, rather than of age, although his dark hairs were largely mingled with white.

The physician bowed, and requested the stranger to take a chair; he, however, nodded slightly and impatiently, as if to intimate an intolerance of ceremony, and, advancing a step or two, said abruptly—

"My name, sir, is Marston; I have come to give you a patient."

The doctor bowed with a still deeper inclination, and paused for a continuance of the communication thus auspiciously commenced.

"You are Dr. Parkes, I take it for granted," said Marston, in the same tone.

"Your most obedient, humble servant, sir," replied he, with the polite formality of the day, and another grave bow.

"Doctor," demanded Marston, fixing his eye upon him sternly, and significantly tapping his own forehead, "can you stay execution?"

The physician looked puzzled, hesitated, and at last requested his visitor to be more explicit.

"Can you," said Marston, with the same slow and stern articulation, and after a considerable pause—"can you prevent the malady you profess to cure?—can you meet and defeat the enemy halfway?—can you scare away the spirit of madness before it takes actual possession, and while it is still only hovering about its threatened victim?"

"Sir," he replied, "in certain cases—in very many, indeed—the enemy, as you well call it, may thus be met, and effectually worsted at a distance. Timely interposition, in ninety cases out of a hundred, is everything; and, I assure you, I hear your question with much pleasure, inasmuch as I assume it to have reference to the case of the patient about whom you desire to consult me; and who is, therefore, I hope, as yet merely menaced with the misfortune from which you would save him."

"I, myself, am that patient, sir," said Marston, with an effort; "your surmise is right. I am not mad, but unequivocally menaced with madness; it is not to be mistaken. Sir, there is no misunderstanding the tremendous and tolerable signs that glare upon my mind."

"And pray, sir, have you consulted your friends or your family upon the course best to be pursued?" inquired Dr. Parkes, with grave interest.

"No, sir," he answered sharply, and almost fiercely; "I have no fancy to make myself the subject of a writ _de lunatico inquirendo_; I don't want to lose my liberty and my property at a blow. The course I mean to take has been advised by no one but myself—is known to no other. I now disclose it, and the causes of it, to you, a gentleman, and my professional adviser, in the expectation that you will guard with the strictest secrecy my spontaneous revelations; this you promise me?"

"Certainly, Mr. Marston; I have neither the disposition nor the right to withhold such a promise," answered the physician.

"Well, then, I will first tell you the arrangement I propose, with your permission, to make, and then I shall answer all your questions, respecting my own case," resumed Marston, gloomily. "I wish to place myself under your care, to live under your roof, reserving my full liberty of action. I must be free to come and to go as I will; and on the other hand, I undertake that you shall find me an amenable and docile patient enough. In addition, I stipulate that there shall be no attempt whatever made to communicate with those who are connected with me: these terms agreed upon, I place myself in your hands. You will find in me, as I said before, a deferential patient, and I trust not a troublesome one. I hope you will excuse my adding, that I shall myself pay the charge of my sojourn here from week to week, in advance."

The proposed arrangement was a strange one; and although Dr. Parkes dimly foresaw some of the embarrassments which might possibly arise from his accepting it, there was yet so much that was reasonable as well as advantageous in the proposal, that he could not bring himself to decline it.

The preliminary arrangement concluded, Dr. Parkes proceeded to his more strictly professional investigation. It is, of course, needless to recapitulate the details of Marston's tormenting fancies, with which the reader has indeed been already sufficiently acquainted. Doctor Parkes, having attentively listened to the narrative, and satisfied himself as to the physical health of his patient, was still sorely puzzled as to the probable issue of the awful struggle already but too obviously commenced between the mind and its destroyer in the strange case before him. One satisfactory symptom unquestionably was, the as yet transitory nature of the delusion, and the evident and energetic tenacity with which reason contended for her vital ascendancy. It was a case, however, which for many reasons sorely perplexed him, but of which, notwithstanding, he was disposed, whether rightly or wrongly the reader will speedily see, to take by no means a decidedly gloomy view.

Having disburdened his mind of this horrible secret, Marston felt for a time a sense of relief amounting almost to elation. With far less of apprehension and dismay than he had done so for months before, he that night repaired to his bedroom. There was nothing in his case, Doctor Parkes believed, to warrant his keeping any watch upon Marston's actions, and accordingly he bid him good-night, in the full confidence of meeting him, if not better, at least not worse, on the ensuing morning.

He miscalculated, however. Marston had probably himself been conscious of some coming crisis in his hideous malady, when he took the decisive step of placing himself under the care of Doctor Parkes. Certain it is, that upon that very night the disease broke forth in a new and appalling development. Doctor Parkes, whose bedroom was next to that occupied by Marston, was awakened in the dead of night by a howling, more like that of a beast than a human voice, and which gradually swelled into an absolute yell; then came some horrid laughter and entreaties, thick and frantic; then again the same unearthly howl. The practiced ear of Doctor Parkes recognized but too surely the terrific import of those sounds. Springing from his bed, and seizing the candle which always burned in his chamber, in anticipation of such sudden and fearful emergencies, he hurried with a palpitating heart, and spite of his long habituation to such scenes as he expected, with a certain sense of horror, to the chamber of his aristocratic patient.

Late as it was, Marston had not yet gone to bed; his candle was still burning, and he himself, half dressed, stood in the center of the floor, shaking and livid, his eyes burning with the preterhuman fires of insanity. As Doctor Parkes entered the chamber, another shout, or rather yell, thundered from the lips of this demoniac effigy; and the mad-doctor stood freezing with horror in the doorway, and yet exerting what remained to him of presence of mind, in the vain endeavor, in the flaring light of the candle, to catch and fix with his own practiced eye the gaze of the maniac. Second after second, and minute after minute, he stood confronting this frightful slave of Satan, in the momentary expectation that he would close with and destroy him. On a sudden, however, this brief agony of suspense was terminated; a change like an awakening consciousness of realities, or rather like the withdrawal of some hideous and visible influence from within, passed over the tense and darkened features of the wretched being; a look of horrified perplexity, doubt, and inquiry, supervened, and he at last said, in a subdued and sullen tone, to Doctor Parkes.

"Who are you, sir? What do you want here? Who are you, sir, I say?"

"Who am I? Why, your physician, sir; Doctor Parkes, sir; the owner of this house, sir," replied he, with all the sternness he could command, and yet white as a specter with agitation. "For shame, sir, for shame, to give way thus. What do you mean by creating this causeless alarm, and disturbing the whole household at so unseasonable an hour? For shame, sir; go to your bed; undress yourself this moment; for shame."

Doctor Parkes, as he spoke, was reassured by the arrival of one of his servants, alarmed by the unmistakable sounds of violent frenzy; he signed, however, to the man not to enter, feeling confident, as he did, that the paroxysm had spent itself.

"Aye, aye," muttered Marston, looking almost sheepishly; "Doctor Parkes, to be sure. What was I thinking of? how cursedly absurd! And this," he continued, glancing at his sword, which he threw impatiently upon a sofa as he spoke. "Folly—nonsense! A false alarm, as you say, doctor. I beg your pardon."

As Marston spoke, he proceeded with much agitation slowly to undress himself. He had, however, but commenced the process, when, turning abruptly to Doctor Parkes, he said, with a countenance of horror, and in a whisper—

"By ——, doctor, it has been upon me worse than ever, I would have sworn I had the villain with me for hours—hours, sir—torturing me with his damned sneering threats; till, by ——, I could stand it no longer, and took my sword. Oh, doctor, can't you save me? can nothing be done for me?"

Pale, covered with the dews of horror, he uttered these last words in accents of such imploring despair, as might have borne across the dreadful gulf the prayer of Dives for that one drop of water which never was to cool his burning tongue.

When Rhoda learned that her father, on leaving Gray Forest, had fixed no definite period for his return, she began to feel her situation at home so painful and equivocal, that, having taken honest Willett to counsel, she came at last to the resolution of accepting the often conveyed invitation of Mrs. Mervyn and sojourning, at all events until her father's return, at Newton Park.

"My dear young friend," said the kind lady, as soon as she heard Rhoda's little speech to its close, "I can scarcely describe the gratification with which I see you here; the happiness with which I welcome you to Newton Park; nor, indeed, the anxiety with which I constantly contemplated your trying and painful position at Gray Forest. Indeed I ought to be angry with you for having refused me this happiness so long; but you have made amends at last; though, indeed, it was impossible to have deferred it longer. You must not fancy, however, that I will consent to lose you so soon as you seem to have intended. No, no; I have found it too hard to catch you, to let you take wing so easily; besides, I have others to consult as well as myself, and persons, too, who are just as anxious as I am to make a prisoner of you here."

The good Mrs. Mervyn accompanied these words with looks so sly, and emphasis so significant, that Rhoda was fain to look down, to hide her blushes; and compassionating the confusion she herself had caused, the kind old lady led her to the chamber which was henceforward, so long as she consented to remain, to be her own apartment.

How that day was passed, and how fleetly its hours sped away, it is needless to tell. Old Mervyn had his gentle as well as his grim aspect; and no welcome was ever more cordial and tender than that with which he greeted the unprotected child of his morose and repulsive neighbor. It would be impossible to convey any idea of the countless assiduities and the secret delight with which young Mervyn attended their rambles.

The party were assembled at supper. What a contrast did this cheerful, happy—unutterably happy—

gathering, present, in the mind of Rhoda, to the dull, drear, fearful evenings which she had long been wont to pass at Gray Forest.

As they sate together in cheerful and happy intercourse, a chaise drove up to the hall-door, and the knocking had hardly ceased to reverberate, when a well-known voice was heard in the hall.

Young Mervyn started to his feet, and merrily ejaculating, "Charles Marston! this is delightful!" disappeared, and in an instant returned with Charles himself.

We pass over all the embraces of brother and sister; the tears and smiles of re-united affection. We omit the cordial shaking of hands; the kind looks; the questions and answers; all these, and all the little attentions of that good old-fashioned hospitality, which was never weary of demonstrating the cordiality of its welcome, we abandon to the imagination of the good-natured reader.

Charles Marston, with the advice of his friend, Mr. Mervyn, resolved to lose no time in proceeding to Chester, whither it was ascertained his father had gone, with the declared intention of meeting and accompanying him home. He arrived in that town in the evening; and having previously learned that Doctor Danvers had been for some time in Chester, he at once sought him at his usual lodgings, and found the worthy old gentleman at his solitary "dish" of tea.

"My dear Charles," said he, greeting his young friend with earnest warmth, "I am rejoiced beyond measure to see you. Your father is in town, as you supposed; and I have just had a note from him, which has, I confess, not a little agitated me, referring, as it does, to a subject of painful and horrible interest; one with which, I suppose, you are familiar, but upon which I myself have never yet spoken fully to any person, excepting your father only."

"And pray, my dear sir, what is this topic?" inquired Charles, with marked interest.

"Read this note," answered the clergyman, placing one at the same time in his young visitor's hand.

Charles read as follows:

"My Dear Sir,

"I have a singular communication to make to you, but in the strictest privacy, with reference to a subject which, merely to name, is to awaken feelings of doubt and horror; I mean the confession of Merton, with respect to the murder of Wynston Berkley. I will call upon you this evening after dark; for I have certain reasons for not caring to meet old acquaintances about town; and if you can afford me half an hour, I promise to complete my intended disclosure within that time. Let us be strictly private; this is my only proviso.
"Yours with much respect,
"Richard Marston"

"Your father has been sorely troubled in mind," said Doctor Danvers, as soon as the young man had read this communication; "he has told me as much; it may be that the discovery he has now made may possibly have relieved him from certain galling anxieties. The fear that unjust suspicion should light upon himself, or those connected with him, has, I dare say, tormented him sorely. God grant, that as the providential unfolding of all the details of this mysterious crime comes about, he may be brought to recognize, in the just and terrible process, the hand of heaven. God grant, that at last his heart may be softened, and his spirit illuminated by the blessed influence he has so long and so sternly rejected."

As the old man thus spake—as if in symbolic answering to his prayer—a sudden glory from the setting sun streamed through the funereal pile of clouds which filled the western horizon, and flooded the chamber where they were.

After a silence, Charles Marston said, with some little embarrassment—"It may be a strange confession to make, though, indeed, hardly so to you—for you know but too well the gloomy reserve with which my father has uniformly treated me—that the exact nature of Merton's confession never reached my ears; and once or twice, when I approached the subject, in conversation with you, it seemed to me that the subject was one which, for some reason, it was painful to you to enter upon."

"And so it was, in truth, my young friend—so it was; for that confession left behind it many fearful doubts, proving, indeed, nothing but the one fact, that, morally, the wretched man was guilty of the murder."

Charles, urged by a feeling of the keenest interest, requested Dr. Danvers to detail to him the particulars or the dying man's narration.

"Willingly," answered Dr. Danvers, with a look of gloom, and heaving a profound sigh—"willingly, for you have now come to an age when you may safely be entrusted with secrets affecting your own family, and which, although, thank God, as I believe they in no respect involve the honor of anyone of its members, yet might deeply involve its peace and its security against the assaults of vague and horrible slander. Here, then, is the narrative: Merton, when he was conscious of the approach of death, qualified, by a circumstantial

and detailed statement, the absolute confession of guilt which he had at first sullenly made. In this he declared that the guilt of design and intention only was his—that in the act itself he had been anticipated. He stated, that from the moment when Sir Wynston's servant had casually mentioned the circumstance of his master's usually sleeping with his watch and pocketbook under his pillow, the idea of robbing him had taken possession of his mind. With the idea of robbing him (under the peculiar circumstances, his servant sleeping in the apartment close by, and the slightest alarm being, in all probability, sufficient to call him to the spot) the idea of anticipating resistance by murder had associated itself. He had contended against these haunting and growing solicitations of Satan, with an earnest agony. He had intended to leave his place, and fly from the mysterious temptation which he felt he wanted power to combat, but accident or fate prevented him. In a state of ghastly excitement he had, on the memorable night of Sir Wynston's murder, proceeded, as had afterwards appeared in evidence, by the back stair to the baronet's chamber; he had softly stolen into it, and gone to the bedside, with the weapon in his hand. He drew his breath for the decisive stroke, which was to bereave the (supposedly) sleeping man of life, and when stretching his left hand under the clothes, it rested upon a dull, cold corpse, and, at the same moment, his right hand was immersed in a pool of blood. He dropped the knife, recoiled a pace or so. With a painful effort, however, he again grasped with his hand to recover the weapon he had suffered to escape, and secured, as it afterwards turned out, not the knife with which he had meditated the commission of his crime, but the dagger which was afterwards found where he had concealed it. He was now fully alive to the horror of his situation; he was compromised as fully as if he had in very deed driven home the weapon. To be found under such circumstances, would convict him as surely as if fifty eyes had seen him strike the blow. He had nothing now for it but flight; and in order to guard himself against the contingency of being surprised from the door opening upon the corridor, he bolted it; then groped under the murdered man's pillow for the booty which had so fatally fascinated his imagination. Here he was disappointed. What further happened you already know."

Charles listened with breathless attention to this recital, and, after a painful interval, said—

"Then the actual murderer is, after all, unascertained. This is, indeed, horrible; it was very natural that my father should have felt the danger to which such a disclosure would have exposed the reputation of our family, yet I should have preferred encountering it, were it ten times as great, to the equivocal prudence of suppressing the truth with respect to a murder committed under my own roof."

"He has, however, it would seem, arrived at some new conclusions," said Dr. Danvers, "and is now prepared to throw some unanticipated light upon the whole transaction."

Even as they were talking, a knocking was heard at the hall-door, and after a brief and hurried consultation, it was agreed, that, considering the strict condition of privacy attached to this visit by Mr. Marston himself, as well as his reserved and wayward temper, it might be better for Charles to avoid presenting himself to his father on this occasion. A few seconds afterwards the door opened, and Mr. Marston entered the apartment. It was now dark, and the servant, unbidden, placed candles upon the table. Without answering one word to Dr. Danvers' greeting, Marston sat down, as it seemed, in agitated abstraction. Removing his hat suddenly (for he had not even made this slight homage to the laws of courtesy), he looked round with a care-worn, fiery eye, and a pale countenance, and said—

"We are quite alone, Dr. Danvers—no one anywhere near?"

Dr. Danvers assured him that all was secure. After a long and agitated pause, Marston said—

"You remember Merton's confession. He admitted his intention to kill Berkley, but denied that he was the actual murderer. He spoke truth—no one knew it better than I; for I am the murderer."

Dr. Danvers was so shocked and overwhelmed that he was utterly unable to speak.

"Aye, sir, in point of law and of morals, literally and honestly, the murderer of Wynston Berkley. I am resolved you shall know it all. Make what use of it you will—I care for nothing now, but to get rid of the d——d, unsustainable secret, and that is done. I did not intend to kill the scoundrel when I went to his room; but with the just feelings of exasperation with which I regarded him, it would have been wiser had I avoided the interview; and I meant to have done so. But his candle was burning; I saw the light through the door, and went in. It was his evil fortune to indulge in his old strain of sardonic impertinence. He provoked me; I struck him—he struck me again—and with his own dagger I stabbed him three times. I did not know what I had done; I could not believe it. I felt neither remorse nor sorrow—why should I?—but the thing was horrible, astounding. There he sat in the corner of his cushioned chair, with the old fiendish smile on still. Sir, I never thought that any human shape could look so dreadful. I don't know how long I stayed there, freezing with horror and detestation, and yet unable to take my eyes from the face. Did you see it in the coffin? Sir, there was a sneer of triumph on it that was diabolic and prophetic."

Marston was fearfully agitated as he spoke, and repeatedly wiped from his face the cold sweat that gathered there.

"I could not leave the room by the back stairs," he resumed, "for the valet slept in the intervening chamber. I felt such an appalled antipathy to the body, that I could scarcely muster courage to pass it. But, sir, I am not easily cowed—I mastered this repugnance in a few minutes—or, rather, I acted spite of it, I knew not how; but instinctively it seemed to me that it was better to lay the body in the bed, than leave it where it was, shewing, as its position might, that the thing occurred in an altercation. So, sir, I raised it, and bore it softly across the room, and laid it in the bed; and, while I was carrying it, it swayed forward, the arms glided round my neck, and the head rested against my cheek—that was a parody upon a brotherly embrace!

"I do not know at what moment it was, but some time when I was carrying Wynston, or laying him in the bed," continued Marston, who spoke rather like one pursuing a horrible reverie, than as a man relating facts to a listener, "I heard a light tread, and soft breathing in the lobby. A thunderclap would have stunned me less that minute. I moved softly, holding my breath, to the door. I believe, in moments of strong excitement, men hear more acutely than at other times; but I thought I heard the rustling of a gown, going from the door again. I waited—it ceased; I waited until all was quiet. I then extinguished the candle, and groped my way to the door; there was a faint light in the corridor, and I thought I saw a head projected from the chamber-door, next to the Frenchwoman's—mademoiselle's. As I came on, it was softly withdrawn, and the door not quite noiselessly closed. I could not be absolutely certain, but I learned all afterward. And now, sir, you have the story of Sir Wynston's murder."

Dr. Danvers groaned in spirit, being wrung alike with fear and sorrow. With hands clasped, and head bowed down, in an exceeding bitter agony of soul, he murmured only the words of the Litany—"Lord, have mercy upon us; Christ, have mercy upon us; Lord, have mercy upon us."

Marston had recovered his usual lowering aspect and gloomy self-possession in a few moments, and was now standing erect and defiant before the humbled and afflicted minister of God. The contrast was terrible—almost sublime.

Doctor Danvers resolved to keep this dreadful secret, at least for a time, to himself. He could not make up his mind to inflict upon those whom he loved so well as Charles and Rhoda the shame and agony of such a disclosure; yet he was sorely troubled, for his was a conflict of duty and mercy, of love and justice.

He told Charles Marston, when urged with earnest inquiry, that what he had heard that evening was intended solely for his own ear, and gently but peremptorily declined telling, at least until some future time, the substance of his father's communication.

Charles now felt it necessary to see his father, for the purpose of letting him know the substance of the letter respecting "mademoiselle" and the late Sir Wynston which had reached him. Accordingly, he proceeded, accompanied by Doctor Danvers, on the next morning, to the hotel where Marston had intimated his intention of passing the night.

On their inquiring for him in the hall, the porter appeared much perplexed and disturbed, and as they pressed him with questions, his answers became conflicting and mysterious. Mr. Marston was there—he had slept there last night; he could not say whether or not he was then in the house; but he knew that no one could be admitted to see him. He would, if the gentlemen wished it, send their cards to (not Mr. Marston, but) the proprietor. And, finally, he concluded by begging that they would themselves see "the proprietor," and dispatched a waiter to apprise him of the circumstances of the visit. There was something odd and even sinister in all this, which, along with the whispering and the curious glances of the waiters, who happened to hear the errand on which they came, inspired the two companions with vague misgivings, which they did not care mutually to disclose.

In a few moments they were shown into a small sitting room up stairs, where the proprietor, a fussy little gentleman, and apparently very uneasy and frightened, received them.

"We have called here to see Mr. Marston," said Doctor Danvers, "and the porter has referred us to you."

"Yes, sir, exactly—precisely so," answered the little man, fidgeting excessively, and as it seemed, growing paler every instant; "but—but, in fact, sir, there is, there has been—in short, have you not heard of the—the accident?"

He wound up with a prodigious effort, and wiped his forehead when he had done.

"Pray, sir, be explicit: we are near friends of Mr. Marston; in fact, sir, this is his son," said Doctor Danvers, pointing to Charles Marston; "and we are both uneasy at the reserve with which our inquiries have been met. Do, I entreat of you, say what has happened?"

"Why—why," hesitated the man, "I really—I would not for five hundred pounds it had happened in my house. The—the unhappy gentleman has, in short—"

He glanced at Charles, as if afraid of the effect of the disclosure he was on the point of making, and then hurriedly said—"He is dead, sir; he was found dead in his room, this morning, at eight o'clock. I assure you I have not been myself ever since."

Charles Marston was so stunned by this sudden blow, that he was upon the point of fainting. Rallying, however, with a strong effort, he demanded to be conducted to the chamber where the body lay. The man assented, but hesitated on reaching the door, and whispered something in the ear of Doctor Danvers, who, as he heard it, raised his hands and eyes with a mute expression of horror, and turning to Charles, said—

"My dear young friend, remain where you are for a few moments. I will return to you immediately, and tell you whatever I have ascertained. You are in no condition for such a scene at present."

Charles, indeed, felt that the fact was so, and, sick and giddy, suffered Doctor Danvers, with gentle compulsion, to force him into a seat.

In silence the venerable clergyman followed his conductor. With a palpitating heart he advanced to the bedside, and twice essayed to draw the curtain, and twice lost courage; but gathering resolution at last, he pulled the drapery aside, and beheld all he was to see again of Richard Marston.

The bedclothes were drawn so as nearly to cover the mouth.

"There is the wound, sir," whispered the man, as with coarse officiousness he drew back the bedclothes from the throat of the corpse, and exhibited a gash, as it seemed, nearly severing the head from the body. With sickening horror Doctor Danvers turned away from the awful spectacle. He covered his face in his hands, and it seemed to him as if a soft, solemn voice whispered in his ear the mystic words, "Whoso sheddeth man's blood, by man shall his blood be shed."

The hand which, but a few years before, had, unsuspected, consigned a fellow-mortal to the grave, had itself avenged the murder—Marston had perished by his own hand.

Naturally ambitious and intriguing, the perilous tendencies of such a spirit in Mademoiselle de Barras had never been schooled by the mighty and benignant principles of religion, of her accidental acquaintance at Rouen with Sir Wynston Berkley, and her subsequent introduction, in an evil hour, into the family at Gray Forest, it is unnecessary to speak. The unhappy terms on which she found Marston living with his wife, suggested, in their mutual alienation, the idea of founding a double influence in the household; and to conceive the idea, and to act upon it, were, in her active mind, the same. Young, beautiful, fascinating, she well knew the power of her attractions, and determined, though probably without one thought of transgressing the limits of literal propriety, to bring them to bear upon the discontented, retired rout, for whom she cared absolutely nothing, except as the instrument, and in part the victim of her schemes. Thus yielding to the double instinct that swayed her, she gratified, at the same time, her love of intrigue and her love of power. At length, however, came the hour which demanded a sacrifice to the evil influence she had hitherto worshipped on such easy terms. She found that her power must now be secured by crime, and she fell. Then came the arrival of Sir Wynston—his murder—her elopement with Marston, and her guilty and joyless triumph. At last, however, came the blow, long suspended and terrific, which shattered all her hopes and schemes, and drove her once again upon the world. The catastrophe we have just described. After it she made her way to Paris. Arrived in the capital of France, she speedily dissipated whatever remained of the money and valuables which she had taken with her from Gray Forest; and Madame Marston, as she now styled herself, was glad to place herself once more as a governess in an aristocratic family. So far her good fortune had prevailed in averting the punishment but too well earned by her past life. But a day of reckoning was to come. A few years later France was involved in the uproar and conflagration of revolution. Noble families were scattered, beggared, decimated; and their dependants, often dragged along with them into the flaming abyss, in many instances suffered the last dire extremities of human ill. It was at this awful period that a retribution so frightful and extraordinary overtook Madame Marston, that we may hereafter venture to make it the subject of a separate narrative. Until then the reader will rest satisfied with what he already knows of her history; and meanwhile bid a long, and as it may possibly turn out, an eternal farewell to that beautiful embodiment of an evil and disastrous influence.

The concluding chapter in a novel is always brief, though seldom so short as the world would have it. In a tale like this, the "winding up" must be proportionately contracted. We have scarcely a claim to so many lines as the formal novelist may occupy pages, in the distribution of poetic justice, and the final grouping of his characters into that effective tableau upon which, at last, the curtain gracefully descends. We, too, may be all the briefer, inasmuch as the reader has doubtless anticipated the little we have to say. It amounts, then, to this:—Within two years after the fearful event which we have just recorded, an alliance had drawn together, in nearer and dearer union, the inmates of Gray Forest and Newton Park. Rhoda had given her hand to young Mervyn, of ulterior consequences we say nothing—the nursery is above our province. And now, at length, after this Christmas journey through somewhat stern and gloomy scenery, in this long-deferred flood of golden sunshine we bid thee, gentle reader, a fond farewell.

ACCOUNT OF A "REAL LIFE" VAMPIRE: ARNOLD PAUL OR ARNOD PAOLE

Johannes Fluckinger

Many different countries have vampire mythology. The myth of a bloodsucking soul stealing creature exists in almost all countries around the globe. The most famous case of a "real" vampire account is that of Arnold Paul. The account of Arnold Paul is most striking in that it was documented by an official in the army and filed in an official report.

Do vampires exist? Most would say no, but the case of Arnold Paul does give one pause. No one today can say what happened in that far away country in that far away time, but whatever transpired was enough to convince an Army surgeon to file an official report on the unusual case of vampirism.

In the Austrian Empire, near Medvegia, 1732 Arnold Paul was working out in the farm, when suddenly he fell from his wagon, and died shortly after from a broken neck. Unknown to most of the townspeople, while Paul had served in the armed forces, he had encountered a vampire in Greece, where he was stationed. The only person he had revealed this information to was his young fiancé. Weeks after his death, reports began to surface from all over town that Paul had returned from the dead and was bothering the locals. Many people reported Paul was actually seen in their homes. Within a few days of reporting seeing Paul in their homes, several individuals died unexpectedly. Frightened townspeople and government officials marched on his grave. Soon it was opened, and all in attendance deemed that Paul had become a vampire, and therefore had to be destroyed. Paul was immediately staked, decapitated, and burnt to ashes. This was most famously documented by an army surgeon named Johannes Fluckinger hired by the emperor. His report was published in translated English and titled, "Seen and Heard."

This is a transcript of the orignal Document written in 1732 by the Regimental Field Surgeon Johannes Fluckinger To the Emperor
Visum et Repertum
Seen and Discovered
1732

After it had been reported that in the village of Medvegia the so-called vampires had killed some people by sucking their blood, I was, by high degree of a local Honorable Supreme Command, sent there to investigate the matter thoroughly along with officers detailed for that purpose and two subordinate medical officers, and therefore carried out and heard the present inquiry in the company of the captain of the Stallath Company of haiduks (a type of soldier), Gorschiz Hadnack, the standard-bearer and the oldest haiduk of the village, as follows: who unanimously recount that about five years ago a local haiduk by the name of Arnold Paole broke his neck in a fall from a haywagon. This man had during his lifetime often revealed that, near Gossowa in Turkish Serbia, he had been troubled by a vampire, wherefore he had eaten from the earth of the vampire's grave and had smeared himself with the vampire's blood, in order to be free from the vexation he had suffered.

In 20 or 30 days after his death some people complained that they were being bothered by this same Arnod Paole; and in fact four people were killed by him. In order to end this evil, they dug up this Arnold Paole 40 days after his death—this on the advice of a soldier, who had been present at such events before; and they found that he was quite complete and undecayed, and that fresh blood had flowed from his eyes, nose, mouth, and ears; that the shirt, the covering, and the coffin were completely bloody; that the old nails on his hands and feet, along with the skin, had fallen off, and that new ones had grown; and since they saw from this that he was a true vampire, they drove a stake through his heart, according to their custom, whereby he gave an audible groan and bled copiously, Thereupon they burned the body the same day to ashes and threw these into the grave. These people say further that all those who were tormented and killed by the vampire must themselves become vampires.

Therefore they disinterred the above-mentioned four people in the same way. Then they also add that this Arnod Paole attacked not only the people but also the cattle, and sucked out their blood. And since the people used the flesh of such cattle, it appears that some vampires are again present here, inasmuch as, in a period of three months, 17 young and old people died, among them some who, with no previous illness, died in two or at the most three days. In addition, the haiduk Jowiza reports that his step-daughter, by name of Stanacka, lay down to sleep 15 days ago, fresh and healthy, but at midnight she started up out of her sleep with a terrible cry, fearful and trembling, and complained that she had been throttled by the son of a haiduk by the name of Milloe, who had died nine weeks earlier, whereupon she had experienced a great pain in the chest and became worse hour by hour, until finally she died on the third day. At this we went the same afternoon to the graveyard, along with the often-mentioned oldest haiduks of the village, in order to cause the suspicious graves to be opened and to examine the bodies in them, whereby, after all of them had been dissected, there was found:

1. A woman by the name of Stana, 20 years old, who had died in childbirth two months ago, after a three-day illness, and who had herself said, before her death, that she had painted herself with the blood of a vampire, wherefore both she and her child - which had died right after birth and because of a careless burial had been half eaten by the dogs- must also become vampires. She was quite complete and undecayed. After the opening of the body there was found in the cavitate pectoris a quantity of fresh extravascular blood. The vessels of the arteries and veins, like the ventriculis ortis, were not, as is usual, filled with coagulated blood, and the whole viscera, that is, the lung, liver, stomach, spleen, and intestines were quite fresh as they would be in a healthy person.

The uterus was however quite enlarged and very inflamed externally, for the placenta and lochia had remained in place, wherefore the same was in complete putredine. The skin on her hands and feet, along with the old nails, fell away on their own, but on the other hand completely new nails were evident, along with a fresh and vivid skin.

2. There was a woman by the name of Miliza (60 years old), who had died after a three-month sickness and had been buried 90-some days earlier. In the chest much liquid blood was found; and the other viscera were, like those mentioned before, in a good condition. During her dissection, all the haiduks who were standing around marveled greatly at her plumpness and perfect body, uniformly stating that they had known the woman well, from her youth, and that she had; throughout her life, looked and been very lean and dried up, and they emphasized that she had come to this surprising plumpness in the grave. They also said that it was she who started the vampires this time, because she had eaten of the flesh of those sheep that had been killed by the previous vampires.

3. There was an eight-day-old child which had lain in the grave for 90 days and was similarly in a condition of vampirism.

4. The son of a haiduk, 16 years old, was dug up, having lain in the earth for nine weeks, after he had died from a three-day illness, and was found like the other vampires.

5. Joachim, also the son of a haiduk, 17 years old; had died after a three-day illness. He had been buried eight weeks and four days and, on being dissected; was found in similar condition.

6. A woman by the name of Ruscha who had died after a ten-day illness and had been buried six weeks

previous, in whom there was much fresh blood not only in the chest but also in fundo ventriculi. The same showed itself in her child, which was 18 days old and had died five weeks previously.

7. No less did a girl ten years of age, who had died two months previously, find herself in the above-mentioned condition, quite complete and undecayed; and had much fresh blood in her chest.

8. They caused the wife of the Hadnack to be dug up, along with her child. She had died seven weeks previously, her child—who was eight weeks old- 21 days previously, and it was found that both mother and child were completely decomposed, although earth and grave were like those of the vampires lying nearby.

9. A servant of the local corporal of the haiduks, by the name of Rhade, 21 years old, died after a three-month-long illness, and after a five week burial was found completely decomposed.

10. The wife of the local bariactar, along with her child, having died five weeks previously, were also completely decomposed.

11. With Stanche, a local haiduk, 60 years old; who had died six weeks previously, I noticed a profuse liquid blood, like the others, in the chest and stomach. The entire body was in the oft-named condition of vampirism.

12. Milloe, a haiduk, 25 years old; who had lain for six weeks in the earth, also was found in the condition of vampirism mentioned.

13. Stanoika, the wife of a haiduk, 20 years old, died after a three-day illness and had been buried 18 days previously. In the dissection I found that she was in her countenance quite red and of a vivid color, and, as was

mentioned above, she had been throttled, at midnight, by Milloe, the son of the haiduk, and there was also to be seen, on the right side under the ear, a bloodshot blue mark, the length of a finger. As she was being taken out of the grave, a quantity of fresh blood flowed from her nose. With the dissection I found; as mentioned often already, a regular fragrant fresh bleeding, not only in the chest cavity, but also in ventriculo cordis.

All the viscera found themselves in a completely good and healthy condition. The hypodermis of the entire body, along with the fresh nails of hands and feet, was as though completely fresh. After the examination had taken place, the heads of the vampires were cut off by the local gypsies and burned along with the bodies, and then the ashes were thrown into the river Morava. The decomposed bodies, however, were laid back into their own graves.

Visum et Repertum
Seen and Discovered
1732
Regimental Field Surgeon Johannes Fluckinger
To the Emperor

www.ingramcontent.com/pod-product-compliance
Lightning Source LLC
Chambersburg PA
CBHW021446240626
47153CB00001B/314